WHERE THE BEAUTY IS

a true north novel by

LARA ALSPAUGH

ISBN: 978-1-7337678-0-4

Book design and editing by Poole Publishing Services LLC

Cover photo courtesy of Kate Novikova

Other books by Lara Alspaugh:

Love, Red

Last Turn Home

To my mothers...

My mom: moxie and wisdom
My stepmom: humble resilience
My mother-in-law: grace and class

Thank you for teaching me to look for the beauty within the struggle, and for helping me to raise my boys to do the same. And to George, for raising E.

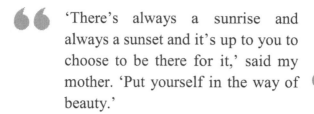 'There's always a sunrise and always a sunset and it's up to you to choose to be there for it,' said my mother. 'Put yourself in the way of beauty.'

— Cheryl Strayed, *Wild: From Lost to Found on the Pacific Crest Trail*

Nora Phillips's life is perfect. Well, she wants you to believe it is. One girl, one boy. A nearly-thirty-year marriage to her plastic surgeon husband, Joe. Their dream home on the crest of a hill overlooking the Little Traverse Bay.

Other than losing her beloved father to cancer two years ago, there wasn't anything that Nora would ask to change.

Well, of course, she would have liked to lose a few pounds (no matter how many sets of burpees or box jumps she paid her trainer Jordan to make her do, her robust middle wouldn't budge)—but what nearly fifty-year-old, premenopausal woman didn't want to do that?

And if you could have asked and she could have been honest, she would have said she wanted to have sex with her husband more often than she did—but was that so uncommon?

Despite this, Nora Phillips was certain her life was perfect.

But Nora wasn't paying attention.

No, Nora was too busy trying to make everyone believe her life was perfect to realize perfect isn't real.

MAY 26, 2018

PHE

Phe Sullivan watched her daughter tip her head back, laughter melting across her face like frosting on a warm brownie as she gently held her glass of red wine in both hands. Pinot noir, Phe knew. Phe smiled and tugged the shoulders of her cashmere sweater toward her middle, fending off the early summer chill as the sun went down. Sullivan's graduation party was perfect - "Nora Perfect." Of course, Phe knew it would be. Nothing Nora did was without panache, and her only son's graduation party was no exception.

Phe twirled her empty champagne glass between her fingers, her restlessness settling in her hands. She looked out over the bay—the large expanse of water changing with the shifting light. The sun slipped toward night letting the magic hour between day and night soak into her skin. The beacon at the end of the pier left its outline on the horizon. This was the time of day she felt closest to William; it was also in these moments where his loss was sharp—cutting and fresh.

The bells from the clock tower outside the city marina signaled 9:00. She'd lived here her entire life and never grew tired of the chimes. Petoskey and Harbor Springs were sister cities on the same bay, each unique, each special. Phe had lived in one and worked in the other. The familiar sights of the bay, the mountains, the sand, and the church steeple were home no matter which town she was in.

Still, Phe felt invisible. As if losing her husband had made her transparent, as if it had been his soul that had brought her to life, given her color and breath and spirit. She wanted to feel the depth of excitement and anticipation and energy a party for Sullivan's graduation should bring. Instead, she felt dull, muted. Sad.

Sadness was her constant companion.

Her attention gravitated toward the dance floor set up in front of the band. Her granddaughter, Samantha, was in the middle of a gaggle of friends, laughing and singing the words of a familiar song back to the lead singer of the band. Samantha's smile stretched wide as she lived easily in the moment. Her slender frame was perfectly suited for the white linen romper and floral print sash she'd tied around her waist. A stack of bangles decorated her right wrist while a Petoskey stone pendant hung in a deep V around her neck. Her toes peeked out of her navy-blue wedges. Sammy reminded Phe of herself when she was young, their looks were reminiscent and Sammy's elan mirrored her own. She also held the strong profile of her grandfather, another point of affection for Phe. Sammy was always surrounded by a crowd, always the life of the party and the sunshine in the room.

Phe's granddaughter had chosen her grandmother to be her confidant. Samantha's trust and robust restlessness for life was a balm on Phe's grief. The fire in Sammy's belly was the same ember Phe had when she started Josephine's, her upscale, boutique clothing shop downtown Harbor Springs. Sammy and Phe shared the same discontent, it was part of their DNA. A restlessness that was soothed by hard work, accomplishment, and success. Sammy was a risk-taker, an adventurer. Sammy was the opposite of her mother—Sammy and Phe's closeness had buoyed Phe in these past years without William.

Samantha smiled and waved at her grandmother from the dance floor. Sammy was unhappy in Lansing. She'd told her grandmother what she hadn't been able to tell her mother: that she hated the monotony of her insurance job—there was no room for her to create or be independent. She was weary of the drama of living with roommates. She wanted to *do* something, *create* something. She felt she was bigger than what she was doing now.

For years Phe wished for Nora—her only daughter— to find passion and interest in fashion, in owning the store. She taught her about line sheets and fashion trends, designers and profit margins. She took Nora to work with her, let her play with the jewelry pieces, experiment with dressing the mannequins and design the window displays. She loved to play with "The Ladies"—Josephine's floor sales staff. During high school, Nora was content to work hourly at Josephine's, and at the time, Phe had taken that as a sign of interest. Looking back now it was clear the job had been easy and safe for her daughter, Nora hadn't had to risk much to walk into Josephine's every day. After graduation, her part-time status melded into a full-time position as one of The Ladies on the floor. Phe had secretly been thrilled to have her daughter with her every day. She gently tried to show Nora the ropes, to expose her to all sides of the business without pushing her prickly teenage daughter away. Nora had been excellent with the customers. She understood what women wanted and had a keen eye for finding it amongst the racks. She also was gracious and tactful in steering women away from what might not be the best look.

Phe had remained hopeful that Nora would want to take over Josephine's, despite Nora's decreasing interest. Then her daughter had fallen in love. When Nora announced she was marrying Joe and moving to Ann Arbor until he finished medical school, Phe had been crushed. It hadn't been what she wanted for her daughter. She'd wanted her to take over Josephine's, or at least to have a career, to work and be independent. She'd tried to disguise her feelings, but Phe had never been a good actress. William had warned Phe not to push. He tried to get Phe to understand that Nora was her own person, different from her mother. She hadn't listened and the chasm between Phe and her daughter only grew. Just another regret Phe revisited now that she was a widowed woman in the twilight of her life.

When Phe was a young business woman she would not have believed she would come to be governed by regret. Even so, the regrets came quickly now like the waves of the lake, licking the sand and stones, wearing them down. Phe had always prided herself on aging gracefully—she had been successful and worked hard, she was proud of her life and her business. Aging well was another thing to do well—until she lost William. It seems now aging was more about loss and less about the wisdom, peace and the gentle comfort she'd believed she'd earned. Age—and loss—was softening her edges like the first warm day after a cold northern Michigan winter. In between her regrets, Phe also had real worries, tangible concerns that she needed to deal with, that needed answers now.

Three years ago, Danielle, Phe's store manager, had purchased Josephine's on land contract. Phe hadn't wanted to sell Josephine's, but William had been patient with his wife's ambition and business long enough. He wanted to travel to Greece, to winter in Florida, to eat grapefruit together for breakfast every morning. She had assumed they had time. She had assumed they would see Santorini and rent a home in the Keys. She had been wrong. Just twelve months after Josephine's changed hands, William was diagnosed with pancreatic cancer and Phe's life took on a landscape she never anticipated.

Now, Josephine's was in trouble. Danielle had been excited—she had a lot of ideas but too little experience in the market. She tried to change too much, too soon. She hadn't been in touch with her customer base—both the wealthy ladies of the season and the women who made Harbor Springs their year-round home. She didn't have Phe's business savvy or Nora's intuitive sense of style and design. Because Danielle had bought the store on land contract, Phe was in line to have the business back in her lap within the next few months.

Phe, who had been reluctant to sell—even bitter at times—would have never believed that the thought of Josephine's returning would exhaust her. She didn't have the desire to run Josephine's again, and that broke her already sad and wounded heart. She took a deep breath. Josephine's was a problem for another day.

Tonight, her plate of problems was already full.

Something was going on with Joe and Nora. Her daughter's smile, as perfect as it was, didn't reach her eyes. Joe was distracted, distant.

The invisibility of widowhood had given Phe the superpower of observation. People were worried about her—but also discounted her in some ways. So much so they forgot to disguise their own secrets, to veil the looks on their faces or pretend with their body language. But Phe wasn't invisible, and she wasn't asleep or hard of hearing or blind. She'd been widowed. Instead of making her unseen, that grief had made her astute, her feelings as vulnerable as a newborn. She had become a lightning rod for emotion. Phe's relationship with her daughter may be prickly at times, but Nora was her daughter. And that, as far as Phe was concerned, was the greatest love there is.

Phe stood up and headed toward the bar to refill her champagne flute. She rarely allowed herself more than two glasses of anything— but tonight... tonight she deserved a third. Walking carefully across the lawn she looked in the direction of Joe. He caught her glance as quickly as a new dad caught the tail end of the string of a balloon before it drifted away from his toddler. Joe smiled at his mother-in-law. Phe looked away, tucking her small hand in the pocket of her pantsuit, catching her wedding ring on the cusp of the opening.

Nora knew the embarrassment of having your marital trouble be public knowledge. A sharp pang jabbed Phe. She had longed for a way to connect with her daughter, to overpass the gap that William had bridged over for so long. Maybe the trouble in her daughter's marriage could be the conduit that would finally reconnect Phe and Nora? Was it wrong for Phe to feel hopeful in the face of her daughter's incoming disaster?

"Hey there, Phe!" The bartender smiled.

"Hello, Gatsby," she answered. Phe tried to keep her

tone light, this was her grandson's graduation celebration after all. "I'll have a glass of champagne, if you please." Gatsby took Phe's old glass and replaced it with a chilled champagne flute filled with sweet bubbly. "Add me a muddled strawberry or two, dear?" Gatsby smiled again and obliged.

The party was on the lawn at The Stafford, perched high in the hills of town the beauty of the Little Traverse Bay carved out in front of the guests. Sullivan, his friends, and their parents were dancing, laughing, and eating under a sparkling, white tent. There were paper lantern lights hanging from the tent ceiling, as well as strings of antique garden lights and dainty Christmas twinkle lights all working together to create a subtle, textured glow. Round tables were draped with white tablecloths displaying all of Sullivan's favorite foods (including hundreds of Nora's World Famous Snickerdoodles and piles of subs he loved from Harbor Springs). His football jerseys were hung up around the tent, hundreds of photos of her grandson, some gracing tables and others tacked to old shutters, window frames and even a door complete with the crystal knob for a handle at the entrance to the party. The space had turned into a shrine for Sullivan. The tables each had a token of Sullivan's childhood as a centerpiece—the wooden train Phe and William had given him for his first birthday, the clock he made in eighth-grade woodworking class, a vase full of home run baseballs.

The DJ was playing all the kids' favorites and the adults were enjoying the open bar.

Phe sipped her champagne and walked toward a crowd of people. Better to chat with others and get her mind off her family's troubles than sit alone and brood. Phe surveyed the party, momentarily closing her eyes trying to feel the love she knew was surrounding her. Oh how she wished William were here.

She had so much to tell him! Sullivan graduating. Nora and Joe. The trouble with Josephine's. Sammy's confession. Phe had friends who had become widows. She had sympathized and invited them to lunch. She called and checked in and was sure to include them in social events. She thought she had been supportive. It wasn't until she lost William that she realized the epic devastation of losing your spouse. Phe missed her husband every day, she was homesick for him. She missed how he cut up a grapefruit for her every Sunday morning and sprinkled just a touch of sugar. She missed how he bounced his foot over crossed knees as he read *The New York Times* in his favorite chair. She missed how he knew when she was stewing about something and needed to talk.

"A penny for your thoughts?" he would say with a hint of his brilliant, sideways smile.

She missed how he smelled of sandalwood and bourbon. She missed everything about her husband, and tonight she missed having a listening ear and the wisdom of his advice that came with it. Phe didn't know how to fill in all the places that William used to be.

There were moments the loss of him took her breath away. When her eyes sprang open in the middle of the night, her hands grasping the cold space in the sheets next to her, air catching in her throat. His death felt merely seconds away, her memories intense and technicolor. She could feel the warmth from his skin and the hot moisture of his breath on her neck as they slept. Phe held her body still, alone under the covers in those fleeting seconds. Desperately clutching the memories where the presence of the love of her life was real, it was true. She felt alive and loved and safe. The magnitude of those passing seconds left her emptier than before. Her fear of forgetting him exploded as the weight of him slipped back into the darkness, the wrinkles cupping his eyes and the rough edges of his fingers stolen by his passing gone all over again.

William's birthday was coming up quickly, July fourth. How her patriot husband loved sharing his birthday with his country! Phe used to love it too—they would go all out having a large backyard picnic—BBQ spare ribs, brisket, burgers, Koegel hotdogs, and bratwurst from the butcher's shop. She'd serve his favorite coleslaw and always strawberry-blueberry shortcake and Faygo root beer floats for dessert. They would pile into the old woody station wagon with blankets, sparklers, sweatshirts (Northern Michigan weather could surprise you!), snacks and a thermos of William's sidecars to watch the fireworks explode over the bay—mirroring their magic into the inky expanse of the water. Last year she hadn't felt up to celebrating anything—this year she felt the same although she knew William was waiting for her to resume her life. He'd made her promise to enjoy the time she had left in the days before he'd slipped away. She'd promised, but of course, she had no idea how hard that promise would be to keep.

Their marriage hadn't always been perfect and Phe was careful to remember the hard times, too. Not just the fact that he never picked up a pair of socks in his life, or that his towel, newly damp from the shower would inevitably be in a pile on their closet floor. No, she chose to remember in vivid detail their great disappointments. She had no interest in idolizing a man without faults or pretending that her marriage had not had its ups and downs. No, in her old age she relished the good and the bad. She understood, now more than ever, she could not be completely human without both the beauty of their love and the pain of their mistakes. Phe knew she had hurt her husband, as he had her, but somehow the memory of the bad times made the love they shared stronger, more robust. She remembered the pain, and gratitude visited her for the love they had nurtured until the day he died.

William would have been so proud tonight. Phe could see him now, strutting like a peacock with his feathers in full bloom. His silver hair would have been cut and coiffed perfectly, he would have worn his khaki pants and a blue button-down shirt, no tie. He would have his penny loafers on—a shiny penny for luck in each shoe. They would have taken their turn on the dance floor, William would have sung in her ear in his husky bass voice. He would have charmed the guests, and while part of Phe would have been jealous of his command of the room she would have been proud. Proud of her husband. Her marriage. Her family. Phe smiled.

His death had put a spotlight on the third act of her life. With William's death had come the realization that life changes in an instant. Isn't it interesting, she had lived more than seventy years before he died, and still it took his passing for her to acknowledge that life was fluid, that your days may wind in and out of each other, one looking eerily similar to the last, but in reality every day you move through life, changing in small indiscernible ways until the end when the sum of those changes is who you have become. Sometimes those changes are distant, we see them out on the horizon like a storm front marching across the bay: massive, dark and beautiful. We can plan for them and try to be ready, prepare to hold on while our world shifts.

Although she wanted to believe her husband of fifty years would live forever, she knew for two years that his time had run thin. She held his hand as he took his last Earthly breath, and somewhere inside of her she couldn't believe it had actually happened. That the end of their great love had arrived. There were days, even after all this time, that Phe was struck by the knowledge that she lived in a world where there was no William. Sure, she had a measure of faith and believed his soul to be coveted in Heaven, his body healed, and although she knew that should provide her with a selfless solace, it did not.

Sometimes, Phe thought, no matter how hard we try to control or anticipate what happens, we simply do not see the tide rushing in. Sometimes life changes with no warning: the screech of tires and the force of impact, a ringing phone in the dead of night, a door closing behind someone you thought would never leave, a doctor's words delivering the news no one wants to hear. Phe took a sip of her champagne. She hoped Nora could handle the change that was circling around her family. Memories of her daughter wrapped in a pink bundle in William's arms flooded Phe, warming her from the inside the way only private memories can. It seemed like only yesterday, how had an entire lifetime passed?

Phe watched her daughter covering the room in choreographed steps to serve her guests and be the perfect hostess. Would Phe have enough time to heal her relationship with Nora? She hoped so. She also knew—with perfect clarity—that time was a luxury that can be lost in a blink.

The uneven ground under the tent caused Phe to step cautiously as she searched for someone she knew to chat with. She needed to enjoy the evening, William would want that. So she did as she had for the past two years and pretended her darling was sitting somewhere across the room, laughing and holding court, entertaining the guests. The comfort of the lie buoyed her spirits. Denial was a useful skill she had learned.

Her steps felt unsure and she teetered just slightly. Quietly she chastised herself for wearing a cute pair of mules (they were perfect with her outfit!) instead of her sensible shoes better suited for the grass. Forcing herself to focus on walking, Phe reflexively reached out for William's arm to balance herself. She'd already forgotten he was no longer physically able to steady her.

Phe reached for the back of a white folding chair with her free hand but could not quite reach, the fresh glass of champagne slipped through the fingers of her other hand and broke in pieces on the grass. She shifted her left leg toward the chair, hoping to regain her balance, too late to save herself from going down and late enough to feel as though she was falling in slow motion. She looked up in time to see Sullivan's eyes fly open as he watched his grandmother fall to the ground.

"Phe! Phe! Are you okay?" Sullivan's eyes were full of bittersweet fear. "Can you get up? What happened?"

She tried to focus on Sullivan's voice—hearing him

call her by name gave her resolve. He'd given her the nickname after all. When he was just a toddler, "Grandma Josephine" had been too big of a mouthful for him, so he'd shortened it to "Phe" and it stuck. Before Phe could find words to answer Sullivan, Sammy, Joe, and Nora were above her, circling her with worry and help. Phe tried to roll over, the embarrassment washing over her compelling her to stand—but she couldn't. The pain was too great. She took breaths slowly in and out through her lips, forcing her breath through an imaginary straw. She tried to push herself up again but the pain shot repeatedly from her hip up into her ribs. The voices around her sounded muffled and distanced. Phe comforted herself with thoughts of William.

Joe reached for her wrist and began checking her pulse, leaning in closely to hear her breaths with his head cocked to the side. His brow furrowed together, concern knitting his lips into a tight bow. Phe closed her eyes and directed herself to breathe: *in-and-out, in-and-out,* just as she heard Joe command someone to call 9-1-1. If she had wished William had been with her earlier... well she wept with a need for her husband now. The pain continued to come, an all-consuming wave mixed with fear and embarrassment.

And just like that, the change Phe didn't see coming—came.

NORA

Nora shook her head to dislodge the vision of her mom lying on the ground underneath the tent, the glow of the lights reflecting off of her brow, beaded with sweat.

"I better head to the hospital with my mom," Nora told Joe as the paramedics lifted Phe into the back of the ambulance. The music had stopped and the open bar had been put on hold. Her perfect party for Sullivan was dead in its tracks.

"Of course you should," Joe answered. "I'll keep tabs on Sully. Sammy is staying at Kelsey's tonight anyway." It would have made sense for Joe to go too, he was a doctor, but Nora didn't suggest he tag along.

"He has a curfew. One o'clock," Nora reminded Joe, her face knitted tightly in a worried scowl.

"Yes, I know. You've told us both several times."

"I don't want to ride in the ambulance, but if I take the car how will you get home?" Nora asked.

"No problem at all. I'll find a ride." Joe looked around, his gaze settling just above Nora's head. Nora looked up into his eyes. He was nearly a foot taller than she was. In the beginning, she had loved that about her husband, she'd felt protected and safe. Now, his height simply made him feel further away.

"OK then, I'll see you later." Nora could have reached up to her tiptoes to kiss Joe goodbye, but instead she turned and walked away from her husband. A hot flash shot across her heart like a falling star. It was gone before she knew for sure what it meant.

Fifteen minutes later, Nora walked into the Emergency Room, squinting her eyes under the harsh artificial light. She asked the front desk for Josephine Sullivan and was escorted to her mother's room where she waited outside until the X-ray tech finished a bedside X-ray of her hip. Nora clutched her purse to her side, then she slipped her hand in the opening, rooting around for her pill bottle. It was there, in the side pocket where it always was. Her heart beat loudly in her chest.

Nora had learned what her mother needed from her only child was strength and resolve. Phe was not well-versed in nurturing—she had always struggled when her daughter was hurting. Being vulnerable, being human, wasn't comfortable for Phe—if Nora had needed comfort, it was her father she sought out.

The sound of IV monitors and the overhead announcement of a Code Blue somewhere in the hospital disoriented her, the bitter taste of adrenaline on her tongue was soothed only by reminding herself she had hcr pills if she needed them. Never mind that she'd never actually used them.

Nora sucked in a deep breath and walked into Phe's room. The sight of her mother connected to heart monitors, an IV taped on the top of her small, bird-like hand and her hip supported by a large bolster took a sharp gasp of Nora's breath. There was no underestimating the vulnerability that descends the first time you realize your parents are aging. Until this moment—even through the worst of her father's cancer treatments—her mother had been a pillar of strength and reserved resolve. Now, there was no denying that Nora would also lose her mother. Not today, or even tomorrow, but the fact that Nora would eventually be without either parent was undeniable.

The lump in Nora's throat threatened to bubble forward, exposing her fear. Nora shook her head sharply and the emotions of the moment subsided, she'd willed the swell in her chest to quiet with practiced efficiency. How Nora missed the comfort of her father—navigating her relationship with her mother without his steady hand was a difficulty Nora would rather avoid. But, Nora had work to do. Being an only child meant the work of caring for her parents was hers alone. It wasn't the first time in Nora's life she wished for a sibling to share the burden. She took a deep breath now. She could handle this, she *had* to handle this.

"Hi, Mom. I'm here," Nora said as she reached for her mother's hand—the one without the IV—and lightly squeezed it. Phe turned her head toward Nora and smiled faintly through the oxygen mask that was hissing loudly.

"Nora?" Jason Dodds, a friend of Joe's, pushed through the curtain of ER Room 4 and held his hand out to Nora in greeting.

"Hi Jason, how are you?" Nora let her mother's hand

return to the bed, limp.

"Better than you two tonight! Wasn't Sullivan's graduation party this evening?" Jason asked.

"Yes, my mom fell in the lawn under the tent. Joe stayed behind to clean up," Nora replied with a tired smile, unsure of why she mentioned Joe.

"Well, this must be your mom, Josephine—"

"She goes by Phe," Nora interjected. Jason, who was normally James-Corbin-funny (he even looked like him, too!), was all business and his typically warm demeanor was different—if not cool. Nora shook her head. She was tired, it was late—who knows how long Jason has been here. She knew she was being overly sensitive but she could not shake the uncomfortable feeling she was getting from Jason.

"Phe, pardon me," Jason smiled down at his patient. "You did it up good, young lady. You broke your hip."

"Oh shit," Nora said out loud, quickly covering her mouth. Jason looked in her direction and then back at Phe.

"We'll put you back together. Surgery scheduled for 10:00 tomorrow morning. Until then we'll give you some IV pain meds to help keep you as comfortable as we can." Jason directed his question toward Phe and looked at Nora. "Do you remember what happened, Phe?"

"She twisted her ankle on the lawn. I should have taken her home hours ago," Nora answered, tears threatening.

Phe looked up at Jason and smiled, nodding her head. Nora held her mom's hand, rolling her fingers between her own.

"That's what the paramedics reported, I ordered X-rays on both ankles to be sure there isn't a hidden injury there. I don't see anything on the films and can't feel any laxity or soft tissue damage on exam. Looks like we got lucky there. We'll keep our eye on it as you recover to be sure there isn't a subtle injury we're missing."

Phe had closed her eyes as Jason spoke. Morphine finally settled the pain enough to allow Phe to rest.

"Do you have any questions, Nora?" Jason asked as he gently squeezed Phe's shoulder by way of goodbye.

"I don't right now, but give me a minute to Google what I should worry about and get back to you," Nora answered, hoping for a smile from Jason.

"I'm sure you know how us doctors feel about Google medical searches." Jason smirked and stood up and walked toward the door. "It's good to see you, I'm sorry it's in the ER." He smiled without meeting Nora's gaze.

"You too, Jason. Now that Sullivan is graduated, Joe and I will have more time for dinners out—I'll call Shelly and plan something." Nora and Joe had never had dinner with Jason and Shelly with the exception of hospital functions—Nora wasn't sure why she offered now outside the fact that tonight Nora felt the need to win Jason over.

"Sounds good. Young lady, I will stop by and see you after surgery tomorrow." Jason turned toward Phe ending his conversation with Nora.

Nora reached in her purse and dug for her phone to let Joe know about Phe's hip. She considered mentioning Jason's cool vibe, but decided she would ask Joe later—it would be hard to explain over text. Besides, she was probably overreacting.

> Nora: *Not coming home. Phe broke her hip. Will stay with her tonight and be back in the morning. Sully ok?*

The next hour was spent gathering all of Phe's clothes and belongings, traipsing them up to the third floor and settling Phe in for the night. Two hours passed before Nora realized Joe hadn't texted back. Twenty-five minutes later her phone buzzed as she was unsuccessfully rearranging Phe's pathetic hospital pillow under her head trying not to tangle them both in the IV lines.

> Joe: *I suspected. Sully is fine.*

She was irritated it had taken Joe so long to respond—he hardly let his phone out of his sight, but tonight, when Nora was sitting in the hospital with her mom, on Sullivan's graduation night, Joe decides to not respond? Nora shoved her phone back into her purse, an anxious worry creeping into her stomach.

There just wasn't enough of her to go around. She knew her mother needed her, but frankly she wanted to be home to be sure Sullivan made it back and followed curfew. He had danced around trouble these last two years of school. She had caught him sneaking out of the house and drinking, she found weed in his car and he nearly failed pottery. *Pottery?* How does one fail pottery?

Sullivan had been born six weeks early. Nora had pre-eclampsia, her blood pressure had spiked dangerously high when she was thirty-three weeks pregnant. After a week of bedrest in the hospital, Sullivan William Phillips entered the world too early. At four pounds and five ounces, he was half the size of Sammy, who had been eight pounds and eleven ounces. His tiny body scared Nora terribly. He was in the NICU for twenty-seven days, learning to eat, regulate his temperature and grow. Nora had been consumed with guilt, regardless of what the doctors said she was certain his early birth was a result of a mistake she had made.

Sullivan recovered from his premature birth and grew into a strong baby, small but sturdy. Nora obsessed with worry for her son. She'd breastfed him for nearly two years, made her own organic baby food and rushed him to the pediatrician at the slightest hint of a sniffle. In the beginning, Joe had obliged his wife's fears, pulling favors to have his son seen on weekends and the middle of the night. As Sullivan grew, Joe became more confident in his son's health, and therefore became less accommodating when Nora was overprotective. Sullivan continued to develop, to fill in the gaps of missed time. He grew stronger and eventually no one would have known he had a precarious start to his robust life. By the time Sully was in third grade, it was clear that not only had he caught up, his once small, frail body was growing into a strong, self-assured athlete.

While Sullivan was an average student—often bored by the tedium of school—he was skilled at all things physical. Baseball, football, basketball. He loved it all and while they joked his favorite sport was whatever ball was in his hand at the time, eventually it was clear football was his favorite. He loved the contact, the speed, the aggressive play. He loved everything about it.

Nora couldn't argue that Sullivan had found something he loved to do, and that his success was transferring to the classroom, but inside she cringed every time his body was tackled. She couldn't quite get past his fragile beginnings and worried incessantly that her boy would be hurt. Joe, on the other hand, had reveled in it. He never missed a game. Which was saying something. When their daughter Sammy had been in high school, she was on the swim team, but Joe was so busy at the hospital and with patients in his office he rarely made a single meet.

Nora was happy for Sullivan that his dad was

interested and involved, but she resented Joe's involvement on behalf of Sammy. Sammy on the other hand, a full eight years older than Sully, was untouched by her dad's dismissal of her activities. "It's fine, Mom," she would casually say, "it's really not the end of the world. Let it go."

But Nora couldn't. It was just another thing on the list of things that Joe did that she didn't approve of, along with routinely allowing Sullivan to disregard his curfew when he was "in charge."

Nora was exhausted... the party, graduation, Sullivan, Joe and now Phe. So many people wanted a piece of her. The sandwich generation, isn't that what they called this? When you were stuck between caring for your kids and caring for your aging parents? Nora certainly understood that analogy, she felt like a soggy peanut butter and jelly that nobody would want to find in their lunch.

"Momma?"

Nora's head turned toward the door, just as beautiful Sammy peeked around the curtain. "What are you doing here, sweet pea? I thought you were staying at Kelsey's?" Nora smiled at the sight of her daughter. Sammy was the opposite of Nora: tall, thin and blonde to Nora's short, dark, robust physique. Sammy looked like a natural-born ballet dancer—or yoga teacher. She was slender and willowy.

"I couldn't stay there while you were here alone." Sammy smiled.

"Oh thank you. I was just going to ask the nurse for one of their recliner chairs to sleep on, those ones that fold out into a bed." Nora rubbed her forehead with her hands and glanced over at Phe who was finally sleeping, her breaths as rhythmic as a heartbeat.

"Why don't I stay, Mom? You can go home, get a good night's sleep. You said in your text she has surgery at ten a.m., right? You could be back here first thing and not miss much. You have to be exhausted from Sully's party."

Nora adored her children. Sure, there were times they were frustrating or downright maddening, but then there were times like tonight where their maturity and compassion made her proud. "Oh Sammy, those chairs are so uncomfortable. You don't want to do that."

"Yes, actually I do. In fact, I'm going to insist. There's really no reason I can't—at twenty-six-years-old—stay in the hospital with my grandmother before hip surgery. You can go home, get some sleep. I know it's still not easy for you to be here."

Nora took a deep breath and reluctantly agreed. "When did you turn into such a bossy pants?" she teased her daughter.

"Oh, I learned from the best. The very best." Sam laughed.

"I assume you are talking about Phe?" Nora smiled, calling her mother Phe felt more natural for everyone, not just Sully.

"Oh, she's the original, for sure. But I got my bossy

pants straight from you."

With that Nora grabbed her purse and organized her mother's blankets, kissed her on the forehead and hugged her daughter. Sammy's long, slender limbs wrapped tightly around her. Nora was so proud of her girl. She was proud of her for leaving Petoskey and the subtle complexity of family and small-town life and to create something out of nothing. And tonight she was grateful for her, too. Nora did need to be home. She needed to check on Sullivan, and now she could sleep in her own bed and be ready for the long day at the hospital tomorrow.

The hospital still brought a haze of sadness to Nora. All those days and nights spent with her dad before he died. He had spent twenty-three days in the hospice unit on the fourth floor waiting to die. For twenty-three days she watched her father—her mentor, her idol, her best friend—die inch by inch.

There had been no explanation as to why William had hung on so long. When they moved him into hospice the doctor said he was declining rapidly, his organs were shutting down, it wouldn't be long. Still, twenty-three days later he had still been suffering. There never was a formal explanation, why but Nora knew. Her father had known she wasn't ready. Despite the two years of treatments and drugs and side effects and surgeries and procedures and appointments and a diagnosis with a five-year survival rate of a paltry seven percent, Nora still hadn't been ready.

Never once in the two years after he'd been diagnosed had Nora succumb to the fear—or reality—that she would lose her dad. He had been her rock, her steadfast supporter her cheerleader and her best friend. No, Nora knew he had waited every one of those last twenty-three excruciating days for his daughter to tell him she would be okay. He waited for Nora to grant him permission to pass. She hadn't had the courage, not until the twenty-third day.

"Joe, I can't do this. I can't let him go and I can't watch him suffer for one more minute. I'd rather suffocate him with a pillow than watch him drown on his own." Her breath caught. "I just can't."

Joe nodded his head and hugged his wife close to his chest her tears pressed into his crisp, white button-up shirt. "Tell him it's okay to go. You will be okay, we will take care of Phe. Tell him, Nora. He needs to know. You need this, it's time."

So she had. She sat with her dad and held his hand. She rocked back and forth like a child unable to fathom life on this Earth without her father. He passed within the hour. Had she been more courageous, her dad would not have suffered the way he did in the end. That is hard to forgive yourself for. Nora wondered if she ever would.

Nora crossed over the river into town, driving past the city marina following the curve of the bay. Her sweaty palms gripped the steering wheel as her heart began to race. Just a gentle acceleration at first, a subtle shift in gears. She felt the familiar galloping beat of her heart as sure as a racehorse coming down the final stretch. A thoroughbred, strong, tough, aggressive. He thundered through her heart, pulling its rhythm along with him. She wiped her hands down the side of her pants, leaving dark spots where the moisture soaked in. Nora swallowed hard, trying to push the worry that bullied its way into her veins down, out, away. She focused intently on the road, tunneling her vision and breathing through pursed lips—*breathe in for two, out for two, breathe in for two, out for two*. The racing began to slow, her racehorse slowing to take his cool down lap.

Under the quiet cloak of darkness, staring at the midline of the road, she remembered her father's last hours. The fear that shot through her veins, a pain that was as physically real as a broken bone, as he took his last ragged breaths. Her heart ached under the pressure of her grief. The familiar yearning of homesickness for her father as ripe as if he had died just this morning. Life was harder now, without her dad to buffer her time with Phe. Nora and Phe were close, for certain, but that closeness was taunted by a thin shearing of disappointment.

Phe had spent her life working, pursuing her passion of creating and growing Josephine's, while Nora had spent her life pursuing her passion for a perfect family. Logically, Nora knew that Phe was proud of her daughter. That didn't stop the whispers of insecurity that came from Nora believing that inside Phe's heart lived a small bubble of disappointment that Josephine Sullivan's daughter was *just* a stay-at-home mom. That Nora was *just* a mother and wife and not a CEO or entrepreneur or leader in her field was the power behind the rocky undertow of Nora and Phe's relationship.

In so many ways Nora admired her mother, and even envied her life's work. It wasn't as if Nora had never had dreams or ambitions, it was simply that Joe's dreams were bigger, more complex and yielded a greater benefit for their family. Nora never regretted caring for her children and her husband, she had lived her perfect life well. It's just that the restlessness that comes with an impending empty nest has shed light on her dusty, forgotten, decades-old dreams for her future. In moments of hope, where Nora could see a part two, when her children leaving her home didn't feel like someone ripping her heart out of her chest with their bare hands, those dreams bloomed in color in her imagination. But most the time, resignation that she had chosen her path decades ago and those old black-and-white visions in her mind of a path not taken were just that: memories of a choice she didn't make. Tonight, with new worries for Phe's health and memories of her father's death refreshed by time in the hospital, Nora could scarcely remember what those dreams once were. This was her life, her perfect life, there was nothing more to imagine.

Willow met Nora at the back door, sleepy and happy to see her master home. A few sharp barks in greeting until Nora was quick to shush her, hoping to keep her family asleep. Technically, Willow was Sullivan's dog, a four-year-old Goldendoodle, but the truth of a dog is whoever feeds said dog is loved the most. Willow rarely left Nora's side. Nora slipped off her wedge sandals, her feet tired and sore. She kicked them toward the mudroom door. Three pairs of Sullivan's shoes blocked the doorway in a pile. She reached down and lined them all up in front of his cubby, hanging his sweatshirt that had fallen on the ground and putting away two of his baseball hats that were scattered on the bench. She was not ready for him to leave home, not even his messes made her anxious for him to go.

Her friends all agreed with her when she complained about being desperately sad that their kids were graduating and leaving. But Nora was secretly convinced none of them hurt the way she hurt. As egocentric as it was—not to mention groundless—she believed it. After all, Steven and Alicia were planning a trip to Australia after their twins left for school in the fall! Fran was going back to work full time in August and Tara still has three kids at home. None of their friends were facing what Nora was facing: a completely empty nest with no job and a husband who was never home. Nora was petrified for Sullivan to leave, because Nora did not want to be left with an empty house and a lonely heart. She knew in her mind that her baby leaving for college was not everything, but it was not nothing either. It was something, and that something was pretty powerful.

Nora had taken to thinking of Sullivan with a countdown clock floating on top of his head. Like the countdown clocks people created online to measure time until their big spring break trip or to mark time before their weddings. Tonight, the night they celebrated his graduation from high school, that clock hanging over Sullivan's head seemed to start speeding up at an alarming rate. She needed to sleep where Sullivan was, in her home in her own bed.

Nora was pleased with herself tonight. She had successfully managed to sit with her mother in the hospital, talk to the doctors and navigate her mother being admitted all by herself in the middle of the night—after Sullivan's graduation party no less! It wasn't that Nora didn't believe herself capable—it was more than she didn't trust her body to not betray her. Even after nearly two years of sporadic panic attacks—at least that's what the doctor called them—Nora was no closer to understanding what caused them. Dr. Bateman and Joe had both suggested she go to counseling, but Nora refused. She was not interested in discussing her feelings and the fact that her heart sometimes raced, her hands shook and she sweat like she was having a hot flash in the Sahara. Or that sometimes she felt nauseous and vomited after an attack; all of which left her profoundly exhausted when it was over. No, Nora didn't need counseling. There was nothing to talk about! Nothing to panic about! Her life was perfect. Nora had filled the prescription of Xanax that Dr. Bateman had given her as a precaution—she would have been mortified if one of her spells had happened in public! Nora was in the throes of menopause and was certain that's what the episodes were—so she carried the bottle of pills with her everywhere she went *just in case.*

Nora took the stairs two at a time up to Sullivan's room. Her trainer, Jordan, told her once that people thought that running up the stairs helped their overall fitness, but he believed that was a myth. She thinks about this every time she runs up the stairs, but she still does it. Her own personal defiance against Jordan and his insanely hard workouts. Sullivan's door creaked when she pushed it open, clothes on the floor resisting her entrance. She made her way to the side of his bed, climbing over piles of clothes, shoes, and remnants of the past month, his last month of high school. She waited for her eyes to adjust to the sliver of moonlight that had crept into the room to help her see. His room had been the same since he was in the fourth grade. Nora had tried to entice him into new paint and carpet, but Sullivan didn't want anything to change. His walls were gray, the carpet navy blue and his comforter was a well-slept-in, comfy denim with the Detroit Tigers ol' English D in the center. She pulled the covers back carefully so she didn't wake him. She just wanted to see his sleeping face and kiss his forehead.

But Sullivan wasn't there, he wasn't in his bed. Dammit. Joe, like usual, didn't make him follow curfew. It was 4:15 in the morning, there was no excuse for him not to be home! Nora pulled her phone out of her pocket and started typing furiously: *Sullivan! Where are you? You are supposed to be home by 1. It's 4:15 a.m. Seriously? You KNOW THE RULES.*

Nora sat on the edge of her son's bed, tapping her leg up and down, waiting. Tears stung her eyes. Why can't Joe just do what she asks? Why does everyone fight her so hard? He was fine to leave her with the heavy lifting when the kids were little. Now all of a sudden he has an opinion, wants a say? Maybe he should have changed a diaper, or stayed up all night with them while they drooled and cried and writhed in teething pain! He could have held their little heads while they threw up or gone to a parent-teacher conference, he could have given Sullivan The Talk about sex. He could have done any number of mundane, difficult, tedious and boring parenting tasks in the past twenty-six years. But he didn't. He chose to work. He chose to ignore the kids crying, fighting, struggling. He chose to ignore Nora. Now he wants to be the good guy, the one who shows up to football games and doesn't hold Sullivan to his curfew and won't back Nora up when she tries to enforce it? It's bullshit.

Seven minutes passed and still she had no answer from Sullivan. He was probably sleeping. Nora knew he was probably sleeping but still, the anxiety that she worked so hard to keep at bay bubbled like hot bile in her throat. What if he wasn't? If she had been tired when she came home from the hospital, she was vividly alert now. Willow had followed Nora into Sullivan's room and curled up next to Nora's feet, sighing deeply as she adjusted her paws underneath her neck. Nora's foot tapped on the floor, Willow easily ignoring the annoying sound.

Nora checked her text messages again. The iMessage continued to read "Delivered" with no response. Sullivan is supposed to always have his read receipt on, but Nora knows he turns it off. The "Delivered" message did not give her any comfort. Nora opened up FamilyFind—or as Sully called it her "Stalker App"— searching for Sullivan's location. His phone icon showed him at Chase's house up the road. Sullivan hated that Nora tracked him. But after being caught at a party he hadn't had permission to go to, Nora contended that if he was always where he was supposed to be it made no difference and until she knew he would follow the rules, he would be tracked. Sullivan's resistance to it did nothing except flame the mistrust growing between mother and son. Joe sided with Sully, of course.

Last fall Joe and Nora had bickered about the app at

a football game. Alicia and Steve sided along gender lines—Alicia believing tracking her twins was her right as their mother, Steve believing his parents didn't know where he was all the time, why should they know where their kids were now? Stephanie Laredo had been the only woman in the group who *wasn't* tracking her kid. "I don't even *want* to know where Elise is half the time, I'm sure she can handle herself." Nora had felt a sting of uncertainty: not that she would ever want to be a parent like Stephanie Laredo, but she was a touch envious of the freedom not *needing* to know where Sullivan was would bring her.

Nora took a deep breath and laid back, resting her head on Sullivan's bed. Hot tears slid out of her tired eyes, running down her cheeks and pooling on the cool fabric of his pillow.

Nora missed the years when Sullivan and Sammy were young. She felt more confident as a mother when her kids were little; it was easy for her to determine what was right what was wrong, and letting go meant letting them walk across the room while she stood sentry next to them. If she thought the teenage years with Sammy nearly broke her, she was mistaken. Sullivan found trouble at every turn. He was drawn to mischief like a moth to flame. He was impulsive and fearless. A fierce and dangerous combination for any teenager. Nora was certain if she didn't keep a heavy hand on her son he would meet with disaster. Why did Joe not see that? She hadn't spent eighteen years keeping him alive to watch him self-destruct!

Nora looked out the window toward the moon and remembered the first week they had lived in this house. Sully had been just two, and they had used the move as the opportunity to transfer him from his crib (which he had been routinely climbing out of for over a year) to a "big boy bed." He loved the bed for stories and even liked to play on the bed like a trampoline, but when it came time to lay down he was not having it. Nora had spent every day of the first two weeks rocking him to sleep at nap time and bedtime. She had snuggled his sweet body up to hers, grateful for the time to hold him. He finally learned to sleep in his bed and she supposed he would learn to take care of himself, too. What she wouldn't give to go back to nap time and snuggles and controlling his safety.

Nora looked back at FamilyFind, refreshing the screen one more time. Sullivan was still at Chase's. This time she noticed that Joe had turned off his location. A second flash of hot anger seared through her. They had discussed this. How was Nora to expect Sullivan to keep his location on— an argument they routinely have— if Joe wasn't willing to do the same. Joe argued that no one needed to track him, and Nora argued it's easier to get children to do what you *do* not what you *say*.

Nora made her way down the stairs toward their bedroom. She was irritated with Joe. The muscles in her arms ached to rip open the bedroom door and swipe on the lights. Her brow tightened and her teeth clenched. She walked into her bedroom, ignoring Joe's side of the bed as she stomped straight into the bathroom. She flicked on the light, not bothering to shut the door. She turned on the water, washed her face and slammed the cleanser and lotion back down on the granite counter after their use. Catching a glimpse of her face in the mirror she paused for a moment: an angry woman stared back at her. Ignoring her gut reaction of disgust at her own reflection, she brushed her teeth harder than necessary. She was so angry. Angry at Joe. Angry at Sullivan. Hell, she was even angry at Phe for wearing those stupid mules instead of shoes that would have been safer in the grass!

She wanted Joe to wake up. She wanted him to ask her what's wrong. She wanted to scream at him for allowing Sullivan to break curfew. She wanted to scream at him for never helping change a diaper or deal with a teacher, for never coming to Sammy's swim meets. She wanted to scream at him for not coming to the hospital with her and Phe— he's a doctor for God's sakes! Joe didn't respond to her antics in the bathroom, to her childish slamming of drawers and sighs and swearing under her breath. With one last slam of her makeup drawer, Nora stormed into the bedroom, blasting the overhead light on and demanding, "Where is Sullivan? Why is he not home?"

It was then that she noticed what she should have known all along: she was alone. Thoughts darted around her mind like hornets to their nest. Joe is not home. He's not in their bed. His location is turned off. Sullivan is at Chase's. Suddenly Joe's distance these past months descended around Nora like a heavy fog. She could hear the coolness in his voice, see the distraction in his eyes. She pulled her phone out again, desperate to believe she was wrong and that his location was on. It wasn't. She read their last text exchange—she had never responded. He had offered no olive branch for her to respond to, that's true. He hadn't even offered a "Poor Phe," and certainly not "I know you're tired do you want me to come?" The truth of the matter is that Joe hadn't crossed her mind until she had realized Sullivan wasn't at home. Joe hadn't crossed her mind until the red-hot anger of parenting alone had crept up behind her and kidnapped her rational thought. Joe hadn't crossed her mind until he wasn't in her bed.

MAY 27, 2018

JOE

He hadn't meant for it to happen. He realized how cliché that sounded, that he sounded like a spoiled child who simply wanted his way. But the truth is, Joe didn't mean to end up in an unhappy marriage, either. In the beginning, and for most of their marriage, he believed Nora loved him, really loved him. The way Phe loved William. The way his mother loved gin and his father loved women. He thought they would grow old together, hold hands and sit in rocking chairs on their front porch and marvel at the life they created: a gaggle of grandchildren sitting at their feet while their own children rocked in chairs next to them.

Something happened. *Life* happened, he supposed. He was embarrassed that he had become a cliché. The rich doctor with a wife more interested in going to the gym and impressing her trainer (a man younger than their daughter) than she was in impressing her husband. He was the rich doctor having an affair with the divorcée nurse. How basic. He had not intended to become basic, they were supposed to be special. He and Nora were going to be different. It turns out different is difficult.

He found it amazing that Nora didn't know. He saw the other nurses snicker and whisper when he walked into the ICU, he knew the gossip mill that was the hospital. He hadn't done much to cover his tracks. In his heart of hearts he knew what this was about: he wanted his wife's attention. He wondered if Nora would have even noticed or if she would have been too busy tracking Sullivan on FamilyFind, planning his graduation party or heading to the gym with Jordan-The-Ridiculously-Expensive-Trainer-He-Pays-For. Resentment toward his wife swirled in his stomach along with the hangover he was nursing.

In the darkness of the early morning, Joe zipped home from Stephanie's condo to his home of sixteen years to shower before he met Nora at the hospital with Phe. What had sounded so decadent the night before— sleeping with Stephanie nestled in the crook of his arm—made him squirm with disgust as the sun crested the trees behind their home.

He had been so preoccupied with Stephanie at Sullivan's party he hadn't really registered much of his son's night outside of her. They were becoming brazen. He had been excited by her desire for him being displayed in public, the way she touched him when she walked by as if they were the only two at the party, as if Stephanie didn't care who saw that she grabbed his ass when he stood in line for food. For God's sakes he hadn't even gone to the hospital with Nora when Phe broke her hip—he, the doctor—he'd let his wife go to the hospital alone. Of course, Nora hadn't asked for his help and that was a convenient excuse. He was embarrassed to have taken advantage of his mother in law's accident to further his affair.

He let the water of the shower creep toward scalding, both wanting to feel the punishment of the burn and cleanse himself of his decisions. When Nora said goodbye as she left the party she'd given Joe her typical instructions regarding Sullivan's rules, which Joe both resented and disliked. But it wasn't the irritation of his wife not trusting him to parent Sullivan that was haunting him this morning. No, it was the look on Nora's face before she turned to go. There was a flash of emotion that crossed her eyes—sadness? Fear? At the time Joe had equated it to the disruption of her party and Phe's fall, but today, standing under the hot stream of water, Joe knew better. His wife was hurt.

For the first time since his "friendship" with Stephanie began, Joe considered its end. He hadn't thought much about where this relationship would go—in part because he had no right, and in part because he knew he had always known the answer. For months Joe had made decisions based on what was soothing the ache in his heart, not by the difficulty of moral and ethical choices.

Joe stepped out of the shower and dried off his legs

and torso, then wrapped the towel around his middle. He put his hands on the granite counter and leaned into the steam-soaked mirror, struggling to look into his own eyes. When the steam began to clear, Joe was startled to see so much of his father's reflection looking back at him. How had he let this happen?

Joe stopped short when he entered Room 106, swinging open the door and pulling the curtain back as he would for one of his own patients. Sammy had been walking through the door at the same time.

"Hey, Sam. When did you get here?" Joe asked his daughter as he hugged her. Joe was grateful he'd gone home to shower after staying with Stephanie.

"I got here late last night. I knew Mom was tired so I sent her home and I stayed with Phe." Sammy reorganized her purse and belongings on her shoulder avoiding her father's gaze. Joe looked over Sam's shoulder and saw Nora was curled up in the chair beside Phe, sound asleep.

Joe froze.

"I woke up about five o'clock this morning and she was back here already. You know Mom" Sammy smiled. "I'm heading home to shower, I'll come back and sit with mom during surgery." Sammy rubbed her eyes gently and stretched up to her tiptoes to kiss her father on his cheek.

Joe kissed his daughter back and walked through the curtain toward Phe's bed. His heart raced with fear and guilt. His mind tumbled in circles. Nora had gone home. She would know he wasn't there. The mountain of lies that Joe had placed firmly between himself and his wife in the past months began to slide like mud. He looked at his wife, knowing these were the last moments Before. Every moment after this one, once Nora opened her eyes, would be After.

The early morning sun sliced through the blinds and settled in a pool around her, her skin glistened in the light. A thunderbolt of shame seared through him as he watched his wife's slow and steady breaths. In that moment, she looked like His Nora. The Nora who loved him. Not the Nora who resented him and was critical of his every move.

Joe hated to wake her, His Nora. Instead, he wished he had his camera. The light was subtle, gentle; perfect for a portrait. He squeezed his eyes closed briefly, taking a mental snapshot of his wife, peacefully asleep. This was what he had done well in this world. True, he had lost his way, but he would find a way to guide them back to when they were good. And they had been good. The disgrace of becoming his father despite his desperate pleas to the heavens and effort to the contrary for most his life shook Joe to his core. What had he done?

Not wanting to wake Nora yet, Joe whispered as he turned and kissed his mother-in-law on the cheek.

"Good morning, Phe. How are you feeling this morning?"

Nora roused at the sound of his voice. For a moment he thought she might smile at him, at least in his direction, but she didn't. Her gaze cast downward, her eyes blank. "Morning, Nora," he added, tossing a glance in her direction.

"Morning, Joseph," Phe responded first. Her voice thin and scratchy from the dry hospital air and the pain medicine. She was the only one he let call him Joseph. "I'm okay. Ready to get in there and get this hip fixed. I have things to do, you know." Phe smiled and reached for her son-in-law's hand. Nora, for her part, ignored Joe's presence in the small room.

"Nora, did you sleep okay?" Joe looked directly in Nora's direction. Like walking out on a tight wire, he was afraid to look away.

"No, I didn't. I didn't actually sleep at all last night." Nora looked right back at him. "Did you?" Nora's gaze was ice.

"Yes, I slept okay. Willow kept me up all night, she missed you." Joe wasn't sure why he tacked on the lie about the dog, but then he wasn't sure why he did anything these days. Lying had become second nature.

Nora's eyes flashed with anger. "Yes. She was pretty happy to see me when I got there." His pulse quickened and his palms grew sweaty between Phe's long, slender fingers. His mind did a quick calculation, his eyes locked with Nora's and it was clear: she knew.

His hand squeezed Phe's, holding on tightly.

Nora followed Joe out the door of Phe's room. "Where were you?" she hissed when Phe's door was shut behind them.

"Nora, this isn't the place," Joe pleaded.

"This isn't the place? This isn't the fucking place? Are you kidding me? Do you know what's going through my mind? Do you?" She reached her hands up and slapped Joe on the chest with the force of her anger. Her hands recoiled at touching him and he felt the weight of what he had done. She took a long, slow breath and gathered herself. "Tell me where you were. Now. I know you had your location off. The only reason to turn off your location and not come home is obvious. Just give it up."

Joe took a deep breath. "I was with Stephanie Laredo. At her condo. For the night." Joe was contrite as he looked his wife in the eye. He did not want to rub his wife's face in his transgressions, but he also did not want there to be any confusion in his confession.

"Stephanie Laredo?" Nora's lip quivered. "Stephanie Laredo? Elisa Laredo's mother?" Her voice thick with emotion. "You left our son's graduation party with Elisa Laredo's mother while I was in the hospital with my mom?"

It was one thing to relish the thrill of secret meetings

with your mistress, to covet the feel of her skin and the look of longing in her eyes. That, Joe was discovering, was the sweet spot of infidelity. In reality, it was another thing to have your wife suspect you are having an affair and yet another to look your wife in the eye and tell her that her suspicions are true. You have been unfaithful.

Joe expected to feel guilty. And he did. What he hadn't expected to feel was relief. Relief the lying was over, relief that the affair was no longer a secret. In fact, the relief was so strong it flowed out of him like an overflowing glass of water, spilling on the floor of the stark hospital hallway. He was drenched in relief. Oddly, he also felt redemption. Nora was hurting, he had hurt her and somehow that soothed him. He had convinced himself that she would not care if he had an affair. Hell, Nora had convinced him that she would not care. He had not had sex with his wife in months. She had not reached for him in the night or asked for a hug after a long day. She had not asked for help or offered any to him. He may have been the one to have the affair, but she left him first. A long time ago.

A smile escaped his lips as he equated her anger with feeling: she does care about him! For the first time in a long time, Joe felt a spark of hope. What is it they say? The opposite of love is not hate, it's indifference? Nora was definitely not indifferent, and she was definitely angry. There was something here to work with. Joe felt that small spark of hope begin to smolder.

"You're smiling?" Nora was incredulous. She shook her head and walked three steps down the industrial, white-walled hallway and whipped back around, "I have given you nearly three decades of my life and you throw it away on trash like Stephanie Laredo? And then you smile at me?" Her arms flailed around, her face contorted—this person did not vaguely resemble his wife. Anger consumed her like a red tide.

"You know things haven't been right for a long time," Joe began. His response surprised him. In the brief moment he'd had to think through what he should say before Nora had begun yelling, he'd intended to be remorseful. A familiar resentment revisited Joe, years of discontent and anger oozed out from behind Joe's guilt. In an instant, Joe remembered why he had cheated on his wife to begin with, feelings of guilt and relief and remorse cut short.

"Let me ask you a question, Nora. How did you know? When did you realize I wasn't at home? When you didn't answer my last text? When you realized Sullivan wasn't home? Let me guess—you didn't even notice my car was not in the driveway when you got home. I bet you didn't notice I wasn't in the house until you looked to see where Sully was on your phone."

Tears flashed in Nora's eyes. "I have to go sit in the surgical waiting room while my mother has surgery. I cannot talk to you about this right now, she needs me."

"It doesn't even matter if I have an affair— I can't keep your attention!" Joe slammed the wall behind

Nora with his hand, his eyes piercing her anger like daggers, surprising even himself. "You're too busy with the kids, your mother, your phone, Jordan the fucking trainer *I* pay for! So self-important you think the world will fall apart if you don't control it all. Everybody else always needs you more."

"You obviously don't need me," she spit back.

"You are right. I do not need you." Joe turned and walked away from Nora. The strange cocktail of redemption and a numb arrogance of finally pushing Nora too far outweighed the relief or guilt of only moments ago.

JUNE 9, 2018

NORA

Nora's shirt clung to her skin, pulling and hanging awkwardly as she sorted, cleaned, stacked, and organized the guts of her home. Jordan was always talking about functional exercise, she'd have to tell him about this workout if she ever went back to the gym. She'd skipped the last two weeks and had avoided his calls and texts asking where she was.

The front closet was finished—she had piles of shoes for the Goodwill, three bags of trash, some to go to the high school where her friend Karen, a tenth grade English teacher, kept a stockpile of clothes to discreetly hand out to kids in need. She'd dismantled the bookshelf in the front foyer—throwing all of Joe's coveted Tom Clancy novels in the recycle bin and tossing all of the CDs he'd kept from college in the trash. It's not like he'd listened to Joshua Tree on CD in the last ten years. Throwing Joe's stuff away was physically satisfying. With every pile she pounded into the garbage bag she felt a tickle of embellished anger.

Maybe she should break their china dishes from their wedding, or throw their crystal champagne glasses across the room? She contemplated the idea as she moved the leather loveseat and two wingback chairs that were staged around the fireplace and windows looking out toward the bay, dusting and vacuuming around them.

After Phe's first day in the hospital, Joe stayed a few nights at a hotel until Phe was released to Great Lakes Rehab Facility. Nora hadn't spoken to him, not even looked in his direction for the six days Phe was in the hospital. Not when he came to check on Phe. Not when he helped resolve the small infection Phe developed in her incision. Or when he was there to monitor the physical therapist getting her up to walk for the first time. Nora did not look at him. She couldn't. She was afraid if their eyes met, she would become a woman she would feel sorry for. She would beg, she would cry, she would ask why. He had become her kryptonite. Her anger was a shield and she clung to it as a drowning woman to a raft.

When Phe moved into the rehab facility, Joe moved out of the home he had shared with Nora and the kids for sixteen years. Nora kicked him out. There would be no forgiveness, no counseling, no long talks in the night to figure out where they went wrong. No more family dinners or trips to the islands or evenings on their boat. No, Nora deemed Joe's infidelity unforgivable. She had no choice, she said. It was his fault, she reminded herself. He had to leave, she demanded. If Nora thought Joe having an affair was the most embarrassing, painful thing that could have happened she hadn't used her imagination. When she watched her husband and partner of nearly thirty years packing up his bags it became clear, *that* was when her humiliation was complete.

Well, Nora had believed it to be complete. Until Alicia had called to tell her that Joe told Steven he was staying with Stephanie at her condo until he could find a place more suitable. Of course Stephanie, Alicia said, was busy telling everyone Joe had moved in permanently.

So today, Nora was cleaning. The harder she worked the easier it was for her mind to unplug, to dismiss the worry and the anxiety that followed her everywhere she went. She had not been successful at stopping the racehorse thundering in her chest, sweaty hands and nausea—she'd thrown up after the last one. The panic and anxiety sat on the edge of her mind, watching her, waiting for an open door to slide in a sinister foot and slink into her body. What she had been successful at doing was unplugging her mind from all thoughts and ideas that *might* produce a spell. So, she cleaned.

She reached under the master bed and pulled out three large boot boxes. She'd forgotten about those. Joe attended a conference in Dallas, Texas years ago. Long before her dad had gotten sick. Nora tagged along, reading books during the day and joining Joe for cocktails and delicious dinners out in the evening. They'd eaten at Five Sixty in the Reunion Tower, and at Javier's—the famous Mexican restaurant that was part of Dallas's infrastructure. Joe had smoked a cigar with his cohorts in Javier's while Nora drank a heavenly organic prickly pear margarita. The last night of the conference was a cowboy-themed steak dinner and country line dancing. Joe had left his meeting a few hours early and surprised Nora to take her shopping for a pair of boots for the event.

While he'd settled on a pair right away she couldn't decide between a high cut pair with corset-style leather straps up the back that were accented in purple at Cavender's or a deep mahogany leather pair that were as bedazzled as the milky way from Pink's Western Wear—Joe had bought them both and a new dress for each. They'd had such fun that night together. They'd laughed, talked, had sex in the morning before he left and again after dinner when they'd return to their room a little tipsy and a lot tired from laughing and dancing.

Nora sat down on the floor, resting her back against the bed and pulled the purple boots out of the box and ran her hands up and down the intricate cut out designs on the sides. Willow curled up next to Nora, resting her head in her lap with a deep sigh. The smell of leather hit her as her fingers ran along the rugged ridges of the design, coaxing tears from her eyes. If someone had told her that night that she would be here alone, just a few short years later, she would never have believed it.

Embarrassment and anger surged as she shoved the boots back in the box and tossed them in the Goodwill pile.

Nora reached farther under the bed and pulled out an old suitcase and piles of old books—including a coffee table Harley Motorcycle book, a cribbage board and a three random dress socks. More vacuuming, more dusting. She pulled the sheets off the bed and threw them into the wash. The curtains came down and she put them in the dry cleaning bag.

She started on the top shelf of their shared master closet. Teetering on the top step of their four-foot ladder, she pulled down blankets and added them to the laundry pile and piled up old magazines to be recycled. There was a brown archive box she'd saved—letters from when she and Joe had begun dating, letters from her dad after she'd moved to Ann Arbor to be with Joe, letters from her kids when they were young. She cracked open the top, reached in and touched a Christmas card from her dad. Running her fingers over the indentions of his heavy handwriting. She dusted the lid and placed it back on the box. Not today. She wanted to be angry, not sad, not sentimental, not weepy. Angry.

There was another box stacked under the box full of letters. It was black, slim and larger than the one on top.

Nora climbed down off the ladder carrying the box with her. Nora sat down on the floor, crossed her legs and nested the box between her knees.

The top stuck on the corners as she tried to pull it from its counterpart. When the lid finally pulled away from its base Nora was confused. The box was full of pictures. Black and whites, sepia-toned, vibrant, sparkling color. There were small pocket size photos, and larger eight-by-tens and eleven-by-thirteens. Nora picked up a small pile, looking closely at each one.

A black and white of the pier downtown Petoskey in the dead of winter, water thrashing angrily up the sides. The city marina in Harbor Springs, the water washed in the gentle colors of a summer morning. A child eating ice cream sitting outside Yummies—wait, the child was Sullivan! Sullivan eating ice cream sitting outside Yummies in Harbor, the pink building bouncing off his brown eyes, chocolate ice cream dribbling down his chin as he giggled. He's young—maybe ten? Maybe eleven?

Nora picked up a second handful of photos: Sammy fishing off the bridge, Sullivan, Sammy and Nora walking down the Wheelway trail holding hands. Sammy driving a horse and white carriage on Mackinac Island. A sailboat drifting in the bay, her sails quietly at rest. The view of Petoskey and Bay Harbor from Harbor Springs in the height of the summer. A canopy of trees dressed in the peak of their fall colors. There were dozens of photos recounting the past decade of her life as well as photos capturing the beauty and energy of Northern Michigan. They were buoyant in color and subject, their lines sharp and emotion balanced with reality, well... perfectly.

The last photo in the box was a photo of Nora. A black and white eleven-by-thirteen, the largest photo in the box. Her eyes closed with her head tipped back in laughter, her mouth open enough to invite imperfection. It was a close up, her neckline pulled down over her shoulders and her favorite gold necklace lazily lying around her neck. Nora couldn't make out the background of the photo, and she couldn't place the moment in time it was taken.

Joe. *Joe took these?* Nora was stunned at the photographs and their subtle beauty. She had been so caught up in soaking in their details and beauty she hadn't given pause to consider who the photographer had been. It had to be Joe. Sure, she'd bought Joe the camera he'd asked for for Christmas five years ago and she knew he'd had a cheaper version he'd played around with before. Of course she knew he took photos, she was the subject of half of the pictures in the box. But she had no idea he took photos like this!

Why hadn't he told her? Why had she not asked?

Nora cringed feeling another secret exposed between her and her husband. She had always secretly chastised women who had not suspected their husbands of cheating. It's not like it was rocket science, he'll be disinterested, he'll come home late, he'll be distant. Nora hadn't suspected for one second that Joe had been having an affair. Nor had she suspected he had an entire hobby he hadn't shared with her. Or had he?

Hadn't he asked her to walk the Bear River trails with her, camera in hand? Hadn't he asked her to come downtown while he shot a few winter scenes? He had. She hadn't gone. She hadn't since her dad died. Well, she had… early on. She remembers walking the wheel way with Joe and watching him shoot some photos while they skied at Nubs Nob, but that's it. She wanted to text Joe, tell him she'd found the photos. Tell him how impressed she was. He was an artist! But no—

Anger. Isn't that what she had decided to allow today? Anger. No sadness, no sentimental feelings. No nostalgia or sadness. Anger. But how was she to feel angry when the images in this box so brilliantly depicted what she'd thought her life looked like these past years. Her perfect family. Her perfect home. Nora put the photos back in the box and placed the box back up where she found it.

Her life had been busy, she'd been raising two children and maintaining the house. There was the PTO and the football boosters, swim team board meetings. Then there was her dad's cancer—no one could blame her for being distracted while her father died! She volleyed the blame of Joe's affair and the end of her marriage back and forth in her mind—first guilt for not having been more available to her husband, then reminding herself she had been one hundred percent faithful to the vows she'd made. No matter that she had been distracted, no matter that she had not been the best wife—she had been faithful. She had been true. She had cared for Joe's children and his home in the best way she knew how. *He* had been unfaithful. *He* had broken their vows. She would not harbor guilt or sadness about the end of their life together. No, Joe was to blame. Nora shut the door to her closet, sealing in the photographs and the remnants of any guilt she felt and fostering her anger toward the man who had ruined her perfect life.

NORA

If Nora had one wish it would be that she had never met Joe Phillips.

Of course, that wasn't really true. If she had not met Joe she would not have Sammy and Sullivan. And they are reason enough to live through Joe.

No, if Nora had one wish it would be that her perfect family would be put back together again. As long as she was ordering up what she wanted: Nora wanted Joe to come home. She wanted Sullivan to never leave. She wanted Sammy to still be her little girl and she wanted her dad to still be alive and for Phe to never age.

When Joe first left she was mortified. She spent nearly a month hiding inside her home on Trillium Drive, afraid to venture out and see someone who might know about her. Then, her embarrassment was fueled by anger and now... now the rage had descended down the slippery slope of anxiety.

Today, Nora was picking up her mom from Great Lakes Rehab and moving her into Joe and Nora's master bedroom. It only made sense. Phe needed help and couldn't stay alone in her condo on the bay, and Nora had not slept in her bed since she found out about Joe's affair.

Nora would like to say that she was being altruistic. That inviting Phe to stay with her was out of the goodness of her heart and that she had a deep desire to help her mother recover. It was true that she wanted her mother to be better, she adored Phe. But if she was honest she would admit it was because she needed her mother's help. She wanted her mother's sympathy. She was helping her mother to save herself.

And there was the matter of an empty house. Sullivan was rarely home. He had taken the news of his father's affair as most teenage boys would. With outward ambivalence that reared its ugly head as anger far too often. He was always angry. And he was always angry at Nora, she was the heavy. The enforcer of the rules. Yet another injustice Nora must suffer because Joe didn't keep his wedding vows.

Phe was waiting in her room, sitting up in the rocker with a smart blue pantsuit, a floral print silk shirt underneath the jacket. Her hair was coiffed perfectly. Nora's heart nearly broke at the sight of her mom. She'd lost weight. Phe—who stood at only five-foot—looked frail.

"Hi, Mom," Nora said, her dull smile not reaching her eyes. She felt her heart begin to ache.

"Hello, dear. How are you?" Phe asked with concern.

Nora's eyes turned downward as she answered, "I'm fine. Just fine! You ready to come home with me?" Nora tried desperately to display strength, to show that she was handling this crisis with grace and dignity. To give her mother a hook to hang her confidence on. Nora looked Phe in the eye. "I thought we could go to Turkey's in Harbor Springs for lunch!" Nora forced an upbeat lilt into her words.

"That would be lovely. I love their turkey club," Phe said with a small smile.

"Then that's what we'll do!" Nora exclaimed with fake enthusiasm.

"You don't have to do that"

"Do what?"

"Pretend everything is fine." Phe smiled up at her daughter from her chair.

"I'm not pretending. I'm fine. Everything is just fine."

"I'm not sure I would call your husband having an affair, moving out and living with his mistress 'fine.'" Phe patted the seat of the chair next to hers.

Anxiety burned in Nora's belly, the heat rising up through her chest and forming a lump in her throat. Something wasn't right. "I don't want to sit down, I want to take you to Turkey's for lunch and then settle you in at home."

"Nora. Sit down. I need to talk to you." It wasn't a request.

Nora sat.

She perched herself on the edge of her seat like a bird on a telephone wire, ready to take flight at the slightest hint of danger. That's how she felt every minute of the day now, afraid. Fearful. Waiting for the next crisis.

"Thank you. Don't look so worried. I'm not dying." Phe giggled. Nora always loved her mom's giggle. Her shoulders rose up, framing her face and the bright smile that was nearly always there. Today, her giggle was a shadow of the one that usually captivated Nora. "I'm happy to go to Turkey's for lunch with you. I'm just not coming home with you."

It was Nora's turn to laugh. "You have to. Where are you going to go? You already said you aren't dying so that's not an option."

"I'm going home," Phe answered.

"We've been through this. You can't go home. It's not safe!" Nora's voice began to rise in frustration. "We've been over this. You are not going home."

"Nora. I am seventy-five years old. I broke my hip. A *month* ago! I get around just fine. I am going home." Phe calmly folded her hands and rested them in her lap. "And we *have* been over this. The doctors agree— even Joseph agrees— that I am capable of living alone. I have made arrangements to have an alert button and I had a railing put in the bathroom. I will be just fine. You were the only one who did not agree I could go home. And despite what you think, you don't actually make my decisions for me."

Nora seethed at the mention of Joe's name. *How dare*

he. It's not bad enough he has humiliated and embarrassed her in front of the entire town, now he is contradicting the plan she set for her mother! "What does Joe have to do with any of this?"

"I trust him. He thinks I will be fine," Phe answered cautiously.

"Trust him? You trust him. That's rich," Nora spat out.

"I am not married to the man. He's a doctor, I trust his judgment that I will be okay going home. To my house. To live. Alone." Phe took a deep breath. "It's not up for debate. I am going home." It was clear that Phe had made up her mind— thanks to Joe— and it was also clear that she wanted Nora on board.

"This isn't about me, dear. This is about you. You don't really want me to come live with you. You just don't want to be alone."

"That's not true, Mom! It's not. I love you. I want to take care of you. I want you to be safe." Nora cried, not the small manageable tears of a few moments ago. Her heart began to pound, really pound. A gentle shake started in her chest and spread through her fingertips.

"It's just not your job to keep me safe. Not yet, anyway." Phe giggled again.

Nora nodded her head, emotion rendering her silent. She wished she could tell her mom what she was really thinking. *I'm so homesick, Mom. I'm so homesick it hurts. I want my life back. I want my marriage back and I want my son back. I want my daughter back. I want my father back. I want my life back. I don't recognize myself in the mirror, I don't even know who I am or what I'm doing here. And I am so, so sad.* Nora couldn't bring herself to say the words. Nora could not put into words the cruel twist of fate that her father was not here to help her through the loss of her marriage— her perfect family.

"When I lost your father, the second-worst thing that could ever happen to me, happened to me. Second to losing you and your family. And I survived it. That's when I realized, really learned, that the only thing I couldn't survive was death. Everything else... well I've got strength for that. And you do, too. I know you're hurting. But you will survive."

"I want my perfect family back. I want my perfect life back." Her feelings spilling over into words like the hot tears stinging her cheeks.

"I'm sorry," Phe attempted to empathize. She reached for her daughter's hand, embracing it in an awkward, warm squeeze.

"It's not your fault."

"I am sorry. I'm sorry you are hurting, so sorry. I am also sorry you think you had a perfect life. And I'm more sorry you want it back."

Nora took Phe to pick up a few items at Glen's after their lunch at Turkey's. When they got to Phe's condo,

Nora did a quick tour for safety hazards. Phe did in fact have the alert button and the railings in the bathrooms, much to Nora's secret disappointment. She had hoped she could trump her mother's decision if the safety measures weren't adequate. Nora helped her mom put away her groceries, settled her in, and left. She drove around for a while. The views in Petoskey were stunning from nearly every corner. It didn't matter where she went, the bay was always there. Steady. An anchor. The town was tethered to the water. She had always loved that she could do something simple like run to the grocery store, walk out, and the view would take her breath away. Nora hated that Joe's actions had changed everything, even the view of the lake. Where once she saw beauty and felt connected to the world, she now saw melancholy and uncertainty.

When Nora pulled into Joe's office parking lot, she was neither surprised nor certain that this is where she ended up. Everything about the building was familiar. It should have been. Not only had it been her husband's office for most of their married life, she had worked with the architect to redesign it, and the landscapers to develop the garden plan. She picked the color of the brick and the trim on the windows. The carpet inside was called "barnboard" and the wall paint was "dusky bay." Joe had worked with Nora to come up with the design of the patient rooms, nursing station, lab room and triage rooms. They had made it functional together, but Nora had made it beautiful—if a doctor's office could be beautiful—on her own.

Faye, Joe's receptionist, looked up from her desk with a smile that cracked when she saw Nora. Faye and Nora had been friends through their boys for years—Sullivan and Chase had been best friends since the second grade. This reunion was awkward for them both.

"Good afternoon, Faye. Is Joe busy?" She kept her tone formal and her smile steady. Nora knew it was a ridiculous question. Of course he was busy, it was 3:00 in the afternoon, on a Wednesday for God's sakes. He would be busy with patients until 6:00.

"Ummm... yes? He is," Faye answered.

Nora stood tall, all five foot three inches of her, and wished she had worn a pair of heels instead of her ballet flats. "Would you please tell him I'm here to speak to him? I just need a few minutes." Nora smiled and sat down in the nearest chair to the window. She made up her mind she would not leave until she saw him.

"I can try, but he is already overbooked today," Faye said, returning Nora's formal tone.

"That's okay. I'll wait." Nora picked up a *People* magazine and began flipping through the pages.

Nora followed Joe down the short hallway to his office in the back. His steps were quick, his footfalls hitting the ground with more vigor than Nora felt necessary. Once in his office, he shut the door and said not unkindly, "What do you need, Nora?"

"Why in the hell did you tell Phe she would be fine living at home? Her home? Alone?"

"Because she will be," Joe answered. Nora's anger boiled as Joe stayed calm.

"She will *not* be! The woman fell walking out of The Stafford and broke her hip! Are you insane? You know she adores you—even after what you did! You know she listens to everything you say. How could you go against what you know I wanted? *Again!*" Nora spat the words out quickly. Her heart was racing, her hands were moist. He was never on her side.

"Because it's what she wanted. It's what Phe wanted. And I do believe she will be safe. She's not your project, Nora. You can't replace Sullivan with your mother."

"Don't fucking tell me what to do." Nora's anger was red hot. Here they were again, having the same argument they always came back to. Nora wanted one thing, Joe disagreed. No compromise, no discussion, only opposite feelings. It didn't matter if the topic at hand was Phe, or Sullivan's curfew, or Sammy's swim meets. The bottom line was always the same. Joe was never on her side.

"I wouldn't dream of telling you what to do. In fact, what you do is none of my business, unless it has to do with Sully or Sammy. You are the one who came here.

To my office. To my business. I have patients to see. Is that all you came for?" Joe turned toward the door, resting this hand on the knob. The patience Nora had seen just moments ago had evaporated.

"I'm not finished," Nora spat back. Anger flashed in her eyes. "Why are you never on my side? You have never been on my side. How dare you go to my mother and give her advice that directly opposes what *I* want her to do! How dare you!" Nora's voice was hoarse, tears threatening her anger. Her heart began its race—the one that came before an attack. Fear spread through Nora's cells like shards of shattered glass. No—she couldn't have a panic attack here.

"Shouldn't this be about what Phe wants? This isn't about you! This isn't even about us! This is about Phe wanting to live independently, on her own. It's about her *not* wanting to live with you! If you haven't noticed, she's not the only one!" The comment stung just as he'd intended it to. "You can't tell everyone how to live! It's suffocating! Can't you see that?"

"I do not tell everyone how to live! This is not telling her how to live! This is me worrying for my mother's safety and you putting her in danger just to be spiteful to me! As if sleeping with the town tramp behind my back wasn't spiteful enough!" Nora was nearly screaming now, her hands shaking and her voice cracking. Joe motioned with his hand for her to keep her voice down.

"You don't tell us how to live? You don't tell me

when Sullivan's curfew is? You don't tell me whose house he's allowed to stay at and whose he's not? You don't tell me daily how to parent my own son? You don't track his every move? You don't tell your mother where she will live? No wonder Sammy moved so far away!" he whisper-yelled back at his wife.

"It's nice of you to finally take an interest in parenting, Joe. You never stayed up all night with either of the kids. You never changed a dirty diaper. You never went to a single parent-teacher conference. Do you even *know* who Sullivan's doctor is? If you had been around to help parent the kids I wouldn't have had to make all the decisions on my own! You left all the dirty work to me and now that he's nearly grown you have decided to have an opinion? Fuck you, Joe. That's not how it works!" Nora's chest was pounding now—so thick and heavy was her heartbeat she felt the hot thrumming of the racehorse deep in her ears.

"Never changed a dirty diaper? I wasn't *allowed* to change a dirty diaper. I never did it good enough! Besides, he's eighteen-years-old—talk about dredging up old bullshit!"

"It's all bullshit! Never did it good enough? What does that even mean?" Nora rolled her eyes.

"It doesn't mean anything now. Look. I have to get back to work. I sent you an email earlier did you get it?" Nora looked back at Joe and shook her head. "I've scheduled an appraiser to come to the house. We need to know how much it's worth for the divorce agreement. His name is Robert Wolf. He'll give you a call to schedule a time to come by."

Nora looked back at him in disbelief. For the last month she had been denying this was happening. Suddenly she felt exposed, she could have been standing in the middle of Joe's office naked. "I don't have a lawyer," she said by way of answering.

"Well, you need to get one." With that Joe turned and walked out of his office.

JOE

Joe walked into Stephanie's condo and slapped his keys on the brown Formica counter. He looked around the kitchen, two cupboard doors were hanging just left of straight. A basil plant stood dying in the corner in front of the window above the sink. Loneliness was painted on the walls in the dirty beige paint. The edginess that blew in with Nora's visit to his office had yet to soften. He had been sharp with his staff and quick with patients, he needed to clean up his act but couldn't quite pull himself together. He knew what he needed—he'd grab his camera and head into Harbor Springs, try and get some good night pictures of the Pearl Necklace—the lights of Petoskey and Bay Harbor against the bay from the Harbor side. He'd been working on different light settings and wanted to see what he could come up with. He'd grab something to eat, take his camera, and lose himself in the lens.

Stephanie had plans with her daughter Elise tonight, and he was grateful for that. Joe opened the fridge door for a quick bite before he left. There was leftover mac and cheese and two strawberry yogurts, nothing appetizing to him. He and Stephanie ate out most nights. Taking her out to eat felt more like dating and less like living together—and Joe was trying desperately to keep that distinction. He was staying with Steph, yes. But it was not his intention to live here long-term. Yet, he hadn't done much about changing that.

The divorce was in process, the papers had been filed. Yet, Nora seemed surprised when Joe mentioned the appraiser—she hadn't even retained a lawyer. She had been the one to ask him to move out of their home, she'd been the one who said she could never forgive him, she had been the one who started the fights—but he had been the one to file for divorce and he wasn't sure why.

He wasn't ready to end his marriage. The thought was as clear as glass when he was alone and the chatter of the day, his patients, Stephanie, and even Nora was quiet. He realized it sounded ridiculous as he stood in the middle of his mistress's condo—where he was living—but the truth remained. Joe wasn't ready to divorce Nora. So why had he filed?

Joe walked to the bedroom to change his clothes. He was embarrassed of fighting with his wife in his office, of allowing the emotions get the best of him. He was pissed that a conversation about Phe turned into throwing accusations about changing diapers and Nora's control problem. Overwhelming exhaustion consumed him at the thought of divorce proceedings and dividing their assets and the kids and holidays and his practice. If they could not have a conversation about Phe without screaming at each other, how would they ever get through the rest? He was exhausted at the thought of divorce—and exhausted at the thought of fixing the mess they had made.

Joe pulled clothes out of his suitcase. Stephanie had cleared drawers for him but he had been adamant that his clothes stay separated, in their suitcase not mixed with hers. He slid his long, slender legs into a pair of jeans and pulled on a white V-neck T-shirt. He was certain Phe should be living on her own, he wasn't second-guessing his endorsement of her decision. That wasn't what was bothering him.

It was Nora's anger. He knew that she had every right. He had expected her to be angry at first, certainly, he just hadn't expected it to last so long. When Nora first found out at the hospital the morning of Phe's surgery, Joe had taken her anger as a token of hope. He thought it was a reflection of how much she cared. Now, the weight of it hung around his neck like a yolk. He had been flippant in realizing how hurt his wife would be and that was as regretful as the act itself. *How could he have been so wrong?*

The affair had started innocently enough—well, as innocently as a married man flirting with a younger divorcée is. Stephanie's daughter had been a cheerleader for Sullivan's football team. They became friendly watching the games together with other parents. Stephanie had been new in town, having just moved to Petoskey from Cadillac. She always seemed to settle in along the fence where Joe and the other dads stood, not with the other men's wives clumped together up in the stands. The moms rang cowbells and cheered loudly, yelling at the referees even when they made the right call. Later Stephanie would tell Joe in confidence how she'd tried to befriend the other moms but they wouldn't accept her. Other women weren't nice to her, she'd said. Joe had felt the injustice on behalf of his mistress. He'd even felt a surge of anger toward his wife that she hadn't been welcoming and kind. "If you weren't so pretty they would be nice to you," he'd whispered to her one evening during the game. Her smile secretive—they were co-conspirators—she answered, "That's what my momma always says." Joe was beginning to see that differently now.

One night as the dads stood congratulating each other with pats on the back after a particularly close win, Sullivan had jogged to the sidelines carrying his helmet and hugged his dad after the game, as was their tradition. "I can see why my daughter has a crush on Sullivan. Your son looks just like you," she had said. Joe's heart had skipped a beat. Literally, it fluttered.

It had been so long since someone had taken an interest in him. Nora had been preoccupied, since her father passed away. She'd spent months caring for her dad, helping her mom while William underwent treatments for pancreatic cancer. Joe told his wife he understood, William was one of Joe's favorite people, and taking care of her dad was paramount. When William passed Nora had been bereft. Joe gave her time to grieve and heal—after six months Nora was still struggling and Joe had suggested she see Dr. Bateman, perhaps got some medication. She'd been furious—no pill could bring her father back and neither could talking about how much she missed him. Joe wasn't close to his parents, so clearly he couldn't understand what she was going through, she'd said.

So, Joe was patient—or had thought he had been. Looking back now he saw the line in the sand. She thought he didn't understand, she thought he couldn't understand. She'd mistaken his concern—his lame attempt to fix things with a suggestion of a doctor's visit and medication—as a dismissive offer. She hadn't needed him to fix it. She needed him to be on her side. In her corner. A few months before he'd left home he'd found a bottle of Xanax in Nora's purse. He'd been smug that she needed them—he'd been right and she'd been stubborn and didn't want his help when he offered it. He'd withheld his support. The shame was heavy.

You are never on my side.

Slowly, Nora had looked like she was coming around—she involved herself again in the PTA and started seeing Jordan The Trainer. She updated rooms in the house and even re-did the bathroom in his office. She provided a lot of support for Phe, and Joe had been proud of all of that she did. He continued to wait for Nora's time and attention to return. It never came.

Nora did not turn to him. Not in her grief, not in her healing. She became more absorbed in raising Sullivan, guiding Sammy and seemingly forgot about Joe and what he might need. Joe was lonely, he felt abandoned and isolated. Until Stephanie began showering him with attention.

He had smiled back at Stephanie the night she complimented him and he filed the coy look on her face away to bring out when he was feeling down. He had no intentions of moving forward. It was, however, nice to be the object of someone's attention.

Joe began to run into Stephanie at work. She was a nurse in the ER and, as a plastic surgeon, Joe was routinely called in to look at stitches that were in conspicuous spaces—foreheads and eyebrows, chins. Sometimes trauma patients needed his expertise. Steph was always friendly and cute. Squeezing his arm hello, making sure she came to say goodbye before he left the department. If he consulted on one of her patients, she would rave about him. He had basked in her attention, she had been a welcome warmth. They began sharing coffee over her break. Always in the cafeteria. Always in full sight. Joe told himself if he spent time with Stephanie in full view of everyone he could not be doing anything wrong.

Occasionally he wondered if Nora would find out. He often fantasized about her being jealous and angry that he was spending time—at the time *platonic* time—with another woman. There were days he mentioned Stephanie in Nora's presence hoping to get a rise but it never seemed to register with his wife.

When Nora and Joe had first met the summer after their senior years in high school they spent every moment together until Joe went off to college. The two stayed together, Joe at the University of Michigan studying Pre-Med and Nora back at home in Harbor Springs working at her mom's store. Becky, a girl in his anatomy and physiology lab, began calling Joe frequently. Asking for help with homework, asking him to escort her out to her car after dark. Nora had not said a word when he'd mentioned it—she would just send a sideways glance his way when Becky's name came up.

Until Nora had come down to Ann Arbor for the weekend. They were snuggled on the couch watching *Friends* when Becky called asking Joe to come to the bar where she was. Nora snatched the phone from Joe's hand and said, "Hi Becky, this is Nora. Joe's girlfriend.

He's busy tonight, and every other night. With me. Don't call him again!" She had carefully put the phone back on the cradle and kissed Joe fiercely. She was staking her claim. He had never spoken to Becky again. It was that night he knew he would marry Nora, it was the night he knew he was hopelessly in love with his future wife.

Nora's anger over Stephanie was different, it wasn't territorial or out of love for Joe. At least Joe didn't see it that way. It was out of embarrassment, out of loss. She was angry her life had been upended, but Joe was not convinced she was angry or hurt that Joe was gone. Of course, that is an assumption on his part. He hasn't asked Nora how she feels about any of it. She hasn't given him the chance and he hasn't tried.

It wasn't just Nora's anger that was weighing on him. It was something else she said, *You are never on my side.* He knew he changed a dirty diaper, at least with Sammy he did. But truthfully, it wasn't many. And he *didn't* actually know who Sullivan's doctor was, how could that be?

Loneliness ached in the cracks of his soul where Nora's neglect resided. He knew it wasn't fair to say she neglected him, he had never wanted for anything. His clothes were always clean, dry cleaning picked up, house was immaculate, kids were taken care of and dinner was always prepared. Regardless of what she did, he knew how he felt: neglected. If she had asked him he would have told her he would trade all of that for her time, for her attention. He felt juvenile now, thinking about what he didn't get from his wife.

Raising kids isn't easy for anybody, and he knows that raising his kids was harder than some. Eighty-to-ninety-hour work weeks were hard on a marriage, hard on a person. But it was what needed to be done. It just is what it is. Or was it? Had there been another way? Had Joe used work to skirt the parenting duties he didn't want to do? Probably. He rolled the cuffs of his shirt up in frustration.

Joe pulled out his phone and opened up his text messages.

Joe: *Hey how's it going? Just checking in.*

Sammy: *Something wrong?*

Joe: *No! Not at all. Just seeing how you are. Everything going okay?*

Sammy: *Okkkk... yeah I'm fine. What's really up?*

Joe: *I can't just text my daughter to see how she's doing?*

(Joe struggled to find a smirking emoji but his eyes weren't making it easy to see which yellow face was which and he was afraid to send the grumpy or upset emoji instead, so he settled for :-))

Sammy: *You don't do that.*

Joe: *What do you mean I don't do that? Of course I check in on you.*

Sammy: *Scroll back. The last time you texted me was three weeks ago. And even then you were answering my check-in text.*

Joe quickly swiped downward, she was right. He hadn't reached out to his daughter in weeks.

Joe: *I'm going to try and do better at that. I miss you.*

Sammy: *Yeah, I guess divorce does that to people.*

Joe: *What's that supposed to mean?*

Sammy: *It changes you. You never texted me before because Mom always did, you didn't have to. Now you "are going to try and do better."*

Joe: *I'm going to do better. I promise. Can you come up and have dinner this weekend or next?*

(Suddenly, Joe was desperate to see his daughter's face).

Sammy: *Booked up the next two weekends. I'll look and see what I have going on later in the month and let ya know. I gotta run. See ya*

Joe: *Great, let me know please.*

Joe slid his phone across the Formica countertop. Nora was right. He had left all the heavy lifting when it came to parenting the kids to her. She had done the lion's share of the work. At the time, it only seemed fair. Nora wasn't working, she was staying home with the kids—it only seemed right that she would take care of it all. Hindsight is twenty-twenty. He was contributing, but he had participated as a parent in the way he *wanted*, not how she or the kids needed.

You are never on my side.

It was so much easier to stay angry at Nora. Joe could continue this line of thinking—he could do mental gymnastics trying to figure out the *why* of what he'd done—it wouldn't be difficult to draw the line from his alcoholic mother and absentee, womanizing father to his actions but he was tired. He was hungry. He would save further self-loathing and introspection for another day.

For now, Joe gathered his camera equipment and pulled a sweatshirt over his head. Just the thought of snapping a few shots and working on the light settings began settling his thoughts. Distraction. That's what he needed.

When the door swung open Joe was so deep in thought it startled him when Stephanie walked into the room. "Oh, hey," he said. "What are you doing here? I thought you were going out with Elise tonight to the movies?" The disappointment of her arrival was thick in his tone.

"Yeah, I was. But I decided I wanted to hang out with you more. I didn't want you to be alone," Stephanie answered.

"I am nearly fifty-years-old and perfectly happy to spend an evening alone," Joe said. "Where is Elise?"

"Oh well, I am not sure. I just texted her on my way home and told her I wasn't gonna make it to the movies and dinner tonight." Stephanie shied away from his gaze.

"Don't do that. Text her back. I'm fine. Go see your daughter," Joe implored. While he did generally enjoy Stephanie's companionship, tonight he was a far cry from needing it and nowhere near wanting it.

"She'll have changed plans already. It's fine. I promise. Tonight it will be just you and me."

Joe's frustration grew. "You told Elise it would be just you and her tonight. You should do what you said you would. She's your daughter."

"She doesn't care," Stephanie said flippantly as she tugged at the strings on Joe's sweatshirt hood, sliding her fingers around the knots, pulling him closer. She pulled Joe in for a kiss.

I do! thought Joe. *I do care that you just dumped your daughter!* This is something Nora would never do. She would never bail on Sammy or Sullivan to hang out with Joe. Wasn't that the problem? Wasn't that what Joe was complaining about all this time? Nora didn't give him enough attention, she was distracted, she paid too much attention to the kids? He should be loving that Stephanie was so eager to please him. He should be thrilled that she dumped her daughter to spend time with him. But he's not. Instead, the steady trickle of regret he'd known was there since the day he walked out, dripped faster. *Nora would have never done this.*

STEPHANIE

Stephanie saw the shadow cross Joe's eyes. She felt the cool dip in his temperature. She hadn't thought about what to do with the darkness she saw, but her body knew. Sliding her fingers around the knot of his sweatshirt strings and pulling him in for a kiss came quickly—on instinct. She pressed her chest against him, teasing him with just enough pressure—and left him short. She wasn't proud of manipulating her man with her body, so she didn't look at it that way. She decided to look at it as if she was reminding him what a great thing they had. If she was being honest, which she often wasn't, Stephanie would tell you that her greatest fear since Joe walked into her life was coming true. He was preparing to walk out.

NORA

Nora sat in the corner, tucked up against the wall and with her back to the door. The red wrap dress showed a peek of her thigh as she sat cross-legged at the bar. She tugged on the forgiving material, trying to cover a few more inches of her skin. Her hands gently held the stem of her wine glass, she had trouble deciding where to put them. The restaurant was situated on top of a hill in the Gaslight district of town. She chose a barstool positioned to take in the view from the back windows out to the bay, which was a spectacular showcasing of the sun splashing off of the waves, making diamonds dance across the water. Nora took a deep breath. She imagined pushing her anxiety deep down into her belly like the plug in her bathtub drain. *Not tonight,* she thought. Tonight she was taking herself out to dinner— it was the week of July Fourth, and her father's birthday. Where others love Christmas, Nora's favorite has always been this week of summer. The world stops spinning and the magic of Northern Michigan is in full swing—evening fireworks out on the boat, Joe's Famous Smoked Ribs, fresh strawberry and blueberry shortcake (special red-white-and-blue-birthday edition for her dad!), her toes in the sand at the beach and surfing the waves with the kids.

None of those things were happening this week.

So she would start a new tradition with herself, a red dress and dinner out to kick off the holiday weekend.

Joe and Nora always brought the kids to the Twisted Olive for their birthdays. She had no idea why she chose to come here alone. This restaurant held so many happy memories for her and Joe and the kids, perhaps she should have chosen somewhere new, different. Or perhaps the reason she chose the Olive was so that she *could* be reminded. Reminded that she was happy once upon a time and could be happy again. She could have asked Alicia or Fran, both women had offered repeatedly to have a "girls' night" with her—but she didn't. Phe had offered to come, but Nora didn't want that either. Intellectually Nora understood they were all trying to be supportive, but she couldn't bear an evening of questions—or worse yet, pity. It was bad enough she was the woman scorned, she didn't want them to see she was also the pathetic woman who didn't know what to do with herself now that her life was ruined. Their never-ending fountain of positive thinking and cheerleading wasn't what she needed. She needed to sit in her loneliness. Not wallow, per se, but she needed to just be present in the fact that this was now her life. She wanted to be strong. She wanted to do something besides lay on the couch and cry.

Another deep sigh, and then a long sip of her pinot noir. Usually she stuck to a house version—Elouan or Mark West. Tonight she had perused the wine list, scanned for a pinot, evaluated the price, and picked the most expensive glass she could find. She found fleeting hiccups of joy using Joe's credit card. Alicia and Fran were concerned he may turn her credit off although Nora couldn't see Joe doing that. But of course she hadn't seen his affair coming, either.

If it wasn't difficult enough for her to be a single, lonely patron sitting at the bar, Jason and Shelly Dodds came through the door. Nora thought back to Jason's cool demeanor the night Phe was in the ER. He must have known about Joe and Steph. Nora had assumed she had offended him in some way—she was embarrassed now that she realized he couldn't look Nora in the eye because he'd known about the affair. Tonight he smiled warmly with his wife as they exchanged pleasantries with Nora. Her wine glass was filled, compliments of the two of them.

At least the bartender waiting on her was Gatsby. He was the caretaker of Joe's family's beach house in Harbor Springs—"Beachside"—he mowed the lawn, took care of the snow, did spring cleanup and any minor repairs the renters discovered. He was also Sammy's lifetime crush—he was two years older than Samantha in high school—and although he was a nice kid, he hadn't much noticed the cute sophomore to his high-school-god-seniorhood. Nora smiled now at the nights they'd sat up, mother and daughter, analyzing a casual "hello" in the hallway or how Sammy's heart broke and she sat sobbing when The Great Gatsby asked Jewel Gibson to prom. Joe contended that Gatsby wasn't good enough for Sammy anyway, a stance that irked Nora. Yes, their daughter was special. She loved Sammy dearly—but she hated the thought that some father somewhere would tell his daughter that Sullivan Phillips would never be good enough for his crush.

Her phone chimed with a new text.

Sammy: *Hey whats up?*

Nora smiled. There was a guilt she supposed all mothers carried when their children grew up. An echo of every slight she had passed down to her children, every mistake and every regret came back in triplicate when she felt she had no time left to rectify them. Her failures as a mother seemed more brilliant now in light of her pending divorce and Nora was grateful that despite her many shortcomings as a mother, Sammy still reached out to Nora. When Joe left, Sammy began checking in daily—sometimes multiple times a day. Nora knew she should encourage Sammy to keep on with her life, to not look back at her parents with obligation, but the essence of her daughter caring was a narcotic to the anxiety and pain Nora felt. She wasn't strong enough yet to go it alone, she needed her daughter.

Nora: *Hi sweet pea I am having a glass of wine at the Olive.*

Sammy: *Good for you, Momma! Who are you with?*

A pang of embarrassment shot through Nora like a lightning bolt. She could lie. She could say she *was* here with Alicia or Fran—or both! She could pretend Phe was here with her. It would settle Sammy's worry for the evening. Self-pity took ahold of Nora as she answered.

Nora: *No one. I'm alone.*

Sammy: *Oh… are you okay?*

Nora: *okay enough*

Sammy: *Want me to come home this weekend for Saturday night?*

Nora: *I would love that honey, I really would, but you don't have to.*

Sammy: *I will call you Saturday morning! I don't have anything going on here, anyway.*
Love you Mom, hope you enjoy yourself

Nora: *I don't know about enjoying myself, but it's better than sitting home alone I guess*

Sammy: *For sure!!!*

Nora: *Night Sam-I-Am I love you*

Sammy: *Love you tooooo*

Nora rested her phone on the granite bar top next to her wine glass. She knew her happiness was too heavy a burden for her children to carry. Still, she was grateful for the quick lifeline Sammy had thrown her. She swiped through her recent text messages pretending to have business to attend to, to have someone who needed her. She longed for the past, when her phone rang incessantly about missing assignments, canceled practices, changes in the schedule, back-ordered carpet for the office. Sitting alone in a bar drinking wine in a red dress had sounded empowering—in reality she was embarrassed. Another long sip, the wine heating her from the inside out. Flashes of anger toward Joe shot hot, like arrows off of Katniss's bow. Sullivan had loved *The Hunger Games*. She had been unsure he should read them. Joe had insisted she stop babying Sully, so she read them to him. Resentment, anger and humiliation were a powerful cocktail, Nora had drunk enough of it lately.,

Her phone rang. By now she recognized the unknown number: the appraiser. She had pushed him off once today, declining the call immediately. She did so again, silencing the call feeling righteous that no one could expect her to answer a phone call at the bar! In her old life, she would have never procrastinated doing something that needed to be done. She would have added it to her list, called, scheduled and executed the task and crossed it off, moving on. There was a line in the sand—before Joe left and after Joe left. After Joe left she has become a disorganized and passive woman.

"Mrs. Phillips, can I top you off?" Gatsby smiled at Nora. The kid was handsome. Of course, he was closer to thirty than twenty, so he wasn't *really* a kid anymore.

"Sure. Thank you," Nora looked over Gatsby's shoulder toward the bay, uncomfortable suddenly with being called "Mrs. Phillips." Should she change her name? A shudder flickered through her chest. No, she could never do that. The thought of Sammy, Sullivan, and Joe all sharing the Phillips name while she retreated to become Nora Sullivan again spouted anxiety up from the depth of her belly, the adrenaline shooting out toward her fingers, making her limbs tingle. She physically ached at the dissolution of her family. No, she would never change her last name. She would remain Nora Phillips, if only to remind herself, every day, that her perfect family had been real. Joe could take back his marriage vows, his commitment to their family, and her dignity, but he could not take back her name.

"How's Sammy doing?" Gatsby ventured, his eyes trained on the bottle of wine he was opening for Nora.

"She's fine! Great, in fact. She's working downstate in Lansing, at Auto Owners. She just got a promotion and she has a cute little loft apartment with some girlfriends. She's doing well! She loves it there. It's a perfect fit for her." Nora laid on thick Sammy's new life, even if it was an exaggeration, in silent solidarity with her daughter.

"That's great! Good for her. Sully? How's he doin'?" Gatsby handed Nora her newly refreshed glass.

"Sullivan... Sullivan is Sullivan. He leaves for CMU in about a month. He's excited."

"Ahh… last one to leave the nest! Big plans after he's gone?"

Nora felt her cheeks flushed. *Big plans? I barely got myself here tonight.* "No, nothing yet. It will take some getting used to," Nora answered.

"Have you been to Beachside? The yard looks beautiful. And there is a pair of loons who have been hanging out around the house. Looks like they'll be there until they fly south. Pretty neat, you should check them out."

"I'll let Joe know," was all that Nora could say.

Gatsby smiled at Nora and turned his attention toward the newly-seated couple next to her. Nora looked out toward the water, wanting to ignore the street behind her.

That's it then, Nora thought. Life goes on. People came and went through the door of the restaurant, others walked down the street laughing and holding hands behind her. A normal evening in everyone's normal life and Nora sat here alone. Every part of her felt exposed. The peek of her thigh between the slit of her red dress, the dip toward her cleavage where the diamond necklace Joe bought her for Christmas last year was nestled, her knees crossed under the bar top. She was broken and no amount of wine or a sexy red dress would make her feel whole again. Nora made a mental note to talk with Sullivan about being careful with other people's feelings. Hearts shatter like glass when you drop them, they needed to be handled with care.

Wine mixed with simmering anger lead Nora down a road she had been trying to avoid as adamantly as she had the appraisal appointment. What did Joe see in Stephanie Laredo that he did not see in his wife? There was the obvious: Stephanie was younger, tiny, beautiful long dark hair and seductive eyes. There was a reason women were not always kind to the bombshell—she was threatening. She oozed sex. That, and Nora's marriage was not the first one Stephanie had interloped upon. Nora had looked down on Stephanie since she'd moved to Petoskey. She put men ahead of her daughter—and sometimes her career. Nora and Alicia had heard that she had an affair with a doctor at the last hospital she was at in Cadillac—

whose wife was the director of nursing! Of course, it was all hearsay but as they say, "Where there is smoke there's fire." It may not all be true—but what was true was that Joe, Nora's husband of twenty-seven years, was living with Stephanie in her crappy two-bedroom condo instead of with his wife in their home of nearly two decades.

Nora ordered another glass of wine and the cheese plate for dinner. She picked up her phone and scanned down to her last text to Sullivan. He had told her he was spending the day at the beach with Chase and his buddies and then was sleeping at Joe's place. Nora had her suspicions, but didn't she always? It would be nice to trust her son.

Nora: *Hey buddy, how's it going?*

It had been different with Sammy—she had left and gone to school at Grand Valley in Grand Rapids, about as far away as Sully would be this fall. Sammy texted Nora nearly daily—and called when she was walking from one class to the next a couple times a week. Nora didn't feel it was a daughter-versus-son thing as much as it was a Sammy-versus-Sullivan thing. Sammy was inherently independent—school was easy to organize, she never overspent or ran out of gas. She didn't *need* her mom, she *wanted* to talk with her. Nora had *needed* to help Sully—it was not uncommon for Sully to text with an emergency that needed Nora's attention and help routinely. He ran out of gas, forgot his psychology book or his gym clothes. He both appreciated Nora's assistance and resented it. He wanted to be independent, he wanted to remember to fill up with gas or charge his phone on his own.

Nora could see now that every time she saved him she had prevented an opportunity for him to succeed by himself. Her "help" had made Sullivan feel incapable when her intent had been to prevent him from failing. It had been one of the only arguments Joe and Nora had over the past decade—how to parent Sullivan. Nora was trying to see his ignoring her now as a step toward independence. Still, it hurt for more reasons than one. It was ironic, Joe and Nora had largely only fought about Sullivan these past years, now Sullivan was nearly on his own or at least launching his future, and Joe and Nora were over.

Joe's leaving had hit Sullivan harder than it had hit Sammy. He was younger, true, but also he idolized his dad. Sammy had seen Joe for who he was—a good man, for certain—but a good man who didn't always put his family first. Sammy took her dad where he was with no expectation beyond what he could give her. Nora didn't believe that Sammy didn't want for more from her dad, but rather than she had resigned herself to what he was capable of giving. Nora got the idea that Sammy was not surprised at Joe's infidelity, but she had not had the courage to ask Sammy why. Sullivan, on the other hand, had been devastated—and angry.

Stephanie's daughter Elise had graduated with Sullivan, which made things stickier for him. Last week Sullivan and Nora had curled up on the couch, ate popcorn and watched *The Office*—Sullivan's choice! Nora had been so happy he had chosen to stay home with her—out of the blue—she would have watched anything. Sullivan had confessed that he had been handed a healthy dose of teasing over his dad and Stephanie's affair and hadn't wanted to deal with it that night. He was ready to go to college and move past this town and the divorce.

"I'm sorry, Sully," Nora had said.

"It's not your fault my dad's an asshole," Sullivan had answered. She should have admonished him, encouraged him to listen to his dad's side, even given him permission to forgive him. But she hadn't. At the time, hearing her son's anger toward his father had soothed her soul. Later, as she had laid in bed unable to sleep, the weight of Sullivan's unhappiness made it hard to breathe. There was nothing good about Sullivan being angry with Joe, no matter the momentary relief in gave Nora.

Her eyes filled with tears as she sat in her red dress, drinking an expensive glass of red wine she bought with her estranged husband's credit card wishing things were different.

The last of the earthy wine slid down her throat with ease. She raised her glass to Gatsby, silently requesting another. She didn't want to stay, but she didn't want to go home to her empty house, either. One more glass wouldn't hurt, she would just Uber home and walk to town tomorrow to get her car.

The warm breeze of an early July evening blew against her back as the door to the restaurant opened. She shrugged her shoulders hugging herself against the humid air. Nora heard the woman's voice first, and then the man's. She tried not to look, she prayed her heart would refuse to turn her eyes toward the door. The wine had muddied her resolve and her head tipped slightly toward the voices. Standing there, hand-in-hand, were her husband and Stephanie Laredo—in a red dress.

JOE

Stephanie had decided on the Twisted Olive for dinner. It had been one of Nora and Joe's favorite restaurants, not that they frequented it often—but it was the family choice for birthdays and anniversaries. Joe had tried to interest Stephanie in Teddy's or Chandler's, but she wasn't having it. Joe's palms were sweaty as he held the door open for his date. He took a deep breath.

Stephanie looked fantastic. And young. And he looked typical. Basic. The rich doctor with the younger, gold-digging girlfriend. He'd never thought of Stephanie that way before. She had been so intent on listening and understanding him. She had offered him her friendship and attention when he needed it the most.

He hadn't seen Nora right away. He had been busy helping Stephanie with her wrap and advising the maître d' of his reservation. After nearly thirty years together he was not surprised that he had felt her presence before he saw her sitting at the bar. He had gently tugged Stephanie's elbow, his intent to leave written on his face. Stephanie smiled into his eyes and looked over her shoulder toward the bar. If Joe had not been distracted by his wife he would have seen the glint in Stephanie's eye, the competitive drive that had made Steph a survivor.

"Let's go over to the Bistro," Joe suggested, his eyes downcast.

"No. It's fine. We're all adults. She needs to get used to us. I'm not going anywhere," Stephanie answered his request with defiance.

The maître d' ushered Joe and Stephanie to their table for two tucked in the corner with a view of the bay in one direction and a direct line of sight toward Nora at the bar from the other. Joe frantically looked around the room for a free table for two that would keep them out of Nora's view. There weren't any. He offered the seat with the view of the bay to Stephanie, attempting to keep himself as in control as possible. He would keep his eyes on Nora, and keep his mistress happily distracted. He didn't need the drama he suddenly felt certain was coming, his brow collected sweat as if he were three hours into surgery. Stephanie had a glint in her eye, a shine he had not seen before. Her lips were curled in the smallest of smirks and she was definitely arching her back, thrusting her breasts out toward Joe as seductively as she would have if they were alone. This new edge to Steph made him nervous and electrified the air in the restaurant. Joe quickly looked around for people they knew. Jason and Shelley Dodds were sitting in the back corner. He didn't think they'd seen him yet and he hoped they wouldn't.

For Nora's part, she had quietly turned around after watching the pair walk in, taking a long sip of her wine. She hadn't rolled her eyes or cast a voodoo spell on the two of them. She hadn't scathed him with anger or screamed at Stephanie. Nora was the picture of class, he should have expected nothing less.

He hadn't seen her since she'd come by his office. He had texted, called a few times. She had answered in short, curt answers to texts but never to his calls. Bitter remnants of her anger still lingered in his memory. Nora's shoulders rounded gently, her hands fidgeting between her phone and her glass. She self-consciously pulled the few curls that had escaped their place back behind her ears. Her eyes glistened. She looked beautiful, Joe thought.

If Joe had been fortified by Nora's anger in his office weeks ago, he was undone by her sadness tonight. He pulled out Stephanie's chair and offered her the menu as he sat down. How had he gotten to this place and time where his wife was sitting alone at the bar wearing his favorite red dress and his mistress was sitting across the table from him wearing... a red dress.

He couldn't help but watch over Stephanie's shoulder, looking at his wife out of the corner of his eye. For nearly thirty years he had looked at her face every day. He knew her brow furrowed when she was nervous, and she talked too fast when she was excited. He knew tears were slow to come, but that didn't mean she didn't carry sadness. He had touched every curve of her body, she loved kisses behind her ears and wanted her back scratched at night. He had watched her give birth—twice!—and saw her grieve for the two babies they lost in between. He had held her as she heaved with sobs when her father had died. He had held her hair when she had too much to drink on a cruise to the Bahamas celebrating her fortieth birthday with Alicia and Steven. He had worried terribly as he nursed her back to health when she had pneumonia after Sammy was born. He knew she ate Grape-Nuts every single morning for breakfast and her favorite meal was risotto—which she rarely indulged in. He knew this woman as intimately as he knew himself; yet tonight, he had no idea what she was thinking.

"What are you going to order, Joey?" Stephanie asked, her voice tight and demanding. She caught his glimpse with her eyes and pulled his attention back to their table. "The filet," he answered—his standard fare—and put down his menu.

He ordered a martini and Stephanie asked for the same—dirty with two blue cheese stuffed olives. He would drink it in one gulp if he could, he longed for the rounded edges a good buzz would bring.

"I don't know what I want. Can you just order for me?" Stephanie smiled up at him. Her helplessness was a game and he knew it. Still, being needed felt good, like a wool sweater on a chilly November evening.

Justin returned with the cocktails. Joe ordered the steamed mussels for an appetizer and the sea bass for Stephanie. He changed his mind and got the lamb chops instead of the filet, and a second martini. Joe was uncomfortable—Justin had worked at the Olive for years. He'd waited on Nora and Joe and the kids. He'd waited on Joe and Nora alone. To be in public with another woman, all the while Nora sat at the bar alone, was embarrassing. More humiliating than he would have ever thought possible. He'd dreamed of taking Stephanie out to dinner, of parading her in front of his wife and the town. Now that reality was in front of him, and he had the panicked fear that it was all a fool's dream. Regret continued its dependable trickle into the cracks of his heart.

Stephanie talked continuously, not leaving much space for Joe to respond. She was crafty as she wove in and out of each subject, simultaneously ignoring

Nora and becoming hyper aware that her nemesis was behind her. Tonight, Joe found her incessant chatter to be a comfort. The more Steph talked the less Joe paid attention. Instead, he allowed his mind to wander while he created subtle reasons to look in Nora's direction.

Nora continued to sit at the bar, where she smiled now and then and chatted briefly with Gatsby. Her hands were still nervous, her legs crossed and uncrossed.

He was a man of science. He liked facts and data. He enjoyed flowcharts and pie graphs. Nora used to tease him that the reason Pringles were his favorite potato chip is because they were organized. (She had been right, although he would never let her know that.) But tonight his mind wandered to the past. If the walls of this restaurant could talk, would they remember Sullivan's fourteenth birthday dinner? The night Nora had worn the same red dress she had on tonight and Joe had eaten his filet quickly so he could get his wife home and have his way with her? Would the walls remember Sammy's college graduation dinner with Phe and Joe's parents? He and Nora had been so proud, they both had too much wine and had to call a cab home.

"Joey. Are you listening to me?" Stephanie questioned. Her voice piercing his memories like a dart.

"Yes, sorry. I had a complicated case at work today," he lied. His eyes were cast out to the bay, the sun had gone down and he searched to find evidence of the water. He shouldn't have been surprised when he turned to see Nora standing beside their table, her sweater draped over her shoulder. He had conjured her with his thoughts.

"Hey Nora, how are you?" Stephanie asked in a voice that was pleased.

"Doing well, thank you." Nora looked Joe square in the eyes. He wished for her anger to return, the subdued sadness was crushing him. "Joe, is Sullivan staying with you tonight?"

"Not that I am aware of. Why?" Could they have a civil conversation under these circumstances?

"He told me he was staying with you."

"C'mon Y'all, he's fine! He's an adult! So he said he's staying with us and he changed his mind! Good Lord, give the kid some space!" Stephanie, who had lapped Joe on the martinis spat the words out at Nora quicker than Joe could interrupt. Nora glanced in her direction and turned back toward Joe.

"I would like to know where he is, regardless. He needs to be honest." Joe could see tiny beads of perspiration collecting on his wife's brow. He watched her hands shake gently as she clasped them together. Her voice wavered in the smallest way—perhaps only someone who had listened for that voice every day for nearly three decades would notice. She was keeping her composure, and it was costing her. She teetered ever so slightly on her heels, Joe worried for a flash about her ankle. She'd sprained it last summer hiking the Tahquamenon Falls and it'd been a nag ever since. Joe closed his eyes briefly to reset—her ankle was not his problem. How painful it was to let go of all the small nuances of a marriage. How sad it was that thirty years of loving and caring for this woman came down to this.

"I agree, I'll speak with him tonight." It felt good to offer her a token of kindness.

"Just tell Sully to text his mother. Problem solved," Stephanie interrupted. "Then you two don't have to bother each other."

"Stephanie, with all due respect, you can handle Elise how you would like to handle Elise. Joe and I will handle Sullivan our way. Thank you." Nora looked back at Joe. "The appraiser called again today, I'm sorry I haven't had the time to follow up with him. I will get to it this week."

"You really do need to get that done, Nora. Joe can't move ahead with the divorce until that is taken care of," Stephanic interrupted, again.

Nora looked from Stephanie to Joe. "I wasn't aware we were in a hurry."

Joe fumbled with his napkin, placing it in his lap and reaching for another sip of his martini.

"We can't get married until you get divorced," Stephanie answered matter-of-factly. Joe coughed just the slightest bit, his martini suddenly too dry.

Married? he thought.

"Got it. I see, okay. I wasn't aware that you were engaged." Nora glanced at Stephanie's left hand looking for a ring.

Joe tried to interject a refusal, but Stephanie continued to speak.

"We can't live in my little condo forever! There aren't enough bedrooms for Elise, Sullivan, and Sammy when they come home to visit. Once the appraisal is done, we can decide to buy you out or build our own home." Stephanie reached for Joe's hand across the table smiling into his eyes. "We're leaning toward building—that way we can make it our own, for our new blended family."

Before Joe could interject, Nora, in all of her class, picked up Stephanie's martini and sloshed it in his mistress's face. "I hope you'll be as happy as I am," she said as she gently placed the empty glass back down on the table. Her eyes were stone-cold as she looked at Joe one more time, then turned and walked out the door.

NORA

Nora pulled the old red-and-black-plaid, wool blanket out from the back seat of her Escalade. Her father's favorite beach blanket. She tucked it under the crook of her shoulder and grabbed her thermos, filled with pinot noir, to celebrate the Fourth of July and her dad's birthday. She'd packed herself a small Tupperware container full of sliced smoked Gouda and Havarti along with a few grapes and crackers. Joe had loved when she had prepared small plates for dinner—his favorite was brie on a French baguette with fig jam. Nothing fancy tonight, just a little snack as she hadn't eaten all day. She checked—for the third time—that her pill bottle was nestled in the bottom of her tote. It was there—all thirty pills accounted for.

She had confided in Alicia about the panic attacks shortly after her dad passed. Well, she confided a "Nora Perfect" version of the story. She'd had sweaty palms, her heart raced a touch. Alicia had suggested she get a prescription of Xanax just to get through the grief of losing her dad. Alicia used them, Fran had used them. Thirty little pills. Joe had already suggested the same—she'd been angry with him. Somehow, hearing it from Alicia had made it doable. She'd gone to Dr. Bateman, gotten the prescription and hadn't told Joe until just a few months ago when he'd found her pills while looking for a pen in her purse. He hadn't said much—he'd read the bottle and put them back where he found them. She wanted them to bring comfort, but instead, they created a confusing mix of relief and fear.

She walked toward the shore, the sun already sinking toward the watery horizon. Painters dotted the dunes, small portable chairs and easels positioned perfectly for the brilliant display of sunset and fireworks. Their art would be for sale in town at some of the small shops or perhaps at the farmer's market in Harbor Springs. Nora always loved seeing the painters, catching glimpses of their works in progress.

Families with small children were spread out in front of her. Little boys in sagging bathing suits and little girls with damp lake-water-ringlets trailing down their backs. Moms and dads sat on blankets, groups of families huddled together in clumps of beach chairs and coolers. Nora took a deep breath, suntan lotion and the faint smell of campfire filled up her chest. She saw kids drawing chaotic squiggly lines with sparklers. She took in another breath, searching for the predictable smell of scorched aluminum.

There was nothing like the Fourth in Harbor Springs,

and Petoskey was a close second. She'd asked Sullivan and Sammy to join her tonight, but Sammy was in Detroit with friends for a Tigers game and post-game fireworks, and Sullivan had plans with Chase. She'd reminded him about his curfew.

He'd shrugged. "I know, Mom," he'd answered.

Alicia and Steven had asked Nora to join them at their family's annual picnic at their house on the lake. After Martini Night at the Twisted Olive, Nora decided if she were to be alone, she would rather be alone at the beach amongst families she didn't know than to be alone and uncomfortable around people she did. She politely declined every invitation that was offered to her and decided to create new traditions for herself this holiday week.

She opted to turn and go up into the dunes a bit instead of heading closer to the water. She felt the need to be separate, to buffer herself from the intimate sounds of the children and happy families. Perhaps later, after the fireworks and the people had cleared, she'd take a quick walk down the beach where she and her dad had searched for Petoskey stones when she was young.

Finding a secluded "Dune Room," a cozy spot where the dune grass grew in a circle leaving a "room" was always Sullivan's favorite part of coming to the beach when he was young. She found the perfect spot and spread her father's blanket out and sat down, rocking her bottom back and forth to make a sand chair to nestle into. From here she would be able to see Petoskey's fireworks along with Bay Harbor's and Harbor Springs's. She poured her wine from the thermos to her plastic beach wine glass, smelling the rich notes of plum and fig, swirling the wine and watching the legs dance up the sides of the glass.

July Fourth had been her dad's favorite holiday, and not just because it was his birthday. He would have been seventy-six today. He had served in the army—was stationed overseas in Vietnam and done two tours of combat duty. He had taught Nora (and Sullivan and Sammy) to always stand for the flag, hand over your heart, and to sing the national anthem. Every word. Patriotism was a tenet in his life, one Nora was proud of and tried hard to emulate.

She took a sip of the pinot, slipping her toes into the sand—underneath the top layer it was cool and heavy. How she loved this view. She had grown up in Harbor Springs, while Joe had been a summer kid. Coming only in June, July, and August from Chicago with his family to stay at Beachside. Nora and Joe met the summer after they had graduated—she'd been head over heels in love at first sight.

Nora sighed at their young love now. Would she trade all those years to escape the heartbreak of today? Nora considered the moments when life seemed its hardest. When the panic gripped her throat and she felt as though she was choking. When her heart betrayed her and raced down the stretch, or when her hands dripped with sweat at the grocery store. Perhaps in those moments she would trade Joe's love over the panic attacks. But in the quiet moments, when she was left with the empty Joe-sized space next to her in bed, or when she accidentally made dinner for two, and when she reached for her phone to text him to pick up milk and realized that wasn't his job anymore, she was grateful she had known a love like theirs.

Because no matter how it ended, it had been a good life. She chuckled at herself now. Her thoughts on Joe changed like the winds. She had to quickly shift her sails to keep up with her heart. Later tonight, when she crawled into bed alone and thoughts of Joe and Stephanie stormed her thoughts— the two of them cuddling watching the Tigers, eating spaghetti (Joe's favorite meal), making love—Nora will most certainly want to trade those years to escape that pain. She will feel the fire of anger that Joe started with the grenade of his infidelity. But right now, she was content to sit and watch the Fourth play out in front of her, grateful they had had their season.

Shoots of fireworks sprouted out along the bay. Amateurs, excited about the holiday, put on their own shows. The beach was positioned in the neck of the bay, Harbor Springs stretching out to the northwest, and Petoskey and Bay Harbor pulled like taffy to the southwest, with dunes and hills full of hardwood and pine trees tucked the beach in to the east. It was positioned perfectly to catch a Lake Michigan sunset.

From here, it looked like the world was out in front of you. The vision of possibility. Yes, that's what she liked about sitting here on the beach. The subtle feeling of hope she had when she sat her bottom in the sand and tucked her toes under its weight.

Joe's parents were gone now—his mother drank herself to death, dying of liver failure when Sammy was just six. She had never met Sullivan. Joe's dad died a few years later, when Sammy had been nine and Sullivan one. Joe and his sister Alexandra shared ownership of Beachside down in Harbor. She came for one week a year with her family, Joe and Nora went to one obligatory cookout on the beach. Joe never stepped foot inside the house. The rest of the season the house was rented—Nora kept the books and kept the listing for the VRBO up-to-date, and paid Gatsby to mow the lawn and do the spring and fall cleanup. Joe had washed his hands of the property years ago. He'd wanted to sell it, but Alexandra begged him not to.

Before they had built their house, Nora had asked Joe to entertain the idea of living at Beachside. They could renovate it the way they'd like, make it their own. The home was huge—his parents had been well-off and the home had been handed down for generations. They could pay Alexandra out of her half, and it was big enough she could still come spend her one week per summer with them. Joe refused. "I will not raise my family where my parents lived." Nora's heart lurched at the thought.

Joe hadn't had it easy growing up—regardless, and almost in spite of, his family's financial status. She knew his childhood had been a desolate wasteland. Nora had privately long taken pride and credit for his success, feeling as though her love had willed him beyond his parents and above their dysfunction. Of course now that was harder to justify. Joe had turned into a cheater just as his dad had always been. Where maybe Nora should feel angry at that thought, she felt embarrassed. Perhaps she shouldn't have taken credit for Joe's success in building their family. It's not like she had ever told him, "It's a good thing you have me, so you don't turn out like your dad!" But she also didn't give him credit for the work he'd done to grow their family.

Nora pulled out her phone to take a picture of the scene to send to the kids. She'd deleted their family group chat and started one with Sully, Sammy and herself. She added a nice note wishing the kids a Happy Fourth and reminded them to be safe. She tapped out a second text to Phe, who was enjoying an evening of fireworks with the ladies in her condo complex. She had taken to sending her kids and mom small snapshots so that they wouldn't worry as much. The photos didn't always—nearly never—represent where Nora was in life, but they certainly represented where Nora *wanted* to be in life. Happy, peaceful.

The sun was fully under the waterline now, dusk settling down around her. Moments later the sky sprang to life with color, sparkle and light! The children with their families sitting down below her shrieked with delight. They clapped and yelled, "Look at that one!" And, "Oh that one's my favorite!"

Nora smiled softly remembering Sullivan's first Fourth of July. They'd been right here on this beach. Sammy had brought a girlfriend along, the five of them had laid on this same blanket looking up at the sky. Sullivan had giggled and loved the fireworks, the fast-paced show delighting his imagination. He clapped his hands vigorously, and made booming firecracker sounds with his mouth.

That night after he crawled into bed, he clapped his hands and recounted the fireworks with his hands in the air. Darting his fingers up and down, punching the sky. Nora had delighted in his reenactment of the show and had tearily told Joe about it over a glass of wine around their fire later in the evening. She remembered the feeling of sweetness, the feeling of being complete. She had Joe, Sammy, *and* Sullivan. They were building her dream home and her parents were healthy and strong living just a few miles away.

Nora wondered where Sullivan was watching the fireworks on this Fourth of July—seventeen years after his first show. The naivete of his first Fourth coming home to roost. She believed if she worked hard enough she could create a perfect life. What she didn't realize is that life isn't static, it's fluid. It's always changing. She was a fool to believe otherwise—that she could work hard and keep things even, peaceful. Life never stopped changing. Who you are, what you need, what makes you happy changes as you age, as you grow. Old hurts come back to haunt you and new challenges put discomfort in your way. There was no vast sweet spot, no long perfect place of being. There were only perfect moments. Nora and Joe had a lot of those, that is where the heartache began.

In a few weeks Sullivan would leave for school, Sammy was already gone. Joe was moving forward with the divorce and Phe was happily living on her own forging a new life without her husband. Nora felt her heart race, the pounding started in rhythm with the fireworks. At first she thought the percussion of the explosions was what was pressing on her chest and then she realized no, it was her constant companion: panic.

If she'd been at home she would have sat still, taken some deep breaths, and waited for it to pass. She could take a Xanax but, predictably, the thought of taking medication gripped her with fear. She couldn't do it. Instead, she quickly scooped up her dad's blanket. She dumped the rest of her pinot and threw the glass, thermos and untouched snacks in her bag and walked to her car. Her heart pounded in her ears so loud it felt as if they were bleeding. Sweat beaded profusely on her lip and brow, some slipping between her breasts and down the groves of her back.

As she drove away she could see the fireworks pounding into the sky, celebrating her father's day. Celebrating life, liberty, and the pursuit of happiness.

And that... broke her heart again.

JULY 12, 2018

NORA

"Did you seriously dump her martini on her?" Alicia asked.

"I did. I didn't mean to. Well, I mean, I did mean to. I didn't plan to," Nora responded. The story of the jilted wife's revenge had made its way through Petoskey—that small-town thing again.

"I wish I could have been there! I would have given anything to see her face."

"She was surprised." Nora paused. "Not as surprised as I was that they are getting married."

"What did you just say?" Alicia asked, her voice quietly furious.

"Apparently my husband is newly engaged." Nora stuck to the facts.

"What in the actual fuck is going on in his head?" Alicia was indignant. Steven and Alicia had cruised with Nora and Joe in the Bahamas for Nora's fortieth birthday and vacationed at Disney World with their families. They had dinners out and cocktails on the

Phillips's porch. Nora felt the embarrassment of the loss of that friendship as sharply as a knife—Alicia and Steven had invited Nora and Joe to Australia with them this fall—celebrating becoming empty nesters. Joe had begged off, citing the difficulty and unfairness of rescheduling too many planned surgeries. Nora saw that differently now. It wasn't that Joe hadn't wanted to go to Australia. He hadn't wanted to go with Nora.

"Steven hasn't returned any of his phone calls," Alicia added.

"Thank you for that, but I don't want you two to be in the middle. I don't expect him to give up his friendship with Joe because of our divorce," Nora said what she thought she should, although she wrapped Steven's solidarity around her shoulders, it warmed her like a blanket. It served Joe right to lose his friends.

"We aren't in the middle. We are on your side. There is really nothing else for us to do. Hell will freeze over before I ever sit down and have dinner with that tramp. I'm not doing it. And Steven feels the same way." Alicia took a deep breath. "Joe can do what he wants, date who he wants, marry who he wants. I'm not debating that. But he doesn't get to choose her and keep us. Period."

Alicia and Nora made plans to have dinner later in the week. They had made plans two times since July Fourth alone, and still Nora had canceled every time. She hadn't been out in public since Red Dress Night, and even though Nora wanted to spend time with

Alicia, she knew she wouldn't keep these plans either. She'd tried going out—it hadn't worked. She'd tried visiting the beach on her dad's birthday—it hadn't worked. Having a nice time, enjoying herself, smiling all felt like a betrayal of her sadness. And she was hanging on to the sadness—it was the only thing left of her marriage. Moving on, stepping back into life, meant starting a life as a single, empty-nester divorcée. Nora wasn't ready to do that. Alicia would understand. Nora needed more time.

"I've gotta run, the appraiser is here." Nora sighed, hearing the doorbell ring. "I finally called the guy back. Joe has been badgering me for weeks. I can't believe I have to do this."

"I know, Nora. Call me if you need me? Or just shoot me a text?"

"I will. I promise."

The man standing in her doorway was taller than Joe, his shoulders broad and his jawline strong. He resembled Dennis Quaid in the way Joe resembled a middle-aged Adam Levine. His sandy hair was windblown and free—Joe's hair was always perfectly set. This man's eyes, the deep brown of melted chocolate, sloped downward in an endearing, gentleness that spoke of benevolence. He was handsome in a disheveled, friendly way—but he was also curiously familiar.

"Good afternoon, Nora? I'm Robert Wolf." He reached his hand out to shake hers, tucking his clipboard and tape measure under his arm.

"Hi there… I'm sorry it took so long for me to get back with you. I have been so busy," Nora lied. Willow barked at Robert's entrance, her tail wagging, toe-tapping routine of a new visitor in full swing.

Nora took his hand in her own, shaking it firmly, and she looked him right in the eyes like her father taught her. He wasn't just vaguely familiar, she'd seen him before.

His hand was big and strong, the hand of a man who built things. Joe's hands were smaller, softer. Joe had the hands of a surgeon. Nora shook her head side-to-side to rattle away thoughts of Joe—would she always compare men to Joe?

Robert didn't seem to have any recollection of her. Nora was confused by his familiarity, and the startling realization that she felt butterflies in her belly—Robert was a man. A handsome man. Standing in her foyer. It wasn't that she hadn't noticed other men in the last thirty years, of course she had. But it had always been through the shield of marriage. Men were not available to her, they were ancillary to life not essential. This afternoon, she realized for the first time since Joe left that she could date. She could meet another man, she could even get married again someday. Not that she wanted to—but she could. The realization drew in a sadness over her eyes. It should have cracked a window toward freedom from this desperation and grief, but instead it seemed to slam the window closed—if it had been open at all.

"Beautiful day, isn't it?" Robert asked and Nora nodded in rote agreement—although she'd hardly taken notice of the weather. She preened her neck past his shoulder looking out the front toward the bay. It was a beautiful morning. Robert's truck was parked in the driveway, an old, blue Ford. Her dad would have loved it. Nora's eyes squeezed together to shield her from the bright glare of the sun as she took in the view. She had spent many hours rocking on the front porch with a glass of wine and an unspoken certainty that this would always be her home. Lately, she'd avoided taking in the beauty of the bay. Joe leaving had changed everything about her life—even how she saw the water.

"Goldendoodle?" Robert asked, petting Willow's brow.

Nora nodded. She was touched by his gentle manner with her pup, again the feeling of familiarity settled over her anxious shoulders. Where did she know him from? It wasn't through Sullivan, or school or even Joe. No, their connection was an ache, a sadness.

"Yes, she's a sweet, if not overly-exuberant, girl." Nora tugged at Willow's collar to stop her from jumping toward Robert's face.

Robert laughed and crouched down to give Willow a

hearty belly scratch. "You're just excited, aren't you girl?" Robert looked up at Nora. "I won't take too much of your time. I'll be taking measurements of each room, making notes. I need to see the furnace and air conditioner, hot water heater. Those types of things."

Robert's voice was kind, he spoke with a slow pace, enunciating each word—as if he was southern without the accent. He took his time explaining, which gave her time to search his eyes, his mannerisms, his cadence and words for the reason that he was familiar. She couldn't hold purchase on any memory connecting her to Robert—still, she felt it.

"Great. Okay. Well, thank you. I'll just give you a quick tour then?" Nora asked. She led Robert up the staircase off the foyer where Sammy and Sullivan had both stood for prom pictures. Willow followed, her nails tapping on the hardwood floor. Nora showed him the wall-to-ceiling cabinets that her father had made out of Joe's favorite wood (cherry) in the study. Then the playroom turned young-adult-hang-out-loft. After Sullivan's thirteenth birthday party sleepover, Nora had scrubbed an entire bottle of cherry soda out of the new sand-colored carpet—the faint pink hue of the stubborn stain made Nora wistful for the days when the kids were little.

Nora led Robert to their master bedroom where Joe and Nora had spent the last sixteen years making love, sleeping, sometimes fighting, sometimes conspiring or hiding out from the kids. Nora cringed as she saw the piles from her cleaning fit that had *still* not made their way to Goodwill or the trash. Robert measured the room, recorded the information, and swiftly moved on to the next task. He was automatic in his actions. This strange—yet familiar—man standing in her bedroom gave rise to memories Nora had shelved long ago.

When Sammy was a baby and Nora came down with pneumonia, Joe had canceled patients and stayed home for three days to care for her. He gave her medicine, changed her sheets, listened to her lungs and took care of baby Sammy. As awful as she physically felt, she had felt cherished, cared for. She remembered with intense sadness the feelings of gratitude that she had married a man who loved her enough to put her first when she needed it. How had she forgotten that? Her damp, nervous hand smoothed out the cotton-soft eight-hundred--thread count coral and white comforter. Willow leapt easily onto the bed, circled, and sighed as she collapsed.

Robert's easy banter and focus on his work kept Nora calm, if not completely comfortable. She stumbled over her words at times, alternately talking too much and having nothing to say. Her words spilled at times as quickly as a bag of oranges that split open on the side, and then escaped her completely at others. Her steps felt as unsure as her words. She reached for the railing on her custom staircase—the end post built with cedar and rocks mined by her and the kids at the beach—to steady herself.

"You have a beautiful home. It's very unique." Robert said as they came down the stairs together and headed to the backyard to finish up.

"Thank you…" Her voice teetered and she laughed self-consciously. "My husband and I designed and built this home together, I did the interior design and decorating myself." Nora had always loved to create. At first, when she was little, it was with clothes and shoes and jewelry at Josephine's. As she got older, her mind was always searching for ways to change the look and feel of a room.

"It's really something. Where did you go to design school?"

"Oh, I didn't. I just enjoy it, I guess."

"Really?" Robert gently shook his head.

Uncertainty crept into Nora's stomach, she wasn't sure what Robert meant by that. A small, sad smile rose on Nora's lips. "My husband and I are divorcing," she said quietly and quite out of the blue. It seemed important, suddenly to stand in her truth. Nora had yet to become accustomed to admitting that her marriage was over and she was certainly unsure why she had chosen this moment to decide to begin voicing it. The vague familiarity of Robert's eyes had encouraged her.

Robert looked in her direction and the sides of his mouth tipped upward. Not a smile, simply a recognition of Nora's admission. He was kind enough not to acknowledge her with a trite response—no "I'm sorry" or "that's too bad"—because really, what good does that do? Nora took comfort in his absence of response. It felt good to not have to accept someone's sympathy.

She stood quietly and Robert resumed measuring, taking notes on his clipboard and alternately wedging the short, industrial pencil behind his ear while he measured again. She should ask him how she knew him, because she knew that she did. In her old life, she would have done so easily, but that confidence slipped away with Joe.

Her eyes cast downward to her two-carat ring resting on her finger. Joe had upgraded her small half-carat to this gorgeous two-carat teardrop flawless diamond for their twentieth anniversary. She had seen the new set at Northern Lights—her favorite jewelry store downtown—and had dropped a few not-so-subtle hints that she would like to turn in her smaller diamond. He had wanted her to keep the original, the one they used during their vows but she had been relentless. She wanted a new ring, one more reflective of their life now—not the small life they had in the beginning. In the end, he had compromised. He didn't turn in the smaller ring set, he kept it in their safe, and bought Nora the new, bigger one she had coveted.

Now, in the backyard standing next to Robert Wolf the appraiser, looking down on her perfectly cut, perfectly set, perfectly colored diamond, she felt the weight of the trade. Her first diamond had been the promise, the small stone of vague clarity and dim light had been all he could afford at the time and she had loved it when he proposed. It had symbolized Joe's commitment to her, it represented their youth and naivete. It was a sign of their never-ending love and a belief that that love could carry them through any storm. How had Nora ever asked to trade that ring in? What had she been thinking? Why did she not listen to Joe? His sentimental connection to their first ring should have struck her as sweet. It should have warmed her heart. She should have been proud to wear that ring, their first ring, the one Joe worked tirelessly through medical school to take off layaway. Instead, she traded her flawed ring for the perfect set. Look where that got her. Her husband was buying a new ring. And it wasn't for her.

ROBERT

Robert climbed into his baby blue 1957 Ford truck and slammed the door—not in anger, although it looked that way—the old door took just the right touch to get it to latch properly. The satisfying click of the latch when it finally took made Robert smile every time he climbed in the old girl. He swung his briefcase onto the passenger seat next to him. Katie had bought the truck for Robert after her first course of chemo and radiation treatments were complete.

He could still see those eyes dancing when she produced the keys after a scavenger hunt that had ended with him finding "Molly" parked in front of their small cottage sporting a huge red bow. Katie wanted to thank him for taking care of her: for wiping her forehead while she vomited, dispensing pills and sitting in appointments and holding her hand through every blood draw and chemo infusion. He had cared for her through all the things that cancer does to a person. He didn't want any thanks. He would always take care of his best girl—in fact, that's all he wanted in the world. It was only two months later the cancer returned. They thought she'd beat it. They thought they won their life back. They were wrong.

The familiar feeling of homesickness that aches in a way you can't touch and nothing soothes covered Robert like a heavy coat. He twisted the volume up on the AM radio nestled into Molly's wood grain dash. The Tigers had an afternoon game today, he would listen to the last innings on his drive home. His hand draped out the rolled down window, and he let the warm air soften his grip on the day.

Robert was anxious. The kind of anxious that happens when you can't put your finger on what's bothering you—you can't name your frustration. Katie had called the feeling intuition, Robert called it annoying. Still, Robert pursued the feeling, chasing it through his mind like the rooms of an empty house.

What was making him so restless?

He always enjoyed appraising interesting, unique properties and the architectural and design aspects of Nora Phillips's home were special. Every detail had been attended to, down to the Petoskey stone knobs in the kitchen, the handsewn knotty pine lining the half bath and the six individual, gently arched windows that created a cove in the master bedroom showcasing the million-dollar view of the bay. The wood floor in the kitchen was rich walnut, the seeded glass in the cabinets played off the glass of the gas fireplace that was set at eye height and was accented with a bed of large, polished and glossy Petoskey stones. The house was an extension of Northern Michigan, the color palette drawing from the bay and the sand dunes, pine trees, white birch, and stones. Robert made his living looking at other people's houses and this house... this house was perfect in every detail. He was impressed. Impressed enough to find it a shame that Nora had such talent and her home was the only one she had ever designed.

Robert swung Molly's old frame down from atop the Phillips's subdivision and grazed through town, following the water's edge toward Harbor Springs and home.

Robert considered the Phillips's house again. A house like that should be filled with laughter and life. It should be bursting at the seams with sand on the wood floor from an afternoon at the beach and wild flowers in vases filling the air with the sweet scent of their heavy summer blooms. The rare but brilliant January sunshine should pool at the foot of the couch making a warm nest for a winter nap. Instead, the house was empty. The perfection of the house, although beautiful and unique, was stilted.

If there was one thing Katie had taught him it was that perfection came from imperfection. It came from a pile of dirty dishes in the sink left over from a home-cooked meal. It came from muddy clothes in the wash after a hard day's work. It came from sand in the seats of your car in July and soggy clothes drying on the register after a winter hike.

Katie was the queen of imperfection. If her favorite sweater had a stain, she'd still wear it. When their china plates from their wedding that she used daily began to chip, she smiled.

"Finally!" she'd said.

Their small cottage was vintage and full of whimsy, there was no palette of matching colors, only the colors that made Katie happy the day she painted. She was an artist. A painter and a sculptor. A poet and a musician. If there was something to be created, and a mess to be made in the process, Katie would be found in the middle of it.

Nora's home was perfect in its architectural details and design. But not where it mattered. The plush, rich leather chairs, the spectacularly appointed chef's kitchen, the backyard fire pit with the empty wicker chairs all sat suspended and motionless. The house was lonely. Still, there was something about Nora that was curiously familiar.

Robert followed the water around the bend of the bay. The Tigers' middle-reliever struck out the side in the bottom of the sixth—a little late as they were already down 5-0. He meandered down M119 slowly heading toward their little cottage in Harbor Springs, thankful he was done for the day.

He forced himself to focus in on Dan and Jim as they called the game, pushing out thoughts of the house on Trillium Hill and Nora Phillips.

He was certain now he had met her before, perhaps she'd been friends with Katie? Robert couldn't recall, and his unease continued to grow. Was he interested in her? No, not in the way a man should be interested in a woman like Nora Phillips. Logically, he could see she was beautiful. The curves of her body were pleasing and she was gentle and classy in her mannerisms. She had a vulnerability, a sweetness about her. His heart squeezed as remembered her whispered voice telling him she was getting divorced. No, he was intrigued by her familiarity, but not interested. Robert stayed honest to his vow never to be with another woman. He would be true-blue to Katie until he left this Earth, despite his last promise to her.

Robert pulled Molly over at his favorite roadside fruit stand to pick up some fresh blueberries and raspberries. If he picked up two pints they'd be gone before he rounded the corner and reached home, so he grabbed two quarts instead. He made small talk with Anna, the woman who ran the stand, and smiled as he climbed back in Molly to head out—waiting for the *thunk-click* that came when her door latched before starting the engine. He could still hear Katie telling him that Anna had a crush on him. She'd said it every time they pulled away from Anna's stand. Katie found it immensely pleasurable to know that other women found him attractive.

"It makes me feel like I won!" She would smile.

In the end, when the doctors had told Katie she wouldn't survive, she had promised Robert she would speak to him, that she would always be near. He had numbed the pain and shock of the slow loss of the love of his life with that promise. She would be Patrick Swayze to his Demi Moore. The logical side of him never believed, but his heart... his heart couldn't not. He supposed that was another reason to be angry. He'd allowed himself to believe and Katie hadn't come to him. Not once.

The Tigers had already made up two runs in the seventh with only one out. 5-2 with runners on the corners piqued his interest. Robert's pop had taken him to his first Tigers game at Tiger Stadium in 1984. It was the year they won the AL East, and they were off to a 9-1 start. It had been a crisp, sunny day for Michigan in April. He'd had on long jeans and wool socks, he'd worn his favorite blue sweatshirt with his

Alan Trammell jersey overtop. His mom had stashed a blue stocking cap in his pocket but he never took it out, Pop wasn't wearing a hat so he wouldn't either. Robert remembered the feel of his hand inside his pop's as they walked into the stadium, hands rough from working were calloused and dry. Robert knew enough at ten years old to be proud of those hands. He'd felt small but he'd felt safe. They had hot dogs loaded up with onions and chili. Robert hadn't much liked onions but Pop had said it would be the best hot dog he'd ever eat—so he ate it. And it was. His pop worked long and hard as a lineman to provide for their family—and he knew a Tigers game on a sunny Friday afternoon was as good as life could get. The Tigs beat the White Sox with a Lance Parrish walk-off hit. One of the best days of Robert's life.

Robert's stomach rumbled. The raspberries and blueberries weren't enough and he knew his cupboards were bare. He suddenly wasn't in the mood to go home alone so he turned Molly around and headed back to town. He found a parking spot in the front row of the Olive. One wouldn't think this place was necessarily his cup of tea, but he loved the Nashville chicken they served on Tuesday nights and the view couldn't be beat. Plus, Katie had loved it there and they'd frequented it for their sea bass alone before Katie got sick. She'd befriended the kid who bartended, Gatsby, and Robert liked him too. Tonight he would sit at the bar facing the water and chase away the loneliness with a few beers, maybe chat with Gatsby if he was working and try and forget the restless wonder rumbling around his chest.

On nights like tonight, where the loneliness physically ached in a pain so stark it was difficult to breathe, where missing his wife seemed as endless as the Milky Way, Robert resorted to filling his time. He would stall the evening at the Olive and get through until he could go home, close his eyes and go to sleep. Not that sleeping brought any comfort—he'd heard stories of people who swore their lost loved ones visited them in their sleep. He had prayed for that— as adamantly as he'd prayed for Katie to send him her messages—and it'd never happened. No, he never dreamt of Katie. When his wife died, so did Robert's imagination, his love of life. The color had gone out of his days and his dreams fell silent. Without Katie, Robert just got by.

GATSBY

Robert saddled himself on a bar stool looking out at the water. "Gatsby, my man. How are ya?" Robert reached across the bar and shook the young bartender's hand.

"Wolf! Pretty good, pretty good. Can't complain," Gatsby answered. "Oberon?"

"Yes. Please."

Gatsby grabbed a frosty schooner from the cooler and pulled an ice-cold draft off the tap and handed it to Robert. "Long day?"

"No, not too bad. Just not in the mood to go home." Robert shook salt on his napkin before setting his beer down. "Any interesting pieces you've been working on?" Gatsby pulled out his phone to show Robert a few photos of the sofa console he was creating.

"I picked up the wood at an antique store, it's black walnut." Robert looked at the photo, enlarging the picture by spreading his fingers wide. Gatsby smiled as Robert nodded in appreciation of his work.

"That's a beauty, kid. I love it. I really like the live edge." Robert swiped through the handful of pictures of the table and handed the phone back to Gatsby.

"Thanks, man. I think I'll list that one online." Gatsby pulled out a basket of fancy twisted breadsticks and put them on the bar.

"I may be able to help you sell that one, let me know when it's done."

"I will, that'd be great, thanks!"

Gatsby met Robert when he and his wife, Katie, used to come in for dinner several times a month. Katie loved the sea bass and always ordered a Woodford Manhattan: strong on the Woodford, thin on the vermouth. If Robert had asked, Gatsby would have told him he had a crush on his wife, because who didn't love a woman who drank bourbon? Her easy nature, the way she flirted with an honesty that said she adored her husband but enjoyed people, the way she asked Gatsby who he was dating, how her green eyes sparkled with mischief as she tried to set him up with nearly every single girl she knew made her hard not to fall in love with. After she got sick, Gatsby had seen them together once or twice over the several months she received treatment, although Robert would come in now and again and have one beer at the bar alone.

For a while, it seemed she had made it. Her hair began to grow out again, the color returned to her cheeks. Her voice had grown thin during chemo and radiation, but the sing-song lilt that carried her tune was returning and her laugh was stronger. Robert and Katie visited the Olive often, always holding hands, always smiling: they were the goal. Two hearts, one love. That's how Gatsby saw it. And then they had disappeared again.

The day Robert called and made a reservation asking for the private room set just for two Gatsby hoped it was a celebration of Katie finally finishing treatment. When the pair walked in through the front door his heart sank. It wasn't a celebration. It was The Last Time. The Last Time Katie would order sea bass and The Last Time Gatsby would pour her Woodford. Katie was thin as a rail, her hair was gone and her skin was sallow, her eyes jaundiced and flat, her trademark spark muted. Robert had held onto her elbow, slowly guiding her into the restaurant. He placed a pillow on her seat before lowering her gingerly onto her throne. Gone was the vibrant, auburn-haired beauty who captivated everyone around her. In her place was a shell of the person Gatsby had known. Had she not been with Robert, Gatsby would have found her only vaguely reminiscent of someone he should know but couldn't place.

Robert had fed her a few bites of the sea bass and held her Manhattan to her mouth so she could take a few sweet sips. Katie had smiled and the pair held hands throughout dinner. Gatsby had served them himself, wanting to be certain their service was impeccable—if this was goodbye, he wanted Katie Wolf to go out knowing he cared.

There was a time when Gatsby had been envious of the pair. They had the perfect love. It wasn't fair that Katie was sick and it certainly wasn't fair that Robert would lose her—but more than that, Gatsby mourned for Katie. It wasn't right that a woman with such warmth, such love, such kindness, would succumb to fucking cancer. Gatsby felt flares of anger that Katie had been cheated. It would have been one thing to go through the treatments and the storm of side effects that they brewed, but to go through it all and *still* die in the end was bullshit. The world needed more Katies, more of her kindness, the mischief in her eyes and the sparkle in her words. Katie had given Gatsby hope, hope that he still hung on to, even more so now that she was gone.

Gatsby watched the obituaries religiously after their last meal. Seven weeks later Katie's picture was there. Her thick auburn hair and wide smile a stark reminder of who she used to be. Gatsby borrowed a suit from Justin at work and went to the funeral. Robert hugged him in the reception line and Gatsby had whispered, "Thank you." Since then Robert had visited Gatsby at the Olive once or twice a week for a beer or two. Sometimes dinner. The two had struck up an unlikely friendship, bonded by the auburn beauty Robert had loved all his life and by whom Gatsby now measured the world.

"Well, no need to go home when you can come here and keep me company. It's pretty slow tonight. Although last week night it was a little crazy." Gatsby shook his head.

"Why's that?" Robert took a long pull off of his beer and tipped his chin upward in question.

"Do you know the Phillipses? He's a plastic surgeon in town, his name is Joe, his wife's name is Nora." Robert looked up from his beer. "Do you know Nora and Joe?" Gatsby asked again.

"I don't *know* either of them, but I did the appraisal on their house today and met Nora," Robert responded. "I thought I recognized her from somewhere... but I can't place her."

"Joe left Nora a little while back for this woman named Stephanie. The other night Joe brought Stephanie in for dinner while Nora was sitting up here at the bar alone. Everything seemed cool, they pretty much ignored each other, until Nora walked over to their table and talked to Joe—I don't know what happened but a minute later she'd picked up Stephanie's martini and threw it in her face. Shit like that doesn't usually happen here."

"Really? When I met her today she didn't seem like a drink slinger." Robert chuckled.

"She's not, I don't think. I work for them, actually. I do the caretaking of Dr. Phillips's parents' place—Beachside. I went to school with her daughter, she was a couple years younger than me. Mrs. Phillips is always super nice, kind. The whole thing was crazy!"

"You never really know do you."

"No, you really don't," Gatsby answered.

Robert drained the rest of his beer and asked for another.

"Dinner tonight?" Gatsby asked.

Robert paused, looking out at the water, his hands clasped together waiting for his beer.

"Yeah. I'll take the sea bass."

JOE

Joe settled into Phe's couch with a warm cup of peppermint tea. His body relaxed. The familiar surroundings were a welcomed gift. Everything about his life had become unrecognizable. Stephanie's condo was not his own, there was not a remnant of his former life in his daily surroundings. Stephanie had hung pictures—mostly selfies—of the two of them on nearly every wall, and propped photos up on the bookshelf in the foyer and on their bedside table. He hadn't thought they had been together long enough to *take* that many pictures, let alone that many selfies. He missed the photos of the kids when they were little that graced the table next to his bed with Nora. He missed the family photo that hung over the couch in the living room— Sullivan was just one, Sammy was nine. They had been so thrilled to finally have a family of four. Nora had spent a fortune on that photo session and Joe had been irritated at the time. Now, he would have paid twice as much to see it hanging on the wall in Stephanie's condo. He realized that was ridiculous, to want to hang a photo of his wife and kids in the home of his girlfriend. But that didn't make it not true.

Phe slowly walked from the kitchen to the living room, carefully measuring her steps and placing her cane at a precise angle. Joe would have thought she would be moving a bit quicker by now. "Are you feeling okay, Phe?"

"Yes…" Phe smiled. "I'm fine. I'm getting old is all."

"You? Old? Never!" he exclaimed. He had always loved his mother-in-law. He hardly knew his own mother. The few memories of Eleanor Phillips he did have were painful, traumatic. He had been mostly raised by a nanny—to whom he still sent an elaborate Christmas gift every year. Well… Nora did.

"Out with your camera this afternoon?" Phe asked.

Joe had skipped out on the last four patients on his schedule. It was a brilliant August day—sunny and eighty-five. He had told Stephanie that he was working late and instead he grabbed his camera from his car and headed for a walk on the Wheelway and down by the city marina. He supposed it should bother him that he had become accustomed to telling lies, and perhaps it did a little bit. But today, the relief of walking alone with his camera and absorbing his mental energy in finding the perfect shot was worth every untrue word.

Joe was precise. He was exact. He was an excellent surgeon—he was revered by his peers and his patients loved him. He was the perfect mixture of pleasant, confident but humble bedside manner and excellence in the OR. Not many people knew about his fascination with photography. Phe had been the only person he eagerly shared his photos with. Nora had bought him the camera for Christmas five years ago to replace his smaller, less sophisticated one. He'd asked for this specific model and she'd gotten it exactly as he'd asked—but she had never asked if he used it. Certainly she assumed it was sitting in the back of a closet collecting dust. She wouldn't be the only one surprised that it was always tucked away in a climate-controlled box in his trunk at the ready.

Joe's job in the OR was *so* precise he found pause in the lens. He loved the creativity of finding the right subject and the science of adjusting the settings. He had taught himself—though he had thought plenty about taking a photography class at the community college in Traverse City. But doing that would have exposed him, and he enjoyed having this private outlet for himself.

"I couldn't sit in my office another second today. It was too beautiful out," Joe answered. He turned on the display and set it up for Phe to peruse the photos at her leisure while they chatted. He handed the camera over to her gently. Phe smiled as she accepted it. She had always been warm and loving to him, accepted him as her son. He hadn't noticed much difference in the way Phe had treated him since she found out about his affair—until today. Phe had welcomed him in when he stopped by unannounced, but it was without the entirety of warmth Joe had enjoyed since he was a young man.

Joe felt another layer of loss. Earlier he had walked down by the Bear River where the kayakers came through. The view was fantastic—lush emerald, lime, chartreuse leaves hung from the trees, the sun pronouncing their texture in technicolor. Birch bark striped the evergreen and maple woods with character. Last summer, he and Sullivan had gone kayaking together on that same segment of river. Today Joe had gotten a few action shots of some young kids shooting the rapids. He had snapped a picture with his phone and texted it to Sullivan.

God, I miss my son, Joe thought now.

Sullivan had answered a terse: *Cool*

In the past, Joe would have laughed at his son's one-word answer. Today, it brought Joe to tears. Sullivan hadn't answered his texts in weeks and had refused to see him or answer his calls. This one word gave him a chance. Joe knew Sullivan had merely opened the door, just to peek outside. But he had still opened the door. Now Joe needed to be patient. He needed to wait. Joe had hurt Sully's mother and embarrassed himself. It had turned Sullivan's world upside down just before everything was about to change. Sullivan would leave for college and would never be able to come "home." Home would always be different, fractured. He had

had an affair—moved in with!—the much younger mother of a friend in Sully's class.

Sullivan had exploded on Joe the last time he'd stayed with Joe.

"How could you sleep with that bitch?" Sullivan had screamed.

"Don't talk to me like that," Joe had countered on auto-pilot. In hindsight, he should have just let Sullivan give it to him. He deserved it.

"You got some beautiful shots today. Very nice." Phe handed Joe back his camera without viewing all of his photos.

Joe hung his head, turned his camera off, and tucked it into its case. "Thanks."

"Why are you here, Joseph?" Phe asked.

Joe took a deep breath and clasped his fingers together. He leaned forward and rested his elbows on his knees. "I don't have any idea, Phe." He didn't have the right to tell her why he was here. Because he missed her. Because he missed his family. Because he didn't *have* a mother to go to. Because he was lost, miserably, hopelessly, wayward. Because he was looking for a way back and he was hoping Phe had the answer.

"I'm angry with you." Phe had always been direct. One always knew where they stood with her.

"I know. You should be, I suppose." Joe's voice was quiet.

"You suppose?" Phe's eyebrows lifted in question.

"Of course you should be."

"And I hear congratulations of sorts are in order?" Phe questioned Joe, looking straight into his eyes. Joe felt ashamed.

"I haven't technically asked Stephanie to marry me," Joe answered. He felt like a child at the knees of his headmistress after he was caught cheating on a test.

"No? That's not what Stephanie told Nora. Of course, you were there, I wasn't. Did Nora misunderstand?"

"No. That's what Stephanie said." Joe's eyes closed and his head bowed.

"So, I'm confused. Are you getting married?"

"I have never discussed marriage with Stephanie." Joe paused. "Stephanie has mentioned she looked at a few rings. I have not taken her shopping for a ring, and there is no plan."

"You haven't asked the woman to marry you—yet you allowed her to announce to your *wife* that you were engaged?" Phe challenged Joe. "That was a month ago! You've let Nora believe this lie for a month without making it right? Who are you? What the hell did you do with your balls?"

Phe's brash honesty slapped Joe as sure as a cold glass of water across the face. "I have no idea."

"Don't know much, do you?" Phe's irritation with Joe's recent behavior was no longer masked by her good manners. "You need to get yourself together. You do realize Sullivan is watching your every move?

Sammy, too. They are looking at you to lead the family and you are leading them right into the trash. Do you want Sammy to believe that marrying someone who is less than honest, who doesn't stand up for his own truth is what she should do? Do you want Sullivan to treat women the way you have treated his mother? Or even how you have treated Stephanie? Allowing her to believe you will marry her—when we both know that's not your intention. No matter how I feel about the woman."

Joe's cheeks burned red, the heat from his belly seeped up to burn his ears. He wanted to be angry, but he was appropriately chastised. His head hung low. "I don't know how I got here."

"Listen, I know my daughter isn't easy. I know she's stubborn and independent and sometimes downright controlling, but she didn't deserve this. You don't have to love her anymore. But you do have to treat her with respect."

"I do love her." There it was. The truth of the matter. The problem was, when Joe admitted to still loving Nora, his vulnerability showed. He suddenly felt the instinct to defend his actions, to make Phe believe this was at least in part Nora's fault. That she ignored him. That she dismissed his needs for everyone else's. That even though he'd done this horrible thing, Nora had done things too. Phe could not convince him otherwise, even if she'd tried. The problem with cheating on his wife, Joe had learned, was that it was the final, mortal sin. Nothing that transpired between husband and wife before the affair counted. Because nothing was as awful as betraying his wife's trust. No matter how neglected, lonely, sad Joe had felt, he had no right to destroy their family and his wife's trust in him. He had convinced himself that Nora would not care that he slept around. He convinced himself she would be thrilled to be rid of him. He had convinced himself of what he wanted to hear.

"Are you behaving in a way that makes her believe you love her, Son?" Joe set down his empty mug of tea and zipped up his camera case. Phe pulled herself up with some effort from the chair she had been sitting in. "You know exactly why you came here today. You came here because you knew I was the only one who will look you in the eye and tell you the truth. I love you, Joseph. Like a son. I have loved you for thirty years. But you, my son, are acting like an ass. You made a poor, selfish decision and you have backed it up with selfish *indecision* for months."

"I know what I want to do," Joe said. He knew he wanted to fix his marriage, he knew it like he knew he loved his children. But what he didn't expect was to feel guilty about leaving Stephanie—and Elise. What he hadn't expected was to mourn, in the smallest of ways, the loss of excitement and the feeling of being young again the affair had given him. He didn't know he would feel guilty about wanting to return to his family—because even though he was realizing

Stephanie was more cunning than he'd given her credit for, she had still been a friend to him when he needed one. He didn't know he would feel so raw, so exposed at the thought of asking Nora for forgiveness.

"Do the right thing. Not the easy thing. Not the thing that feels good in the moment. Do the right thing. I'm not suggesting you go back to Nora or you stay with Stephanie. I am suggesting you do the right thing for yourself and your children and your family—but do something. Not deciding, not doing *is* deciding. And unless you want to end up with a life you did not choose—you need to start deciding for yourself." With that Phe walked into her bedroom and shut the door leaving Joe with his thoughts and the truth.

STEPHANIE

Stephanie drove around the parking lot of J. Phillips Plastic Surgery, searching for Joe's Jaguar. It's not like he was driving an Impala or a Malibu, something hard to see. He drove a jet-black Jaguar and it wasn't in the parking lot. It wasn't there. He had told her he was working late, but she'd heard that before. *She* was the reason Joe Phillips worked late, and he wasn't with her. Stephanie took a deep breath in and tears stung her eyes. She knew this feeling, the slipping away.

Sometimes she wondered if it would be all she ever felt.

It was always the same in the beginning. The men she involved herself with could not get enough of her. They craved her attention and her body, they lied to their wives and girlfriends, they skipped work and their kids' baseball games. And then, sometimes overnight, it changed. They were busy, they had a family dinner, couldn't miss their daughter's dance recital. She had thought Joe would be different, she had thought he would stay. After all, he's the only man she'd ever been with who left his wife and kids for her! He left Nora! He came to live with her! Still, she felt it. The cool breeze of disinterest.

Why does this always happen to me? she thought. *Maybe he didn't drive the Jag to work today?*

She knew the thought didn't make any sense, it was the only car he owned and he had left the condo hours before she had been up (although she wasn't sure when). Joe hadn't slept in her bed; he'd fallen asleep on the couch.

Maybe the Jag went in for service? Or detailing?

Stephanie made another loop around the parking lot; the Jaguar was still not there.

She pulled into a parking spot, pushed the gear in park and grabbed her purse. Inside the office, the waiting room was nearly empty. One woman sat with bandages around her head while her husband (boyfriend?) sat next to her reading his phone and nodding off. Stephanie wondered what she'd had done. Ears? Facelift? Had the sleeping boyfriend asked her to change? Or had she felt she had to do it in order to keep him?

Faye was standing at the reception window, leaning toward the edge straightening the pens and sign in sheet when Stephanie approached her. Her son Chase was friends with Elise and Sullivan, he'd graduated this year, too.

"Hey there, Faye! How are you?" Stephanie smiled, taking a deep breath in.

"Oh... Hi, Stephanie. Can I help you?"

"I just wanted to drop some things off for Joe, do you care if I put them in his office?" Stephanie reached into her purse, pretending to gather a few papers.

"His office is locked when he's not here, he left a couple hours ago. You can leave them here and I will get them to him tomorrow?" Faye offered, her eyes giving away her confusion.

"Oh no, that's okay! I will just give them to him tonight when he comes home. He needed them here at work so I thought I would save him a trip, but no worries!" Stephanie chirped.

At the mention of Joe "coming home," Stephanie watched a cloud of shock drift over Faye's eyes. She didn't know Joe was living with her. He hadn't told his office staff he had moved in with his mistress.

"I'll just make sure he remembers tomorrow morning before he leaves for work to bring them," she added, looking directly into Faye's eyes before she turned and walked out of the office. She was tired of being the mistress. She was tired of Faye and Nora and Alicia thinking they were better than her. She was tired of being left behind and tired of being hidden. She was living with Dr. Joe Phillips. He left his wife for her! She had seen the scarcely disguised veil of disapproval pool in Faye's eyes.

Stephanie peeled out of her parking spot. She should have realized she had no right to be angry. She should have expected Joe to lie to her. She had encouraged him to lie to his wife, she had even helped him at times. Still, she couldn't help feeling the victim. He had told her he was working late—where was he? He wasn't supposed to be lying to *her*.

Trillium Drive was a quiet, dead-end street on the north end of town that led high up a hill overlooking the bay and Round Lake. Stephanie had tried to stay away. She'd had a Cosmo at High Five Spirits. She shopped for a new bathing suit. She texted Joe, but he didn't answer. She called him, but her calls went straight to voicemail. Now she turned down the radio as she slowly swerved around a woman walking her dog—it was only a few seconds before she realized the woman was Nora. Stephanie, surprised, pulled to a stop outside of Nora's house and looked in her rear-view mirror.

Stephanie had started driving by Joe's house before they began their affair. The house was a magnet, it pulled on Stephanie with the draw of the moon to the surf. In the beginning, before Joe had left Nora it made Joe feel closer, made him feel real and attainable. It should have made her feel guilty, remorseful. But it didn't, and Stephanie didn't know why. Frankly, she didn't wonder much why, either.

She had driven by in the early morning and late at night. She had watched Sullivan leave for school and had seen Nora head to the gym. She had watched Phe and Nora sit on the front porch and share a bottle of wine and she had watched Sammy hug her mom in the driveway before she got in her car and drove away— usually right past Stephanie.

She thought having Joe, finally having Joe, live with her in her home and with her daughter would make her feel safe, secure. Instead, her vulnerability and insecurity flared. Even now as she sat out front, the sadness of the family's dissolution written in the grass that was a touch too long and in the weeds that peppered the landscape didn't faze her. The closed drapes and the shut door, the house held no life. And yet, she still did not feel guilt. What she felt was sadness. She would never have the house on the hill or the kids who grew up with their dad and a husband who adored her. It was simply a fact of her small life.

"For a little while, until you get on your feet," she'd said to Joe to convince him to stay with her. She thought once she had him there, even if it was only for a little while, she could convince him to stay. Joe may have left Nora's home for Stephanie's condo, but Stephanie still didn't feel that she had him.

Stephanie watched Nora in her rear-view mirror. She'd lost weight, Stephanie noticed. She was slim, almost fragile looking, as she reached down to pet Willow with her free hand. Stephanie had always, reluctantly, been fascinated with Nora. She was the woman who had it all. Stephanie had both revered and resented the woman who lived on the hill. Today, it wasn't hard to tell that the confident, focused and driven Nora Phillips that Stephanie knew before was a shell of her former self. Her eyes were vacant, empty. Nora continued walking back toward her home.

Stephanie knew she should start driving, there was no reason for her to be on Trillium Drive except to spy on Nora. She also knew that Joe wouldn't be pleased. In the months leading up to their discovery, Joe had talked openly about his wife's faults and shortcomings. He had told Stephanie he had never come first, that Nora wasn't interested in him. He had complained that she was demanding and bossy, that she was rigid and controlling. Stephanie had listened very carefully. She had taken mental notes of what he wasn't getting from his wife and morphed herself to suit his every need. She tried desperately to become the puzzle piece that fit into Dr. Joe Phillips's life. In the last couple weeks Joe hadn't said a word about Nora, and if Stephanie brought her up, he became vaguely defensive of his wife.

When they'd run into Nora at the Olive, Stephanie had been brazen, she knew. She was fueled by vodka and jealousy—competition. She felt Joe slipping away and had to do something to stop it. Now it seems it had backfired.

Stephanie took comfort that Nora was alone, Joe was not with his wife, but still… she couldn't squelch the bitter tension that reminded her that he wasn't with Stephanie, either.

As Nora walked farther down the hill and toward the Jeep, Stephanie felt something: guilt? Regret? Anger? In the past, seeing Nora had given her a rush, a high. Today, seeing Nora had unsettled her, she knew she should feel responsible for the look on Nora's face, for the weight she lost and the lifeless pallor of their charming home. Stephanie's stomach boiled with tension, her hands began to sweat and her brow furrowed. The look in Nora's eyes stayed with Stephanie as she drove away from her, out of the Phillips's neighborhood. At first, Stephanie wasn't sure why—until she caught her own gaze in the rear-view mirror. The look in Nora's eyes was familiar. It was the same look Stephanie saw in the mirror every morning. Nora Phillips and Stephanie Laredo had something besides Joe Phillips in common: they were both lonely.

NORA

The screen was static black as Nora waited for her computer to jump to life. The piles of clothes left over after her cleaning spree taunted her from across the room. She sipped her pinot noir and sank deeper into her chair. Sullivan was staying at Chase's again tonight. She had reminded him of his curfew as he'd slid out the door, backpack slung over his shoulder and his baseball hat tucked deep over his forehead, obscuring his eyes. She thought briefly to ask more questions, wondered if Faye was home, but she remained quiet. If Sullivan noticed her change in diligence, he hadn't mentioned it. She typed "Facebook" in her browser and waited for the page to load. She'd deleted the app from her phone to prevent herself from stalking Stephanie's page, but it hadn't stopped her. It only made it slightly less convenient.

Willow snuggled into the crook of her bent knees as Nora checked her phone, clicking the home button. No notifications. She had texted Joe a few questions about moving Sullivan in at Central in a few weeks—did he have a truck to use? Did he buy the TV he said he would? Nothing she really needed an answer to, she knew she was fishing, wanting to connect with Joe even if the result was a fight. Sometimes, the fight was as satisfying—even more so—than a respectful exchange of which they had managed to have a few.

Stephanie and Nora had been friends on Facebook

for three years and Nora had not even realized it until a few weeks ago when she looked her up on the social media site. She thought about blocking her, unfriending her, whatever she had to do to make her go away, but in the end, she didn't. Morbid, damaging victim-curiosity got the best of her. She became slightly obsessed with scrolling through Stephanie's page, trying to find the answer to the only question she had: why wasn't she enough? Nora had tried so hard to be the perfect wife. She'd given him everything she had.

Nora would like to say she didn't see much difference between herself and her husband's mistress that a boob job and some Botox couldn't fix (and Joe was a plastic surgeon for Goodness' sakes!) but it wasn't true. Stephanie was beautiful. No amount of torture with Jordan at the gym or CrossFit or yoga or 10K runs could give her the body that Stephanie Laredo had. There wasn't enough Botox to make her look ten years younger or erase the deep "elevens" she had between her brow.

But what about the inside? What about all the years she'd given Joe, their family, his practice, their home, his children? What about how much she loved Joe, what about the fact that she had been faithful and devoted to him every minute of their marriage.

Nora had taken to scrolling through Stephanie's photos in the evening when the house was quiet and dark. When the weight of her grown daughter, absent son, and unfaithful husband threatened to suck Nora into the darkest of holes. Oddly, it was looking at Stephanie Laredo's face that soothed the pain. Stephanie in a sexy one-piece bathing suit, baseball hat on backward and head tipped back toward the sun, aviators sitting perfectly on her heart-shaped face. Stephanie sitting on the lap of a man covered in tattoos, in a pair of bedazzled cowboy boots at a Kid Rock concert holding up a beer, duck lips in full force. Stephanie in her scrubs, a selfie in the ER (and dammit if the woman didn't ooze sex even at work!). Stephanie celebrating the first warm day last spring with the top down on her Jeep, a selfie again. Nora wondered if Joe had ridden in her Jeep with her that day.

Nora searched photos of Stephanie spanning the past year. Looking for signs of Joe's betrayal. Something that gave away the secret hidden behind the photos. Nora couldn't help wondering: had Stephanie slept with her husband before she took that selfie in her scrubs at work? Or maybe after? Had Joe peeled the sexy one-piece bathing suit off of Stephanie while Nora was home taking care of Sullivan and picking up her husband's dry cleaning? Nora's mind was an old vinyl record caught in a skip—where? When? She had become obsessed with wanting details about Joe's infidelity. Her mind scoured the past looking for clues. And while she will admit there were some—Joe and Nora hadn't had sex since... well since Nora couldn't remember. But Nora also couldn't remember smelling a foreign perfume, or finding crimson lipstick on the collar of his shirt. She didn't remember him not showing up where he should be or perpetually coming home late. She didn't remember wondering, or a fleeting thought of concern or suspicion.

These forays into the sticky Facebook web were usually laced with Nora's recurring daydreams about revenge. Slashing Joe's tires. Keying Stephanie's car. Sloshing Stephanie's martini in her face was satisfying (if childish), but sometimes it just didn't feel like enough. Nora laughed at the thought—she wasn't a violent woman, but there were moments the thought of sinking a knife into Stephanie Laredo's chest or strangling her perfect neck with her own two hands gave her a spark of relief from this debacle. She wanted to cause a scene in the epic way of a woman scorned, but she also wanted to hide the truth of her husband's affair from every person she knew. Anger and humiliation were fighting it out on the teeter-totter of her heart.

Damn him, Nora thought.

Willow barked at Nora's feet—it was now well past 8:00 and Nora had yet to feed the pup let alone take her for her walk. "Okay, girl. I'm coming. I get it. I know I'm a bad momma."

Nora loved her neighborhood, on the northeast side, high above town. The views of the bay and Round Lake were extraordinary. She had always been so proud to live here. The beauty of Northern Michigan spread out like a bolt of rich green and blue velvet. The colors blending just as the hills and trees melded together with the beaches and the bay. Maybe she could forget if she tried hard enough. She could let the beauty of this town and these lakes carry her away.

The street lights began to spill puddles of light on the road in front of her feet. Willow danced on the end of her leash, ever curious and joyful to be outside. Nora sucked in a giant breath of air looking out toward the coast and Bay Harbor in the distance. While Nora never tired of the view, again the familiar vista intensified her sadness. She wished for the first time she could hear the power of the waves from her home instead of just see the water. It may have made the perfect view feel more real. Tonight it felt flat and two-dimensional, accompanied by a lonely siren song in her mind.

Nora took another deep breath of the moist, warm August air and waved at Gabby Soren as she drove her Lexus around the corner and into the driveway attached to the home three houses from the Phillips. Gabby had stopped by the house the other day. Nora would love to think it was to support her, but she wasn't that foolish. Gabby was on a fact-finding mission—to see how Nora Phillips was handling the scandal of her husband's affair and her coming divorce. Gabby and Nora had been neighbors for nearly a decade as well as room moms together with the PTA, they'd been in the same book club and co-chaired the Hospital Gala. Until Joe's affair, Nora had considered Gabby a friend. It's true what they say, when life is tough you find out who your friends are. Other than that one visit Gabby hadn't sent so much as a text.

Nora hadn't expected much company on the road tonight, but there were more cars than she anticipated. A second car swerved around the pair giving them a safe, wide berth. Nora belatedly realized she should have attached Willow's collar light before they took off. The sun was beginning to set, she would have to be careful.

A third car came up the road, moving slowly. Nora tugged at Willow's leash and pulled her farther to the side of the road. Fear crept in around the edges of the anger that was her constant companion. She kept her pace swift as the car drove past her. Nora tipped her head to peek toward the car as it moved past—a Jeep Wrangler. Nora kept walking in the opposite direction of the vehicle—Willow leading the way down their nightly path. Nora envied the dog and her confidence that the path would be the same as the day before and the day before—no matter that it was hours later than it should have been.

The Jeep slowed to a stop in front of the Phillips's house. Nora stopped and turned, watching, waiting. She tried to remember if any of Sully's friends drove a Jeep—she thought maybe Justin Martinez did but she couldn't be sure. The Jeep sat outside Nora's house, waiting. Brake lights pushed.

Stephanie drove a Jeep Wrangler.

The thought bolted through Nora like a lightning strike. Paranoia swam with anger and humiliation. Nora felt The Feeling swooping around her. The one that accompanied the thundering gallop of the racehorse in her chest, the one that made her feel defenseless and weak. Sweat gathered at her brow, more fear. Her chest felt heavy, tight. Her heart continued to race and her breathing, ever so slightly, tightened.

Maybe it was Joe driving Stephanie's Jeep? Would Stephanie and Joe come to her home together? Nora's mind grappled with plausible solutions, tumbling and flipping ideas around like a jiu-jitsu fighter. The damn horse racing in her chest and tightness in her throat screamed panic.

Nora checked her pocket for her cell phone, yes it was there. Tucked away where it should be. Nora watched the Jeep as it sat, brake lights assaulting the dusky, quiet of her neighborhood. In her old life, she may have stopped into Gabby Soren's house to say hello, or perhaps stopped to check on Mr. Gardner across the street. Anything to be in the company of another human, to help her racing heart and feeble breath return to normal.

The brake lights lifted and the Jeep carried on down the road and disappeared over the hill. Nora felt oddly invisible, as if her existence didn't matter and wasn't of consequence. She was desperate for anything to prove to herself that she was not unseen, that she was real and not illusory. Nora begged the fear to leave, to return to the fissure deep in her broken heart where she could manage it. Willow tucked herself between Nora's frozen legs, resting her head against her mistress's knee. Gently, slowly, the anxiety began to quiet—like a roller coaster sliding off the last heart-stopping hill and into the gate.

Willow seemed to understand as Nora turned around cutting the dog's walk short and heading home. Nora didn't trust herself to be outside any longer. She needed to get inside, close and lock the doors and hide from this outside world that just couldn't grant Nora peace. The racehorse in her chest slowed to a trot as she reached the end of her driveway. A nice glass of wine and *Grace and Frankie* on Netflix would keep her mind purposefully occupied until she fell asleep. Yes, that's it. Think of *Grace and Frankie*. One foot in front of the other.

The ring of her phone startled her, causing her skittish heart to begin racing all over again.

"Hello…?" Her voice sounded weaker than she'd like, as if it was a thin line disappearing into the horizon.

"Nora. It's me." Joe's voice—so unexpected—was

strained.

"What's wrong?" Nora answered.

"It's Sullivan."

JOE

Nora and Joe walked into the police station at the same time. Joe's elbow brushed against Nora's shoulder, and he felt his skin spark—he wasn't exactly sure if that was the right word, but it felt like electricity. It felt like the beginning. When things were new, different.

How strange was that?

Walking into the police station to pick up their son who had been ticketed for underage drinking, he touched his wife and felt a spark.

Sully, Chase, and two other kids that neither Joe nor Nora knew had been caught drinking in a parked car at the city marina. They were each ticketed with Minor in Possession and their parents were called to pick them up.

The air smelled faintly of booze and oil... maybe grease? Definitely cigarette smoke. The overhead lights were fierce and uninviting, but of course they weren't meant to feel comfortable. Joe sighed as he walked through the long hallway toward the back of the station, following the directions the officer on the phone had given him.

"Mr. Phillips?" A short, stocky man with a rotund chest and dad-sized belly walked up to Joe, hand on his gun holster and what Joe saw as a condescending look on his face.

"Dr. Phillips," he heard himself answer.

"We are Sullivan Phillip's parents, I'm Nora Phillips," Nora said, introducing herself. "We are here to pick him up?" Her words lilting up at the end, Joe could feel the nervousness radiating off of her. He placed his hand on the small of her back—there was that spark again. She turned herself away from Joe, pretending to look toward the door behind the officer, but Joe knew better.

"I'm Officer Gray, I'm the one who found the boys tonight."

"Thank you so much for calling," Nora started. "He's a good kid, he's just... well, we've just had a hard couple of months." Joe cringed as the heartbreak in Nora's voice was palpable.

Joe met Officer Gray's eyes, searing, painfully blue. Perhaps the condescending look was of Joe's creation.

"Teenagers aren't known for making smart decisions, Mrs. Phillips—"

"Call me Nora. Please."

Joe could feel adrenaline squirt into his veins, as if he was mainlining it. It was subtle, his wife's suggestion this man not call her Mrs. Phillips. It could have easily been a polite offering, but to Joe it felt like he was watching his wife cross a bridge leading away from him and their marriage. *Wasn't that what he asked for?*

"Nora, like I said, teenagers aren't known for making the best decisions." Officer Gray's lips turned up at the corners. A gentle, sad smile that never reached his eyes. He chuckled to himself. "You wouldn't believe what I've seen kids do. What I am most concerned with was the fact they were in a vehicle. Kids, they do experiment with alcohol. As dangerous as it is—not to mention illegal, and I am not condoning it at all—but the car? They *cannot* experiment with driving drunk. I am certain at least some of them had been smoking pot in the car as well. I could smell it, but we didn't find any. Although I will admit I didn't look that hard." Officer Gray took a deep breath.

Joe nodded his head, pausing with his chin pulled down toward his chest. This man was trying to help his son.

"Driving under the influence is personal to me. My daughter died in a drunk driving accident three years ago down state." Officer Gray looked at both Joe and Nora. He didn't have the eyes Joe had expected from a cop—they contained no judgment, but instead an offer of understanding and warning.

"Oh my God, I'm so sorry," Nora said, clenching her fists together at her chest.

"That's awful," Joe added, embarrassment at his insistence on being called "doctor" instead of "mister" salty on his tongue.

"What's awful is that *she* was the drunk driver."

Joe and Nora stood motionless.

"In some ways I guess you could say we were lucky, she only hurt herself. I want you to know, I think I scared Sullivan tonight. I was tough with the boys, I didn't give them any benefit of the doubt. I want this lesson to stick. I handcuffed them and brought them in and put them in a holding cell. They've been in there a while now. Officer Landon is getting Sullivan. He should be out in a second."

"We so appreciate that. We really do. I am really sorry for what he did—" Nora began.

"Don't be sorry, Nora. His behavior at eighteen is his to own, but I do understand that feeling. Talk to him. It's been my experience that kids often have something on their mind when they push boundaries this far. If you need any help talking with him, we do have a parent support group and we also have a lot of resources for you. If you need anything else, don't hesitate to call me," Officer Gray with the sad blue eyes hiked up his pants by his belt and shook both Nora and Joe's hands, then ushered them toward the pass-through window to sign papers for Sullivan's release.

Officer Landon walked out with Sullivan, who looked contrite and young under the fluorescent lights. So young. Joe's heart ached. He could see the little boy he had been—the deep brown eyes, just like his mom's, glistened with tears. His shoulders slumped forward, not a hint of the teenage arrogance they'd seen since Joe left. Sullivan saw his mom and his shoulders heaved.

"I'm sorry, Momma." His voice was thin and ragged. His words, slightly slurred, ran together like they did when he was a toddler and just learning to talk.

"Sully…" Nora couldn't continue. Her eyes filled with tears. Joe felt his sadness molt to anger at the sight of his wife's pain.

"Sullivan." Joe reached out to put his hand on Sullivan's shoulder, but Sullivan twisted his body away from his dad and toward his mom. "Sullivan, what were you thinking? Do you see what this is doing to your mom?"

"What were *you* doing? Do *you* see what you did to Mom? Are you fucking serious right now?" Sullivan's shoulders, at first rounded and meek, transformed to the arrogant, defiant teenager Joe had grown accustomed to seeing these past weeks.

"Don't speak to me that way. This isn't about me. This is about you." Joe's voice met Sullivan's defiance with authority.

"You're the one who brought up Mom. You don't have the right to bring up Mom!" Sullivan was yelling now.

"Sully… I'm okay, honey. I am. It's okay, let's just go home." Nora wrapped her sweater more tightly around her chest. "Okay? Let's just go home."

"Mom, I'm sorry. I really am. I just can't deal with

this asshole," Sullivan spat back at Joe.

"Your dad is right. You can't talk to him that way. That's enough."

"After what he did to you and this family, I can talk to him however I want!" Sullivan began to yell. Officer Gray peeked his head back out in the hallway.

"Everything okay out here?" he asked.

"We're fine," Joe responded. "We just need to get my son home."

"I'm not going anywhere with you!" Sullivan yelled.

"Are you sure I can't help?"

"I think we'll be okay, Officer Gray. Thank you. Too much booze, too tired. Everybody's just too everything." Nora smiled sadly.

"You got that right," Sullivan sneered. "I'm too pissed to go anywhere with Joe."

Joe squeezed his fists together tightly. Sullivan was drunk. He was angry. But Joe was angry, too. No matter what Joe did or didn't do as a husband did not mean he wasn't Sullivan's father, and it certainly didn't mean that Sully could speak to him however he wanted. "Do not call me 'Joe.' I'm your father. Be respectful."

"Be respectful? Are you fucking kidding me right now? Because you were so respectful when you slept with Elise's mom? Because you were soooo respectful when you flirted with her in front of everybody at my games? Fuck you, man. I don't respect you and I never will." Sullivan turned and started walking toward the door. "Mom, can we please get the hell out of here?"

Joe stepped toward Sullivan, grabbing his son's shoulder in an effort to turn him around. Sullivan resisted being turned, but suddenly gave way, lurching to face Joe with his fist clenched and arm cocked backward, ready to fight. Officer Gray stepped between the two while Nora held on to Sullivan's free hand, begging him to stop between cascading sobs.

"Sullivan. I can see you're really upset. Do you need to stay here tonight? Or can you quiet down and go home with your mom?" Officer Gray stood toe-to-toe with Sullivan, their eyes—Gray's sad blue and Sullivan's angry brown—only inches apart. Joe was held behind Officer Gray, his head hung down in shame.

Sullivan sucked in two huge gulps of air, intended to fight off the sobs coming with the booze and the sadness. "I can go home with my mom."

"Nora? Are you okay taking Sullivan home?" Gray asked.

"Yes, I am. Come on, kiddo. Let's get you home and to bed. We won't talk anymore tonight about it." Nora took Sullivan by the hand and led him down the hallway with the bright light and out the door.

Officer Gray turned toward Joe.

Joe's feet froze in their spot on the floor. He tried to will them to move, one foot then the next, but nothing. He was stuck. The last thing he wanted to do was to break down in the police station, but the tears were coming and his body had simply betrayed him. Joe's hands were clenched in a circle with fingers entwined as he sat down on the bench outside the open doorway where Sullivan had come through. Officer Gray quietly sat across from him, resting his elbows on his knees and waited.

"I had an affair. I slept with the mother of one of his friends. My wife—Nora—she kicked me out. I should have gone to a hotel, but I didn't…" Joe paused. Gray nodded, understanding. "Sullivan, he's angry. Really angry with me. And honestly, I'm angry with him."

"I'd be angry with my son too if I was dragged down to the police station to pick him up drunk on a Wednesday night."

Joe smiled and nodded his chin up and down. "I'm mad about the drinking, of course. And the car… being in the car drinking makes me want to lock him in a room for life…" Joe paused. "But…" Joe hesitated and couldn't continue.

Officer Gray sat quietly.

"I supposed I'm mad my life doesn't look like it's supposed to. Nora was a good mom. She *is* a good mom." Joe stopped mid-sentence, knowing what he intended to say was wrong. But also knowing he needed to say it. "But I needed her to be a good wife. Maybe if she'd spent as much time being my wife as she did being Sully's mom, I wouldn't have found someone else to spend time with." Joe heard his voice saying the words he'd thought so many times. He hadn't had anyone to say them aloud to: his parents were both gone, and even if they weren't his father wasn't a man to talk about feelings. His mother would have been more interested in her gin and tonic than hearing what her son had to say. He couldn't talk to Steven; Alicia was Steven's wife and Nora's best friend. Jason Dodds at work was a good pal, but not someone to share complicated emotions with. How had Joe created a life devoid of a confidant?

"Parenting takes a lot out of you, a lot out of the marriage," Gray said to Joe. This time, his head was cast down, his eyes following the concentric circle pattern of magenta colored rings on the carpet, the fluorescent light garish and interfering. "My wife divorced me after Sydney's accident. Syd had been in trouble for drinking, pot, skipping school—for over a year before she died. My wife took the soft approach, talking to her, asking her questions, trying to understand why she did what she did. I thought Syd was manipulating her mother. So I grounded her, took away her phone, forbade her from driving her car. I was certain I could demand compliance out of her—I am a police officer after all! The night she died, we had fought, and I'd grounded her. She went out anyway, got drunk, and wrapped her car around a tree. The last thing my daughter ever said to me was, "I fucking hate you!" My wife… she never forgave me for driving her out the door. I think I do understand as much as one man can understand another."

For so long Joe had been afraid to say the words. He'd been jealous of Sullivan. Resentful even. Sullivan took all of Nora's time and attention, there was nothing left for him. And dammit he worked hard every day! He supported this family! He provided everything Sullivan had ever wanted. Now that he'd said the hateful words out loud, he felt relief bubble up from his toes. He didn't really believe Sullivan was to blame for the state of their marriage. No, Joe Phillips knew that he and Nora were the only two responsible for the train wreck they had turned their family into.

"Is that why you said we should talk to Sully?"

"Learn from my mistakes," Gray said. "Not that talking is the only solution, it's not. Neither my way or my wife's way worked with Syd. And now that she's gone, I'll never fully understand why she felt the need to act out so much. I only know I wish I had spent my time trying to connect with her instead of fighting. Maybe if you talk with Sullivan—not talk *at*.... Talk *to* Sullivan—you can find a few more answers than I have."

"Thanks for not thinking I'm an asshole." Joe smiled sideways.

"Oh I didn't say you weren't an asshole." Gray stood and reached his hand out to shake Joe's. "I have no idea if you're an asshole or not. I just met you. I know you acted like an asshole when you cheated on your wife, but I also know people make mistakes. Talk to your kid. And not just once. It's going to take a while. Kids are not that complicated, really. I know that sounds ridiculous after the story I just told you. But it's true. Kids just want to know you love them. They want to know you're there. They want to know you have their back even when they fuck up. They need you to show up. Give it some time. Sounds like you have some making up to do."

"I do. And not just to Sullivan,"

"Funny thing about that. Your wife? She needs you to show up, too. Even if she won't be your wife much longer. The best thing you can do for Sullivan is to treat his mother well, love her if you can."

Joe nodded his head, putting both hands in his pockets, and walked down the same long hallway Nora and Sullivan had just left. When he reached the door to his car, Joe stood in the heat of the July evening, grabbed his phone from his pocket and texted Nora:

Please tell Sullivan I love him. I will talk to you both tomorrow. Let me know if you need anything.

Funny how typing a few simple words could make you feel so much better. No matter what happened, he needed to be a man he was proud of. A man who showed up. It was time for a few things to change.

NORA

Nora walked as Willow forged ahead, sniffing the sidewalk looking for errant squirrel tracks. She snapped the leash a few times in an effort to rein in the pup's enthusiasm—but Willow was not be deterred. It had been two weeks since Joe and Nora had picked Sullivan up at the police station. If she were being honest, Nora would say, "It had been two weeks since Sullivan had been arrested and taken to jail." Because that's what happened. But since Officer Gray had shown Sullivan grace—the definition of which Nora had decided was giving someone the exact opposite of what they deserved when they have hurt you—she was showing herself grace as well. She was doing the best she can.

Nora's feet fell in step quicker than normal, her heel strikes landing with more force than necessary and her arms swinging with intention. She'd continued to ignore Jordan's phone calls and texts asking her when she would be coming back to the gym. She knew he was trying to help—he was a good kid (who was also sad to lose his most lucrative client she was sure). But the gym, the trainer… it had never fit well on her. It was like wearing a dress too tight or a sweater that bagged to your knees. She went because she had to, she went because she should. She went because her body was less than perfect. She went because she wanted it to *be* perfect.

She held her head down, trying to force the relative calm that usually came before a walk. She watched her profile in the mirrored store windows as she passed, hunched forward, a scowl on her face, deepening worry lines as sound as the Grand Canyon. She'd started walking the morning after Sullivan had gone to jail. Her anxiety had propelled her out the door and up and down the hills of her town for two and a half hours—searching for an answer, for some way to make it through the day. Since then, she'd done the same every morning. Outside of the pills hidden in her purse, it had become her only weapon against the monstrous anxiety that had grown from a middle-aged woman's angst to the earth-shattering panic of a woman in a state of upheaval. It hadn't healed her, but it took the edge of the burn away.

Turning her attention away from her reflection and back to the road in front of her, she looked just in time to avoid walking straight away into an open door. Nora stutter stepped sideways, pausing to look around the door that was propped open toward the sidewalk. The building was empty and the hardwood floors ran rough into the exposed brick walls. The ceilings were tall, magnificent even. The building was well loved, something about the space spoke to her, her hand lingered on the handle of the door as she looked inside. What had been here before? Nora tried to remember, but she couldn't. She continued to take in the details of the room until her legs itched to continue moving and she obeyed. The spark of interest in the building was hidden beneath the weight of her life.

Nora replayed the text argument she and Joe had had last night. If she had thought parenting as a married couple had been difficult, she hadn't considered how difficult it would be co-parenting a teenager as a single woman whose husband was living with his mistress. Sullivan had been grounded since the Police Incident—he'd followed the letter of the law at home to a "T." He'd been home when he was supposed to be, hadn't turned off his GPS and had even gotten a job picking up a few hours at Harbor Springs Christmas Tree Farm: trimming trees, cutting weeds, and doing a few maintenance repairs to the buildings and equipment before the cold swept in. Even though it was August, winter was always just around the corner in Northern Michigan.

Nora felt Sullivan wasn't ready to go to school. Joe thought he was. Nora wanted to defer his entrance until January. Joe told her she was being unreasonable. Nora wanted Sullivan to have more time at home to mature.

Joe told her Sully needed to learn to be on his own. Nora wanted to spend more time with him, take care of him and make sure he was following the rules. Joe told her the best thing for Sullivan was for Sullivan to have to take care of Sullivan. Joe wasn't being unkind. He was being honest.

The thing was, Nora agreed. She knew Joe was right. She knew Sully needed to be on his own to grow. But she was governed by fear. Fear of losing Sully, fear of being alone, fear of Sully failing. Fear. Fear. Fear. As Nora walked her throat clenched tighter, the kind of squeezing that comes when tears are imminent and you are trying to hold them down with the weight of your ego and your pride. The tightness continued, the sweaty palms and that galloping racehorse heartbeat followed. Fear. Fear. Fear.

Nora looked ahead. Bay Bean Coffee was only half a block away. They'd let her slip inside with Willow. If she could just get to a bathroom and splash her face off maybe she could pull the reins in. Maybe if she tucked herself into a dark corner for a few minutes and let the tears escape—where no one could see—she'd get control. Her feet quickened pace to meet her pulse. Willow tugged. Her throat squeezed. Heart pounded. Fear. Fear. Fear.

The water felt good on her face. Using her hands as a cup she immersed her eyes, nose and mouth in a birdbath of cold water mixed with her hot tears. She took deep breaths in between the sink baptisms.

Willow circled around her, curious as to why the walk was cut short, knowing Nora was not right. Her pup whined, licking at the droplets of water that fell to the ground and nuzzled Nora's leg.

She could hear the chorus of women standing in the corner of her mind, whispering. *Do you see her? She looks awful. She looks old. She looks depressed. I think she's having panic attacks. And Sullivan—did you hear he and Chase Utley went to jail?* Perfect husband, a lie. Perfect kids, a lie. Perfect marriage, a lie. Perfect life, a lie.

Small gasps escaped Nora's throat. Her pride and ego were no match for the raging fear now. The horse galloped through her chest at Derby speed. She pooled new water quickly, submerging her face again and again. The tears came in small spurts as she refilled her hands. Finally, after what seemed to be a lifetime of repeating the ritual, Nora's tears quieted and the fear was settled into a momentarily manageable fire in her throat. She dabbed her face with a dry, brown paper towel. The scratching and imperfect texture was a relief. She didn't deserve a soft, plush towel. This is what she needed. To be uncomfortable.

Patting her eyes dry as best she could and feeling the strength return to her shaking knees, she led Willow out of the restroom toward the light from the entrance at the front of the building.

"Nora?"

She stopped.

"I thought that was you. Actually, I recognized your dog. Willow, isn't it?" There stood Robert Wolf, the appraiser she had avoided and then overshared with when she finally did grant him an appointment. Again she felt his familiarity, she knew she knew this man—but couldn't place him.

"Hi, Robert..." Nora sucked in a deep breath. "Pardon me, my allergies are awful right now. The ragweed and such." Nora hoped he believed her red-rimmed eyes were a product of the season. Robert hardly gave Nora a glance as he knelt down on his knees to pet Willow. Willow, for her part, leaned into this gentle scratch behind the ears. Robert chuckled as the dog rested her head in his hands.

"She loves attention, that's for sure," Nora said, relying on her impeccable manners to guide her.

"I love dogs. I had to put my Great Dane down a few months ago. Haven't had the heart to entertain the idea of a new puppy."

Nora's love for her pup swelled. Her sweet girl had stood by her in the bathroom while she quietly wailed, and now she showered Robert with affection enough to distract him from Nora's disheveled self. Nora reached down and added an extra scratch to Willow's forehead. Willow stretched her head back and upside down, her version of "you're welcome."

"Oh, that's too bad. It's awful when we lose our pets. They certainly are part of our families."

"Yeah. Lucky was my wife's dog. He was one-of-a-kind. More human than dog. He was a wise old soul, even as a pup. He'll be hard to replace." Robert looked up and Nora saw the flash of recognition behind his eyes. The recognition of sadness, of fear. Nora looked away. She was too vulnerable, too open, too wounded to be in public. She needed to gather Willow and go home. The bubbly vocals of Michael Bublé echoed over the Bean's speakers; the barista behind the counter sung along. Nora felt that new-but-familiar ache, the one that resonated when she was presented with someone else's perfection. Then she remembered, didn't Michael Bublé's young son have cancer? Yes, he did. There was no perfection.

"Are you okay, Nora?" Robert rose from his position with Willow and reached for Nora's elbow.

"You know. Just a hard day today. That's all." Suddenly Nora was happy she had overshared about her divorce when Robert had done the appraisal on the house. It saved her the embarrassment of explaining, lying, or otherwise trying to continue to feebly cover up her red eyes and snotty nose to this man. There was something about Robert she liked. A gentle calm. Her embarrassment slipped away.

"Getting a walk with this girl should help. Maybe walk down by the water? Nothing makes me feel better than that. When my wife died, I think Lucky and I walked ten miles a day back and forth down the Wheel Way trail and through the marina."

And all of a sudden, where once a vague familiarity

lingered, a certainty settled.

Nora remembered.

NORA

William sat snuggled in his blanket, Phe holding his hand in the chair next to him. Typically, he received his infusions in a private room, but today the semi-private was all that was left. It was only slightly larger than the private rooms, with enough room for two nursing carts, the infusion pumps and bedside tables next to each recliner. There were chairs for guests, one apiece. Jill, William's nurse, had already carried in an additional chair for Nora. The walls were soft blue with pictures of seaside landscapes. The air was tangy with the scent of medicine and rubbing alcohol.

Jill worked swiftly preparing the gemcitabine, cleaning William's port, and beginning the hours-long session. William adored Jill. She was older than Nora, but not by much. She wore her required teal-colored scrubs with colorful tie-dyed shirts underneath, a pair of white clogs, and always a myriad of bedazzled lanyards for her hospital ID and keys around her neck.

Her hair was silver and curled in unruly waves, giving her the look of a gentle grandmother, even though her skin and face were much younger. Today her hair was pulled back in a hot pink hair scrunchie. Her manner was gentle and easy, her command of William's treatment plan complete. She gave all three of them a sense of calm and confidence. Nora wondered how Jill did it. How she worked with cancer patients every day and kept her sense of hope and joy.

Nora knew the odds. She knew William wasn't expected to make it. She knew that pancreatic cancer was terminal, a death sentence. Still, she held onto hope as a daughter does and Jill—although always realistic—buoyed Nora's spirits. When Nora would pepper her with questions about long term results, about her father's chances, clinical trials she'd read about online Jill always answered with, "He's here now. I can't tell you what tomorrow holds, but today... today he is here." Even though she wanted to hear Jill say the chemo was working, that William would be the survivor, she understood Jill's gentle urging. Let go, we can't control the future. We can only do today.

William spoke softly, occasionally asking for ice chips. Phe gently spooned them into his mouth one by one. This simple act of care and kindness between her parents both comforted and broke her heart. She sat in her folding chair opposite the two of them and busied herself with recording William's blood work results and today's exact dose of chemo into her color-coded folder in which she kept track of every twist and turn of William's treatment. Sections for medications, appointments, scans, and a journal of how well he was eating, his mood and his energy level were carefully organized. The Book came to every appointment, chemo session, blood draw and ER visit. Nora couldn't control the cancer, but she had to control something. So information was what it was.

The recliner across the room was empty, and Nora was thankful. The hours spent in chemo were a religious experience for her. She protected the time with her father and Phe, the three of them immersed in the business of surviving cancer. Her attention to her father bordered on obsessive and she preferred the process to include only the three of them—and Jill. When the door to the infusion room opened, Nora expected to see Jill checking in on William. Instead, a man opened the door and helped guide a woman in.

The woman was her age—maybe younger? Wisps of auburn hair peeked out from under the wine-colored scarf that wrapped around her head to the nape of her neck, its tails trailing down her small back. She wore a cotton caftan in a floral print that matched the scarf. Her eyes, brilliant moss-colored green, were sallow and deep-set, a telltale sign of the loss of health. Nora smiled quietly.

"Good morning," the auburn beauty said as she smiled at William first, and then Phe and Nora pointedly. Her head nodded as she smiled, an acknowledgment that she and William belonged to a club no one wanted to be in.

"Good morning..." her father responded. Nora smiled. He hadn't spoken much since the infusion started. The sound of his voice—although it was weak and thin—wrapped around Nora like a favorite blanket. She squeezed her eyes shut, holding every syllable her dad spoke tightly, imprinting it into her DNA. Fear of forgetting. Forgetting the timbre of his voice, the calluses on his hands, the wrinkles around his eyes were her searing fears.

The gentleman helped his wife—at first Nora assumed it was his wife because they both wore wedding rings, but it was soon obvious in his affection and care of his wife that the two were bound by love—into her chair, tucking the edges of her hand-knitted afghan of many colors around her small frame. He adjusted her pillow and his hand touched her cheek as she settled back and closed her eyes. Nora ached a bit as she watched the husband and wife and her father and mother.

Was it crazy to feel envious of a woman ravaged by cancer? Because she was. It had been a long time since Nora had felt cherished by Joe the way this woman was cared for by this man. Would Joe care for her this way? Would he spoon-feed her ice chips and gently hold her hand while she slept through hours of poison being poured into her veins? Would he carefully settle her into her chair and quietly consult with Jill about this week's lab results? Nora knew he would. Joe would care for her out of duty and obligation. But would he care for her out of love? Nora wasn't sure anymore.

"How are you feeling?" William asked the woman.

Her eyes fluttered open, a smile slowly rising to her eyes from her lips. "I am here today. So it's a good day."

"Yes, it is a good day if we are still here," he answered.

Nora's eyes filled with tears. She had nowhere to look where her father or Phe or the wife and her husband could not see her. She could not hide her emotion or disguise it as anything other than what it was: grief and guilt. Grief for the impending loss of her father and guilt for her anger toward the world that her father had to suffer in this way, guilt that this woman sat racked with illness while she herself was bathed in health.

She was angry her father was sick, despite having lived a long, happy and healthy life. She wanted more time with him. He had a family and a wife he adored, a career he had been both successful at and enjoyed. And here sat this sprite of a woman whose life was draining from her as sure as the water from an emptying tub. Her life was far more difficult than it should have to be, and likely profoundly shorter. She watched the woman's fingers turn into each other on top of the blanket. The worry, the anxiety, the pain, the fear, the side effects all exiting her body by way of her fingertips, like energy shorting out a line.

The husband reached and quieted his wife's hands, cupping them both inside of his. Her slender, long fingers curled and settled quietly in the nest of his warm hands. She smiled up at him, her eyes fluttering open just for a moment. She was so tired. Nora watched as the husband bowed his head in resignation before he reached to kiss his wife's forehead.

When he looked up, he caught Nora's gaze. A small, resigned smiled whispered across his lips. Loving someone who was dying was perhaps the most painful thing in the world and for a moment, Nora and the husband were bound by their shared ache of loss, grief, guilt and sadness. Nora turned back toward her binder, not wanting to intrude and the husband's regard returned to his wife.

While originally she had felt slighted with the semi-private room, now she found strength in the solidarity of her father and the woman walking their way through another chemotherapy treatment, while Phe, Nora and the husband held them up however they could.

William's transfusion was complete before the wife's and Phe and Nora prepared him to go home. Phe helped her husband slip on his shoes, then she folded up his blanket and helped him pull on his jacket. Nora gathered The Book and tidied up the bay they had been sitting in. She pulled her own coat on and sunk her hands deep into her pockets, her hand landing on her worry stone.

When Nora had been young, she and William had spent hours on the beaches of Petoskey State Park and Wilderness State Park, searching for treasure: Petoskey stones. They would get up at dawn, traversing the beach as the sun rose so that they could have the first pick of the lake's nightly offerings. Nora loved the predictability of the pattern on the rocks, the spider web of delicate shapes connected to each other. She loved the way they looked like other rocks when they were dry, and when they were wet their pattern sprang to life. She loved the way each rock looked exactly alike and completely different.

As long as Nora could remember William had carried a Petoskey stone in his pocket. His fingers fiddled with the rock, twirling it about and rubbing his thumbs over the smooth texture. They helped him think, he said. Kept him focused. Even brought him good luck! When Nora had been anxious as a girl William had taught her to do the same. She would rub her thumb over her stone—back and forth—to soothe her troubles.

"It's a worry stone, Norie. Keep it in your pocket and when you are worried or nervous, hold it in your hand and remind yourself you can do hard things," he said.

He never kept the same one long. William believed in leaving his stones with those who needed them—the waitress at breakfast as a topper to her tip, Sullivan after a good football game, Sammy when she moved to Lansing. He gave one to Joe when he opened his new office. They were his calling card, his gift of admiration and love and respect. Jill was the latest to receive one. She'd gushed when he gave it to her, and Nora noticed her handling the rock in her pocket today.

The morning after William had been diagnosed, Nora drove out to the State Park and walked the beach just as the sun was coming up behind the hills. The curve of the land that led toward Petoskey and away from Harbor Springs was ripe with Petoskey stones that morning. She'd kept only one—while she liked to find them, she only kept the ones that spoke to her. The ones that felt right in her hand, the ones that gave her energy and hope. As she had aged it had become more about the discovery and less about the bounty. This morning as she had walked a perfectly heart-shaped stone with a dip in its middle, the perfect size for her thumb, washed up between her feet.

Its pattern was dense and vibrant when wet, and when it had dried, its shape—the heart—spoke loudly to her. She'd kept the stone, taken it home and varnished it so it would carry its hidden pattern always, its sheen would always be perfect. She harbored the rock in her pocket with her everywhere she went, just as her dad taught her to do. When she began to feel anxious or fretful, she'd tuck her hand into her pocket and turn the stone around, letting the motion and energy from the stone comfort her.

She pulled the stone out of its hiding place and bridged the few short steps between herself and the wife and husband with a knowing in her heart. The wife lay sleeping, her head tipped back and the blanket pulled to her chin. The husband looked up and smiled softly.

"I'd like your wife to have this," Nora said quietly. Tears stung her eyes as she handed the stranger her rock. "It's a worry stone. My dad…" Nora looked back at William. "He always carries one. I picked the habit up from him. He carries one until he sees someone who needs it more than he does. Then he passes it on and looks for a new one."

"Thank you," he said as he held the stone in his hands.

Nora knew she should say, "You're welcome." She should wish them well, she should wish the wife health and recovery. Instead her lips fell quiet and she was covered in an overwhelming sense of dread. The wife would not make it. And this man, her husband, would never be the same.

JOE

The decision to drive together to take Sullivan to school was based one part on convenience and one part on what Sullivan needed. Joe and Nora both wanted to be with Sullivan, they both wanted to move him in. Drawing attention to their separation by driving separate cars to the same destination wasn't going to help anybody. They were adults, they were civil, they could ride in the same car and move their son into his freshman dorm together. They were still a family, at least that's what they had told Sully. Joe couldn't help feeling a bubble of hope—he would have his wife and his son together for a few hours. Maybe he and Nora could find a common ground to talk. Maybe Joe could finally have the talk with Sullivan that Officer Gray had urged him to have. He hoped so, he was running out of time.

Joe pulled up to the house in the borrowed F-150. Steven, who hadn't taken his calls all summer, finally answered a text and had agreed to allow Joe to use his truck to move Sully to CMU. Joe had been embarrassed at how excited he was to see his friend—until he realized that Steven was no longer friendly. Steven had texted Joe to tell him the truck was in their driveway with the keys in it and a full tank of gas. Read: don't bother coming to the door, we're doing Nora and Sullivan a favor, not you.

The ride down to CMU had been uneventful. Nora read a book, and Sullivan plugged in his head phones and watched *The Office* on his phone. The quiet was occasionally punctuated by Sullivan laughing at his show.

Joe was silent as he drove, the monotony of the highway and the absence of chatter or stress was quiet and peaceful. Yes, they were dropping their son off at college—something Nora had dreaded doing for months—but they were doing it together. No matter the circumstances, Joe was happy to have both Nora and Sully in the car with him. Sure, it was a little awkward, and the ache for his old life was heavy on his heart, but it was something.

Stephanie had been relentlessly texting since he'd left that morning, hardly an hour had gone by without her checking in, asking how it was going, asking for pictures of Sullivan's room. Joe couldn't help the feeling that she was invading his family's time—and that invasion was calculated. She knew he couldn't ignore his phone—he would always be available to his patients in case of emergency. She used that to her advantage—disrupting his time with Nora and Sully with constant reminders that she should be his focus now. Nora had turned her head when his phone rang the first several times, the chimes distracting her from her book. He'd been stupid enough to leave his phone in the cupholder, where she could easily see that it was Stephanie. Nora hadn't said a word—after the first handful of texts even Nora quit acknowledging them.

Standing in his son's dorm room, watching Nora hang shirts on hangers—her hands shaking and her voice quiet—Joe felt the ache of losing his family grow. He remembered the strange cocktail of excitement and sadness in his heart when he got to his new dorm at U of M. He'd met Nora a few months before he started college. She had framed a small picture of the two of them out on the end of the dock in Harbor Springs for him to take with him to school. He'd propped it neatly in the corner of his desk, her smile and the memory of the sun on their carefree shoulders had gotten him through many tough days and nights at school. Nearly every memory he has in his adult life is tied to Nora in some way, forever woven together.

Sullivan chatted easily with his new roommate. They'd met via Instagram and bonded over Michael Scott and "Fortnite"—for what that was worth. He wasn't sure his boy was ready for this step—but he was ready to *try* and that gave Joe comfort.

"Well, that's about it, kiddo," Nora said. "I think

everything is unpacked." Beads of sweat collected on her brow, her cheeks were flushed red with the heat of the day—it was eighty-nine degrees and there was no air conditioning! She'd propped a fan up in Sullivan's window, facing it toward his bed, and turned it on. Joe watched his wife. Her shorts were baggy and her arms, which had always been strong and muscular, were now willowy and thin. She looked more like Sammy now than ever. She had lost weight. Joe had never minded her healthy physique, he'd always thought she was beautiful no matter her size, which frankly wasn't considered big by anyone's standards but her own. Nora had never believed him. Joe always suspected Nora couldn't bring herself to trust him that she was good enough. He had always thought her capable, strong, independent and beautiful. He wasn't sure when the words he used to describe his wife turned to: cold, indifferent, exclusive and bitchy—but he regretted them now. He had been so myopic in his view, so self-centered. What was it that they called teenagers? Egocentric? Only able to see things from their view? That was Joe Phillips all right, at least for the past year.

"Thanks, Momma," Sullivan said as he hugged his mother in a moment of tenderness. Nora rested her head on their son's shoulder and Joe's throat grew tight. He and Nora had a running dialogue about becoming empty nesters over the years, but never had that dialogue included Nora returning home to an empty house and Joe returning to his mistress's condo. Nora had always cried when she talked about the kids leaving—Joe had always been pragmatic, it was what was supposed to happen, did she really want them to live with them forever? He'd thought his wife's sentiment was sweet, if not a little irritating that she hadn't been more excited to have the freedom of focusing on each other back as it had been in the beginning. But now, standing in this room with his only son, watching his wife gently weep into his shoulder, Joe carried the weight of destroying his family and the sadness of a future that should have been.

Nora stepped away and into the bathroom to gather some Kleenex to dry her tears. Joe stepped toward Sully to hug his son. Sullivan put his arm around his dad's shoulders and said, "Thanks, Dad, for moving me in." The tenderness he'd shown his mother was not shown to Joe. If Sullivan had been trying to hurt Joe—he succeeded. Joe found relief in the pain brought to him by his son's half-hearted goodbye. He had made a colossal mistake and he deserved his son's reproach.

"Okay then, kiddo," Nora managed to speak. "We'll see you later? Please don't forget to text me every now and then, maybe call? Let me know you're alive." She smiled.

"I will, Mom." Sullivan was already pulling up a chair to the television with his roommate—Brian—to start a new round of "Fortnite."

"Go to class. Don't skip. You know how hard that will be for you," she reminded him.

"Yep, I got it. Don't skip. Go to class. Text you every now and then." His attention now fully on choosing his skins for the game and discussing which map he and Brian would drop into.

Joe stepped toward the door, opened it and held it for his wife. This woman he'd loved all his adult life. This woman he'd destroyed by breaking her trust. This woman who was being gutted by leaving their child at college. He put his hand on the small of her back and she flinched under his touch. Joe felt his heart twist into a knot so tight he thought he might lose his ability to see. His wife couldn't stand to be touched by him. What had he done?

Nora slept cuddled against the door of Steven's F-150—curling into a space so tiny Joe didn't think she could get any smaller. She had placed herself as far away from Joe as she could get, any illusions he'd had that they might be able to talk on this drive home were squashed when she got into the car.

"Do you want to stop and eat somewhere?" he'd asked.

"No, I'm not hungry."

"Are you sure? You haven't eaten all day," he'd asked again.

"I'm sure. I just want to go home."

So Joe had driven while Nora slept. They'd left at a reasonable time, but still they were an hour out of

Petoskey and daylight was nearly gone.

He pulled off the highway. He'd grab a quick bite and be back on the road quickly. Nora may not have been hungry, but he was starving. While he had envisioned taking Nora out to eat on their way home, talking over what they should do next was clearly overzealous. He still needed to eat, and McDonald's wasn't going to cut it. He'd run into J Dubbs sub shop in Alanson and grab a quick club—he'd ordered a turkey no cheese, light mayo for Nora even though she hadn't asked for anything.

He checked his phone. There were seven texts from Steph since he'd left CMU. He clicked on her name, opening up the messages. The last one was a picture of her wearing nearly nothing and holding a bottle of champagne.

When will you be home? I'm ready to celebrate becoming empty nesters!

Joe typed back: *Stopped to eat. Be a while yet.*

When they had been sneaking around behind Nora's back, Stephanie had sent nude pictures of herself regularly. Joe would open them in his car when he was alone, study them and delete them immediately. At the time he'd found it thrilling—sexting certainly wasn't something Nora would have done. But now he found Stephanie looked desperate and, frankly, a little trashy in her red bustier, her eyes heavy with smokey eye shadow and her red lips puckered in a pouty smile that was supposed to be sexy. Joe shook his head at how easily he had been distracted from his marriage, deleted the string of texts and slid his phone into his jeans pocket.

Nora woke up when he hopped back in the car, and he quietly handed her her favorite sandwich. She thanked him softly. Joe felt his heart skip. She hadn't spoken to him directly much today—other than to orchestrate and organize the move—and her acknowledgement of the simplest gift, a turkey sub, was less than he'd hoped for but surrounded him with comfort.

"Hey Joe, I have been wanting to ask you something." Nora's opened the wrapper on her sub, avoiding looking at him.

Joe took a deep breath. He wanted nothing more than to talk with Nora, but he also knew it wouldn't be easy. "You can ask me anything," he answered.

"Stephanie drives a Jeep, right?" Nora continued fussing with her sandwich wrapper.

"Yes she does," Joe had promised himself that he would be as forthright and upfront as he could be. His desire to defend himself and to tell Nora how much her inattention and neglect has hurt him these past few years was raw—and unpredictable. If Joe had any hope of talking—really talking—with Nora he cannot allow his hurt and anger to seep forward before his remorse and sadness.

"I think she's been driving by the house. My house. A Jeep drove up past me the night Sully went to jail. And again the other day when I got home from running errands she was parked outside my house across the street." Nora took a deep breath. "I guess I shouldn't say 'she.' A Jeep that looks like the one your girlfriend drives was parked outside my house. It drove off when I came up."

"Really? That's strange," Joe replied for a lack of a better answer.

"Is it?" Nora looked up at Joe as he drove.

"I'll talk with her."

"I don't know what good that will do, she won't admit to it. I just wanted you to know. It scares me. If it happens again I'm calling the police. Officer Gray gave me his cell phone number. Maybe I will just call him."

Officer Gray. Joe felt his cheeks flush. Nora was a beautiful woman, and she had made it clear to Officer Gray that she and Joe were separated. Was he imagining his wife's interest in another man? Regret plunged into Joe's chest as he realized, again, the depth of pain he had caused his wife.

"I'll take care of it. I'm sorry…"

Nora nodded in response to Joe's apology, a small, sad smile playing at the corners of her lips. She returned to eating her dinner and Joe worried.

He would have to be careful leaving Stephanie. And although the decision to leave her had started out as a murky, foggy idea, the sharp edges of the plan had become crisp and clear in his mind—until now. Above all else he must protect Nora. It would take a while to ease Stephanie out of this fantasy, the fairytale ending she has constructed for the two of them. Joe fantasized about walking into the condo and packing his bag as soon as he returned home tonight—but no, he will have to take Stephanie's temperature. If she is already driving by the house, and Joe is certain she is, Joe must tread lightly, work slowly and quietly to end his relationship. Patience was never his strong suit, but he would have to find some now.

The rain had started to fall when they were only twenty minutes outside of Petoskey, nearly home. It was coming down in sheets—a welcome break to the drought they'd been having but still, Joe would have preferred not to be on the road. He slowed down to forty-five mph. Texts continued to come from Stephanie. He'd pulled his phone out of his pocket and slipped it into the cupholder again. The constant vibrating against his leg was distracting. Not just the physical annoyance of a continually vibrating phone, but the constant intrusion into the quiet cab of the truck where Joe was safely tucked in with Nora. He opened the phone, clicking on the "Do Not Disturb" button and set his phone back down.

He hadn't seen the car coming until it was too late. Regardless there wouldn't have been anything he could have done. The red Cherokee hydroplaned, careened through the intersection and slammed into Nora's door, where she had just returned to sleeping after finishing her sub. The crunch of the metal was excruciatingly loud, the screech of the truck's tires on the wet pavement were long and fruitless, the rain and the weight of the truck were unrelenting. The distance they traveled after they were hit seemed miles. Joe wrestled the truck trying to regain control, desperately attempting to steer them away from the oncoming tree. It was too late, Steven's F-150 hit the tree head-on.

"Nora!" Joe yelled. "Nora!" She didn't answer. When Joe was able to gain his bearings and find his phone to turn on the flashlight, fighting with the airbags that had deployed into his chest, he looked at his wife.

"Nora! No!" He dialed 9-1-1, his hands shaking and his mind numb. *Please, please, please don't let this be how this ends. Please!* He quickly gave the dispatcher their location and Nora's condition. She was unresponsive, they needed to hurry.

Nora sat silently, blood dripping down her forehead, He reached for Nora's hand, squeezing it. "Please baby, wake up, Nora! Come on you have to wake up!" He began to cry and his body shook.

The weight of the last year, the lies, the broken trust, the bad decisions, the selfish indiscretion, the pain, the hurt hurdled itself at Joe soaking him in regret. He was paralyzed in fear. He checked for her pulse, first at her wrist and then at her neck. He couldn't find a heartbeat.

How many times would he hurt this woman? Joe Phillips had killed his wife.

JOE

Nora Phillips didn't die on the side of the road. Not the way Joe feared. She had hit her head and was unconscious for quite some time. Seventeen stitches were required to close the gap over her right eye.

When Nora came to, she had been disoriented, obviously. She looked between Joe and Jason Dodds (was he ever not on call?), both doctors leaning over the slim ER bed, checking her pupils and reflexes. Joe had smears of blood across his cheek and was soaked to the bone, his eyes as big as saucers.

"Nora, baby you scared me to death," Joe said, squeezing her hand. Nora shook her head side-to-side, trying in vain to shed the oxygen tubing placed around her face and into her nose.

"Joe?" she questioned.

"I'm here, Norie. I'm here," Joe answered. His hand in hers felt achingly familiar and painfully uncomfortable.

"Why are you here?" Nora asked.

Joe didn't answer, he simply kissed his wife's forehead. Jason clapped Joe's back twice as he stepped away from the bed to check Nora's heart monitor readings.

"You two were lucky tonight," Jason said.

"Yeah. I know." Joe's voice was thin, weak. His body shivered with fear and chill. He'd nearly walked himself straight into traffic when he couldn't find Nora's pulse in the car. When the ambulance had arrived, he'd warned them she was coding—but they'd found a pulse immediately. Joe insisted she hadn't had a pulse moments earlier, the paramedics guessing perhaps Joe's hands weren't steady enough to detect it. Joe didn't buy it, he knew her pulse had been gone. Nora had left this world, just for a moment, in search of peace she hadn't had in years.

"Why don't you let me examine you? She's sleeping again, she's hooked up to the monitors. Kelly is monitoring her vitals from the desk. We can slip in the room next door."

"No, I'm not leaving my wife," Joe said, his eyes not leaving Nora's.

Jason nodded. Joe's words meant far more than leaving Nora in this room to have his own health checked out. "I'll be back in a little bit. Let me know if she becomes agitated or irritable at all." Jason swept the curtain back and headed toward the adjacent room to check on the young kid who'd hit Nora and Joe. He was immediately met with Stephanie Laredo standing just outside Nora's door.

"Stephanie, what are you doing here?" Jason asked.

"I came to check on Joe! Have you seen him, is he okay?" Her words were quick, spilling out quickly, tumbling over each other like an awkward teenager dancing with two left feet.

"He's fine. He's with his wife," Jason said.

"His ex-wife," Stephanie answered, her voice icy.

"I can't give you any details. HIPAA. You know that. You aren't family or on any release forms." Jason walked back toward the nurses' station leaving Stephanie standing in the hallway.

Stephanie waited outside Nora's room, where Joe was watching Nora with hawk-like vigilance. Jason had checked on Nora twice. She was easily aroused and answered all his questions: what day is it? What year is it? What did you do today? She didn't remember the accident, but according to Joe she'd been sleeping so that wasn't concerning. The CT scan was negative. He still decided to keep her overnight. She would be transferred to the floor within the next hour.

Joe called Sammy and texted Sullivan, letting his kids know they'd been in a car accident. At first he debated telling them, but a fear that somehow the kids would find out through social media propelled him to let them know. Sullivan texted back immediately (so he does read his phone!) and was a little freaked out. Sammy offered to come be with her mom, but Joe didn't want her driving in the storms that had been covering the state. After the near miss tonight, he didn't think he could handle worrying about his daughter driving all the way home. Plus, the idea of sleeping in the same room as Nora, even in the recliner by her hospital bed, brought him a comfort he hadn't felt in months.

Next, he'd let Phe know was going on. She had become the littlest bit weepy, which was unlike his mother-in-law. But after William died, Joe understood her fear of loss. Phe insisted she could Uber to the hospital, to which Joe giggled. The only septuagenarian around with wicked technology and Ubering skills. No, he'd urged her to stay put. He promised Phe he'd stay with Nora, would take care of her and not let her be alone.

Jason finally talked Joe into stepping into a second examination room to be checked on himself. He'd sent a med tech down to Joe's locker and had come back with a pair of Joe's own scrubs for him to change into. His clothes were still soaked and had a fair amount of blood streaked across his chest. He had a few sore ribs—probably cracked, although he declined an X-ray. With clear lung sounds and an oxygen level that was above ninety-eight percent, Jason would keep an eye on them rather than treat them in any way.

"Stephanie's waiting to talk with you," Jason said as he pressed his hands into Joe's belly, checking for internal injuries. Joe ran his hands through his hair. "I don't think she's going to leave without seeing you," Jason continued. He had dismissed Stephanie several times, reminding her that he could not give her any information and she should go home and check in with

Joe later. She hadn't budged. She was sitting in the waiting room, refusing to leave.

"Is Nora sleeping?" Joe asked.

"I'm not sure, she's up on the floor now. Room 325. She's not in the ER anymore."

Joe nodded his head slowly. "You can let Stephanie in."

"Joey! Oh my God, you scared me to death!" Stephanie rushed into his small cubicle, throwing herself on his bed, wrapping her arms around him sucking the air away from him. He winced in pain as she put pressure on his ribs. Her eyes were wet, smoky with anticipation.

"I'm fine. Just a few broken ribs that would really appreciate you not laying on them." His voice was colder than he had intended, and Stephanie paused, momentarily.

"Oh, I'm so sorry. You poor baby. I'm going to take you home tonight and take care of you. I can be your own private nurse—"

"I can't leave. I need to stay here with Nora."

"Joey, I have been waiting all day for you to get home. I made dinner, I had plans for us to celebrate our empty nest! I have been sitting here all night waiting to see you—Jason wouldn't let me in!"

Joe nodded his head, acknowledging that he knew

she'd been there. Stephanie's eyes filled with tears.

"I was so scared when Kelly called me to tell me you were here! I was so scared. I had texted and texted you—I called you three times and never got an answer—I should have known it was because you're hurt. I don't know what I would do without you, I really don't. I don't know how I'd go on…" Stephanie poured tears like a daytime-soap-opera-Emmy-award-winning actress. Joe was tired, he didn't have the energy to deal with this kind of emotion from Stephanie. His mind was on the third floor with his wife. He'd made such a mess of things, he really had. His wife was suffering from a concussion as a result of a car accident he caused, that was a direct result of the affair he had carried on for months. Stephanie stood before him with tears running down her face, not innocent in the carnage they'd caused—but he could not deny she was also collateral damage.

He knew she was manipulating him. The adrenaline from the accident and fear of losing Nora has seeped from his veins. All that was left was a carved out feeling of fatigue and sadness. Stephanie was actively trying to keep him from being with Nora, from reconnecting with his wife, from allowing this near-tragedy to lay new bricks in a crumbled pathway. And yet, Joe felt obligated. She had befriended him when he was lonely. When he had felt sad and rejected by his wife—Stephanie had become his friend. And he had become hers.

It wasn't always about sex with Joe and Stephanie. The two had bonded over past hurts. Over fathers who had neglected and abandoned them as young children—something Nora could never fully understand. Her father had doted on her; Stephanie never knew her father. And while Joe had known his dad, his womanizing ways had left Joe lonely and responsible for his mother and sister when he was too young to carry that burden. Stephanie had understood that pain. She'd taken a piece of it and carried it for him. He couldn't just walk away from her in the middle of the ER without an explanation, without a conversation that did not have the hospital staff listening in.

Joe felt incredibly guilty leaving Nora upstairs alone. He wasn't prepared to feel guilty leaving Stephanie, also. Moving Sullivan in to his dorm with Nora confirmed what Joe already knew: he wanted his wife back. He wanted his family and his life back. He knew that Nora may not forgive him, she may have moved far past a desire to reconcile—but he now knew without a doubt that he needed to try. He needed to tell Stephanie he was leaving—but he couldn't do it tonight.

Joe listened as Stephanie asked Jason for Joe's release papers. Jason had resisted at first, citing HIPAA regulations, until Joe relented that, *yes, she could be present.* Joe's thoughts drifted to his wife upstairs. He had promised Phe he'd stay with her. He'd told Sammy he would be sure she was okay. How could he leave? How could he stay?

"Steph, I do need to talk with Jason privately. Could you give us a minute?" Joe asked.

"Oh. Well, yeah. I will go pull the car up. You are coming home with me, right?" Stephanie asked, her eyes wet with tears.

"I will go back to your condo, yes." Stephanie turned and walked out. Joe was certain she knew what he was thinking. Along with sharing with Joe the hurts her father who had never been a part of her life, Stephanie had told him of the others. The other married men. The men she thought loved her. The men she thought would stay. None of them did. She had been so sure that Joe would stay, and he hadn't argued with her. He'd been paralyzed by fear. He'd been embarrassed at what he had become. He had made a decision. Stephanie had been his choice. Or had he decided? Had he really been the one to choose what his life would look like? Or had the choice been made for him by default?

No more. He would go back with Stephanie and leave her in a way that respected the confidences she had given him. He would ask for forgiveness, he would tell her she was worth more than being the second choice of a man with a family and wife. He would remind her of the fire in her belly that had helped her survive the abandonment of her father and the loose parenting of her mother. He would leave her with dignity—he would not leave her the way he had left

Nora with selfish disrespect.

And then, he would go to his wife.

"Jason, I can't just leave her in the ER," Joe said.

"Leave who? Your wife with the concussion or your girlfriend in the lobby?"

"Either. Neither. I can't leave Stephanie in the lobby of the ER. I already left Nora in a way that was incredibly selfish. I can't do it twice. I need to go back, be a man, and tell Stephanie we're done. I just can't do it in the lobby. I don't expect you to understand— you're a far better man than I am. You wouldn't be in this position to begin with, I know. But I'm trying to do the right thing. I'm trying to do right by Stephanie *and* Nora." Joe's eyes begged for understanding. "I need a favor."

"You're right, I wouldn't be in this situation." Jason pulled a deep breath, resting both hands on either end of his stethoscope around his neck. "What do you need me to do?"

"Keep an eye on Nora. Let me know the minute something changes. I'll be back first thing tomorrow morning."

"Yes, I can do that," Jason answered. "Do right by yourself, will you?"

"Thank you. I really appreciate it. I will. I promise."

"Hey, Joey... you ready to go home?" Stephanie peeked her head around the corner of the curtain.

"Yeah, I'm ready to go." Joe gingerly pulled himself off the gurney, adjusting the binder Jason had insisted he wear around his fractured ribs. He crossed his arms around his chest, trying to stave off the pain that the chest binder didn't fix: the pain of his broken heart.

NORA

Nora woke to the strange feeling of an IV in the crook of her elbow. The green and red lights blinked beside her bed, a subtle grinding of the pump pushing the fluid into her veins drowned out the voices in the hallway. The air smelled vaguely of antiseptic and sickness. It was dark, she searched for a clock on the wall—2:30? It must be the middle of the night. Confusion floated through Nora's thoughts like cotton candy. Was Joe here? Why had he been holding her hand? Was he holding her hand? Weren't they getting divorced? Or had she dreamed that? She looked down at her hands, her wedding ring still resting on her ring finger.

No, she knew they were getting divorced. The stone in her stomach that had been her constant companion since June was still there. Panic brushed her chest like feathers touching her skin, just skimming the surface. Her hand reached up to the bandage on her forehead. She remembered the sirens and the ambulance, waking up and seeing Joe holding her hand. He was crying. *He called me "baby,"* she thought. They'd moved

Sullivan! Yes, that was it. They'd driven to CMU, moved Sully in. She ate a turkey sub, fell asleep... the accident. The day's events unfolded in small shards of memory, like the glass from the windshield splattered across the inside of the truck—Steven's truck!—when she woke up. She knew all the pieces were there, she just couldn't quite get them in order to make sense.

Where was Joe now? Nora looked around the room, hoping to see her husband sleeping in the convertible chair in the corner. No, she was alone. The sadness that had descended on her in June pulled tightly against her chest. Slipping her arm out from under the covers, Nora rooted around on the bedside table for her phone. Certainly it would have come up with her from the ER? She had been so sleepy she hardly remembered the ride in the stretcher up here to her room. Finally, her fingers found purchase and she grabbed her phone.

Five text messages:

Sammy: *Momma! I hope you are okay!!! Daddy wouldn't let me drive up in the rain but said he would stay with you! I took the day off and will be there tomorrow to see you! I LOVE YOUUUUU! Text me when you get this.*

Sullivan: *Hey momma hope u r ok I feel so bad you got hurt going home from moving me in. Hope you are okay. Love u*

Phe: *Nora, honey I am so sorry you were hurt. I*

spoke with Joe. He said he would stay with you tonight otherwise I would have been up.

616-452-8763: *Nora, this is Stephanie Laredo. Joe is here at home with me. Just wanted you to know he's fine, a few cracked ribs but nothing I can't take care of! Hope you are feeling better!*

Nora tucked her phone under her pillow. Joe had left her here in the hospital alone and gone home with Stephanie. Stephanie was cruel enough to be sure Nora knew. As if stealing her husband wasn't punishment enough. Nora knew she hadn't always been kind to Stephanie Laredo, but sending that text was vicious. She had no energy to be angry. She pulled the stiff hospital sheets up around her chin. They smelled like bleach, sterile and scratchy. Still, she created a cocoon to insulate herself, trying to feel safe. This wasn't what she had envisioned her first night without Sullivan would be like. Although she had a headache worse than any of her life, and although she had stitches closing the gash in her forehead, she was thankful to not be at home on Trillium Drive alone. She was thankful to be where voices could be heard in the hallway and there were sounds and signs of life—no matter what they were.

She had felt such comfort when she woke after the accident, holding Joe's hand. Being in the presence of his love and care. His hand had been warm, familiar. The pieces of her broken heart reached for Joe. Nora couldn't understand why that would be. He cheated on her. He'd left her. How could she possibly forgive him, allow him back in? It wasn't what you do. Still, Nora felt a tug, like a child pulling on her apron strings.

But what did it matter? Joe wasn't here now.

Nora squeezed her eyes and tried desperately to not think of Joe and Stephanie. She tried not to worry what Sullivan was doing on his first night on campus. Maybe she should ask for some pain medicine to dull both the roar in her head and the anxiety in her chest. Tears stung her eyes. Why she felt disappointed, she wasn't sure. She knew she and Joe were getting divorced. She knew he was living with Stephanie, of course he would have gone home with her! Still, she couldn't help feeling as if she'd been left again. The familiar thundering of the derby horse echoed in her chest. She pulled herself down under the covers, not wanting anyone to suspect.

It wouldn't have mattered if Joe had stayed tonight. She couldn't forgive him. That's not how this worked. Nora wanted to be married. But she wanted to be married to a man she could trust and Joe had ruined that. No, forgiveness wasn't in Nora's repertoire, she wouldn't—no that wasn't it, it wasn't that she wouldn't, it was that she *couldn't*—even consider it. Her two-carat ring, the one she'd bargained her future and family for. The ring she'd traded the promise of their lives together for. The ring that reminded her of her failed marriage every day suddenly became too much to look at. Her hands shook as she twisted and turned the never-ending circle off of her finger. A tender indentation was all that remained on her hand, a quiet reminder of what they had lost. She touched the naked space where her promise to Joe once lived, her heart finally broken in ways she couldn't imagine.

Lying in the dark under the hospital sheets, tears rolling down her cheeks, Nora closed her eyes and the sound of her heart thudding in her chest got louder. She knew what she needed. She grabbed her phone and tapped out a text.

Mom, can you come?

Nearly instantly came the reply.

Phe: *I'm on my way.*

AUGUST 24, 2018

JOE

Joe was furious.

It was eleven in the morning, five hours—five hours!—after he had set his alarm to get up and head to the hospital to check on Nora. He'd been so tired when he arrived at Stephanie's condo from the ER, he'd barely made it into the house. The physical fatigue of moving Sullivan, and the accident, combined with the emotional exhaustion of dropping his son off at college and believing his wife had died on the side of the road, left him profoundly exhausted. He'd crawled into a recliner in front of the television and had set his alarm for 6:00 AM, not having the energy or ambition to explain to Steph he wasn't sleeping in her bed.

His alarm never went off.

The four-mile trip to the hospital felt like forty. Traffic, lights, rain. Joe slammed the palm of his hand onto his steering wheel three times as he waited to turn into the staff parking lot at the hospital. The pain reverberated down his arm and into his chest, his broken ribs ached with each pound.

Joe raced up the stairs in the back hallway, taking the stairs by two when he could stand the pain. His phone vibrated in his pocket. He didn't need to look at the screen to know it was Stephanie. She would call incessantly until he answered. And he wasn't answering. Not now anyway.

The back staff elevator was hot. Sweat dripped down Joe's back under his shirt. He'd forgotten to wear the binder they'd given him in the ER to compress his ribs and decrease the pain. He hadn't wanted to take the time to put it on and adjust it—now, standing in the elevator heaving deep breaths, he wished he had. Joe watched the elevator lights ding as he passed the second floor, finally landing on the third.

Room 325. The door was cracked open just a touch. Joe heard chatting as he breezed in, and he smiled. He'd made it in time!

"Hi, Dr. Phillips!"

Startled, Joe answered, "May? Hi there... I must be confused I thought my wife, Nora Phillips was in this room?" Joe turned to look at the paperwork still in the file folder inside the door. The bed was empty

"Oh she was, but she left about an hour ago. Sampson did rounds about seven and signed her discharge papers. Her mom was here with her. She was headed home, I know." May had been talking with Michael, the head of maintenance. Both of them looked at Joe now, just as confused as Joe felt.

"Shit," Joe whispered under his breath. His ribs ached, his head was throbbing. His phone was continuing to vibrate relentlessly. Phe had picked up Nora. Joe had promised Phe that Nora wouldn't stay the night alone, promised her he'd watch out for her. And instead, he'd headed back to Stephanie's. At the time, it seemed like the right thing to do. His intentions were good—he was trying to do right by both women. This morning, it became clear to him that doing right by both his wife and his mistress was self-serving. Was he afraid to leave Stephanie without knowing if Nora was willing to try again? Perhaps he had been. His phone vibrated in his pocket again and this time he pulled his phone out and turned his phone off.

How would he fix this now?

AUGUST 30, 2016

ROBERT

As Katie's time had drawn thin, she encouraged Robert to pay attention, to keep his eyes open and look for love. She didn't want him spending his life alone, she couldn't bear it she'd said. He was young, she'd said. He had so much to offer another woman, she'd said. He'd told her he could never replace her.

She smiled and said, "I don't want to be replaced. But I won't be here, Wolfy. You can find somebody who is good and honest and fun. Who's healthy. I don't want you to be alone." He would smile but never agree. If he couldn't be with Katie, alone was where he wanted to be.

In the end it had been Katie, Robert and her older sister Laurie. Katie was snuggled under her favorite colorful afghan—they could never get her warm enough—her breath ragged and uneven. The doctors had told them there was nothing more to do. Nothing more to say. Katie wanted to die at home, in her cottage by the lake with her husband and sister by her side.

They'd turned the office into a makeshift hospital room. Laurie had worked tirelessly to find her every convenience and comfort she could find - a hospital bed, a bedside commode, hot water bottles, cold packs, ice chips, and Chapstick. They had brought her home from the hospital. She'd had thirteen days inside their cozy cottage. Thirteen days to see the sliver of the lake from her hospital bed perched in the office near the front of the house.

Her eyes were mostly closed, her face childlike with no eyebrows or lashes. To Robert, she was the most beautiful woman on Earth, even in the end when she was seventy-eight pounds, with her beautiful auburn hair gone and yellow-toned, hollow cheeks and dry skin. Her moss green eyes shimmered beneath the dull exterior when she was awake—they were a portal into the real Katie, the woman who had given him all she had in this world.

Eric Clapton played in the background, "You Look Wonderful Tonight" on repeat. Katie loved that song, and Robert often sang it to her in their eighteen years together. If she had to leave this Earth, and it appeared she did, he wanted her to leave knowing she was wonderful. She was beautiful. She was his girl.

She winced from time to time, her brow furrowing together, her shoulders pinching in pain. The hospice nurse kept enough morphine on board to keep her fairly sedated and hopefully pain-free. Laurie wept openly. Robert remained still.

Around 1:00 a.m. the last night, Robert sat holding his wife's hand. He was studying each finger, trying to memorize each crease and wrinkle, the shape of her nails and the fading warmth of her touch. Her time was nearly over. He could feel it, his heart raced agonizingly as her breaths grew further and further apart. Laurie had fallen asleep in the chair next to her sister, tears staining her cheeks and her arm draped across Katie.

So much heartbreak, Robert thought. And for what?

Grief disguised as anger hid around every moment. He tried to push it away again now, he wanted to be present, to be with Katie in every moment, and he did not want their time to be poisoned by his fury. Tonight he was tired, the kind of tired only a man whose wife is dying would understand, and his anger broke through and began to roll in like the fog off the lake.

As if Katie could feel the change in her husband, her eyes fluttered open. "Wolfy…" she'd said.

"I'm here, baby. I'm here." His tears—finally—would not be held back.

"Hold me." Her voice was so frail, so thin. "It's time."

Robert's every instinct was to yell, "No! It is not time!" But he didn't. As much as he loved his wife, he was prepared to let her go to release her from the hell that was her body. He looked toward Laurie and Katie gently shook her head no.

Robert slid himself beside his wife, careful to not

hurt her and cradled her body in his arms. Where they had once fit perfectly, their physical differences now pained Robert. His body was strong, able and vibrant. Hers was whittled away, her health gone, nothing left except what remained of her spirit. She held her worry stone in her hand. She'd been clutching it for days. Earlier today Laurie had feared her hand had contracted around the stone. Robert nodded in acknowledgement, reminding her that it no longer mattered. Her hands were of no use to her anymore.

"Promise me…" Katie whispered.

Robert knew what she wanted. Katie wanted Robert to live. She wanted him to find a new life and a new love. Perhaps a woman with children she said, he was meant to be a father and it was her greatest sadness that she could not give that to him. No matter how many times Robert repeated that he would not trade being Katie's husband to be someone's father—Katie still felt guilty.

"I don't need anyone but you, Katie Girl," he answered. His voice thick with love, pain, grief. In all the moments of his life, he had not felt the depth of emotion that consumed him now. The pain was unbearable, and yet the relief he wanted for his wife was so close it tasted sweet on his lips.

"Promise me…" she repeated a little louder. The sound of her sister's voice had woken Laurie. She quietly sat up in her chair, reached over, and kissed her sister's forehead. She rested there for a moment, savoring the warmth of her sister's skin under her lips. Her tears falling, staining Katie's face as if they were her own. Katie looked up and blew Laurie a kiss.

"Make him promise, Laur…" she said. Laurie looked over at Robert and squeezed her eyes together, nodding her head, imploring Robert to give her sister her dying wish.

Robert's heart felt as if it would explode. He pushed the anger back, he would not allow it to color these last gentle moments, the last breaths of his wife's life. He would never love another woman, of that he was certain. But he could also not deny his wife, his love, his best friend, her deepest desire as she left this world.

"Okay, you win. You always do," he conceded. "I promise."

"Finally." She smiled. Her eyes danced for a moment in the dim light of the room. "I love you more," she whispered to her husband and her sister. "I'll always be near. And when you find a new love, you will know I sent her to you." She took Robert's hand in her own and pressed her worry stone into his palm, closing his fingers around the rock.

At 2:37 in the morning, his Katie Girl left this world.

ROBERT

Tonight, Robert picked up his wife's worry stone off the windowsill and tumbled it around in his hand. He kept it on the windowsill facing the lake where the sun spilled in and would keep it warm. Robert rarely touched it. He liked to believe a part of her was still there, her DNA embedded in the stone. He was afraid if he touched it too much her magic would wear away and he would lose the only physical connection he had left to his wife.

Katie had jars full of the rocks. She stored them in mason jars and pottery dishes. She loved to polish and varnish them. She believed in their energy, the power they brought to a room. This worry stone hadn't been one of hers, though. During Katie's last chemo treatment (they'd moved from treatment to palliative care shortly after), a woman in the infusion room with her father gave Robert the stone to give to Katie. When Katie woke up, he pushed it into her hand. She'd been so tired she hadn't asked where it came from and

Robert hadn't explained. Katie never left the house without it again.

Robert caressed the dip in the stone, rubbing his thumb over the place where Katie had rested hers. He wanted to feel her, he wanted to know she was there. He ached to feel the warmth of her hand on his shoulder or the dampness of her kiss on his cheek. He squeezed the rock tightly and wiped away the tear rolling down his cheek. The little seed of hope his wife had planted—*I'll always be near… you'll know I sent her to you*—echoed in his heart.

He turned the worry stone over again. It felt light in his hand. He longed to feel a connection to Katie, to feel her with him as she'd promised. Maybe if he carried the stone with him, he could feel his wife. The sun pooled on his shoulders, the warmth melting into the sadness on his skin. Robert slipped the stone into the front pocket of his jeans. Certainty came to him as the weight of the stone left his fingers and he realized what he should have remembered long ago.

NORA

The text came as a surprise. After she'd seen Robert at the coffee shop a few weeks ago she hadn't run into him since. She'd remembered in detail the morning she gave the stone to him. Nora had thought about reaching out. She had his number from the house appraisal. She wanted to let him know she had been the gifter of the worry stone to his wife. But how did one do that?

Do you remember me? I gave your dead wife a rock once.

In the end, she'd decided against it, if only out of fear of further rejection. But still, she'd thought about Robert. She'd thought about Katie. She'd thought about his sad, brown eyes and the old blue truck he drove. She'd thought about her father and then she'd thought about Joe.

Robert: *I remember. I never did say thank you. Thank you.*

He'd included a picture of the worry stone sitting on a windowsill, the lake in the background and the sun shining. After sitting with her phone in her hand for nearly ten minutes, Nora answered.

You're welcome. She was a beautiful woman. I wish I'd known her.

Nora took a deep breath, touched the bandage on her forehead with her fingertips. It felt foreign and familiar at the same time. She and Robert continued to text over the afternoon and eventually agreed to have coffee at Bay Bean. Their texts were honest and real, a friendship blooming two years after it was planted.

Was this what it felt like to have a friend? Sure, she had friends. Fran and Alicia were her friends, she knew. But not like this. She wasn't pretending with Robert. She wasn't perfect. Was this what it felt like to start over? Was this what it felt like to be real, to not be perfect? Was it because of the worry stone? Or because of Katie or her dad? Was it because of Joe?

Nora wasn't sure, but she was eager to find out.

SEPTEMBER 5, 2018

NORA

Nora was having trouble deciding what to wear. The long Labor Day weekend was finally over—it had stretched out in front of her in a pool of sadness and loneliness. She'd had coffee with Robert and she'd enjoyed that. She'd talked to Sullivan who had stayed at school, and Sammy had checked in after going to a music festival in Nashville with her girlfriends. She met Phe for dinner at Chandler's on Sunday evening. Other than that, she'd tried to walk—but the celebration of the weekend, the close of summer coming had a bittersweet end for her this year.

The summer had started with Sullivan's graduation—Nora had been dreading this fall and his impending departure for college—but she couldn't have imagined then what her Labor Day weekend would look like. The town had been full of last-minute summer tourists—little kids eating drippy ice cream cones, live music in the park, the marina full of boaters in sweaters sharing cocktails on the bows of their boats. Nora had tried to include herself, she tried to join in, but in the end she'd largely stayed home with Willow.

Today, nothing she owned seemed to suit the woman that looked back at her in the mirror. She had always been confident in her role in her family, she was certain of who she was: Sullivan's mom, Sammy's mom, Joe's wife, William's daughter. She was the finder of lost items ("Mom, where's my tennis racket? Mom, where's my psychology book? Nora, where are my keys?"). She was the maker of dinners and the chauffeur to practice. She was the one with the answers.

Now, she was both all and none of those things.

Sullivan was gone.

Sammy was gone.

Her father was gone.

Phe was doing just fine living in her condo alone.

And Joe. Joe was living with Stephanie. He'd left her. Left her in their home, left her in the Twisted Olive, left her in the hospital. She was alone. More alone than she had ever been.

Joe wasn't there to care if she had a clean house, if she was fit, if her roots were gray or her wrinkles returned (she hadn't bothered to get her Botox injections since Joe left either—what did that matter? He still left her for a younger woman). No one cared if she carefully prepared a meal or had healthy food in the fridge. Her volunteer work for the school had ended with Sully's graduation. Nothing she had prided herself on in her old life mattered.

She had nowhere to go, no one to take anywhere or any appointments to keep. She kicked aside the bags that were *still* waiting to go to the trash or Goodwill and sat down on the floor in her closet in her bra and underwear. The pounding was back. She tried to take deep breaths in an effort to stop it, make it go away. She had been so afraid to be left with an empty house and lonely heart, but that would have been a blessing. Instead, she was left with an empty house and a *broken* heart.

Dozens of hangers were draped with workout clothes and jeans, cocktail dresses for galas, and sundresses for picnics. She had shorts and T-shirts, yoga pants and sweatshirts. She had long sweaters and bathing suits. She had a plethora of clothes and nothing that suited her.

Her waist was thin. For the first time in her life she could see the smallest hint of an hourglass. Her arms and legs had always been muscular and strong —now her arms hung at her sides like branches, limp from a drought. Her cheekbones were high, and her dimples highlighted her lips—but now they were subtle, not the deep, robust accents to her smile they used to be. In many ways, the body she saw in the mirror reflected the ideal she had wished for the whole of her adult life. She was thin. She was more than thin, she was svelte, willowy, enviably skinny. She stepped on the scale.

Fifteen pounds. She had lost fifteen pounds since Joe left. She laughed out loud. She'd been trying to lose fifteen pounds for fifteen years. Irony.

Justine Nevins had seen Nora yesterday at Glen's. Nora was picking up a few groceries: a small package of strawberries, an avocado, and two individual servings of rice. There wasn't much that whet her appetite and she'd largely spent the forty-five minutes she was there wandering up and down the aisles, aimlessly looking for food for one. She didn't know how to shop or care for just herself, nor did she have much ambition to do so.

"Nora! Wow! You look fantastic!" Justine had gushed.

"Oh… thank you?" Nora had been taken aback at the comment. No one else had commented on her appearance, other than to note her fresh scar from the accident. Before leaving for the store, she had put on one of Sully's baseball hats, pulling it tightly over her ears and hiding the purple line. She certainly didn't feel fantastic. She felt small, weak. Wounded. Just the sound of Justine's voice had sent Nora's racehorse heart pounding in her throat again. She'd clasped her hands together on the handle of her small basket as Justine spoke, trying to hide the shaking.

"How is everything? Joe? The kids?" Justine had asked.

Nora couldn't believe her luck, had she run into the one woman in town who *didn't* know Joe was sleeping with Stephanie? That Sullivan had gone to jail? Or was Justine baiting her, looking for information?

"Everyone's really good. Busy! Sullivan is at CMU and Sammy is still living in Lansing. Working at Auto Owners Insurance. She loves it."

"Oh my gosh, already? You and Joe are empty nesters! How exciting. Do you have any plans now that Sully is gone?"

Plans? Nora couldn't even plan what she would eat for lunch today. "Oh… we may travel a bit. We're not sure yet. Joe's still working a full schedule so we'll have to work around that." The balm of denial and pretending her family was intact had been heady.

Now, Nora leaned into the mirror in her closet, examining the scar over her right eyebrow. It was healing nicely, it was still a dusky purple, and raised to the touch. She knew from years with Joe that there were treatments that could smooth out the texture and color of her scar. Joe had offered her any help she needed, but Nora wasn't interested in that. The scar fascinated her. She'd tried all her life to be perfect, and now right in the middle of her face was the scar that proved her wrong. She actually looked on the outside like she felt on the inside. Damaged. Wounded.

As much as she had always fought her body and the robust curves she'd been born with, she had always been (at least mostly) happy with the features of her face. Her eyes were brown as coffee and showcased by long, black lashes. Her nose was petite and blended into her face seamlessly. Her lips were full and cupid-shaped. She outlined the length of the scar, seventeen stitches' worth, and felt a strange satisfaction. It had been satisfying for people to ask how she was—to inquire if she was healing from her visible injury. She could answer honestly. It hurt, she was scarred, but it would heal. She wanted to feel empowered by being vaguely honest—even if it was trickery, trading her injured face for her injured heart—but the effort of constantly keeping her panic at bay, of fearing an attack, of keeping it to herself, of being alone had broken her down.

Her phone rang from atop her dresser. She glanced quickly: Jordan. She hadn't been to the gym with Jordan since Joe left, just over three months. Jordan hadn't given up, he continued to call even though she hadn't answered once. She should answer the kid. She will, the next time he called.

She carried the hurt around in her body, the shame and embarrassment. It was heavy, it was debilitating. Clutching her knees to her belly she curled back up on the floor. Her body felt strange to her own hands, these slimmer hips, a waist she could feel. Tears came slowly as she rocked herself back and forth, her heart pounding harder and faster. Sweat pooled on the small of her back, her hands clasped around her knees just like she had wound them together on the handle of the basket at the grocery store when she'd run into Justine. Weaving her fingers together to keep herself small.

Her bottle of pills. They were in her purse. Her purse was in the kitchen—a lifetime away. There was no way Nora could reach them now. The pounding from the thoroughbred horse beating through her heart boomed in her ears. Her pulse bounding, like a river overflowing its banks after a storm. Her body felt stiff, unable to move. She felt herself begin to choke. Her fingers were numb, her arms tingled. She looked to the top of the dresser where her phone was. *I need help,* she thought. *I need help.*

She grabbed her phone and tapped out a text.

I need help. Can u please come?

She rocked back in forth in an attempt to soothe herself in any way. The fear descended like a deep wave, her desperation to breathe as real as if she had been dragged beneath the water by the undertow of the lake. Pounding. Crushing. Pressure. Shaking. Fear—primal, profound fear. Skin crawling. Nausea. Minutes traded time with hours and just when Nora wasn't sure she could endure a second longer her heart began to slow. The racing gallop of her pulse quieted in her veins, the desperate, heavy pressure of trying to breathe slid away.

Nora's heart continued to slowly return to a normal rhythm, the attack was fading. She was chilled from the fresh sweat dripping from her skin, her legs and arms tired in a way that only a woman who thought she had lost everything could feel. She was too tired to get up, too defeated to dress herself. Laying here on the floor, curled as small as she could be. This was all she could do.

Nora pulled her hands up under her chin and wept.

She felt him before she heard him. His familiar hands, gently, quietly touched her back. She thought to be embarrassed that she wasn't dressed, but the panic attack had left her nearly lifeless—her vanity discarded with her clothing.

"Nora, baby, are you okay?" Joe asked.

"No... no, I am not okay. I don't know if I'll ever be okay again." Her voice was thin, quiet. She wasn't melodramatic or exaggerating. She was simply stating her truth as she saw it in the moment.

"Did you take a pill?"

"No, they're in the kitchen in my purse. I... I couldn't reach them," Nora answered his question with her eyes closed.

Joe stood and disappeared for a moment—Nora wondered if he'd left again but no, he returned with her favorite soft, slate-blue blanket. He gently pulled her up to a standing position, swaddling her in the blanket and lifting her in his arms. He gently carried her to their bed.

Joe had pulled the corner of the covers back and

gently laid Nora in a nest of blankets. He was careful to keep her covered, and Nora appreciated his efforts to respect her modesty. The comforter was heavy. The kind of heavy that feels safe. Her body sunk into the rich pillow-top cover of the mattress.

"I haven't slept here since you left," she whispered.

Joe closed his eyes and nodded his head in response. He gently climbed on the bed next to Nora—she nestled deep in the covers, he laid on top of the comforter and held her in his arms until she fell deeply asleep.

And while she slept, for the first time since his death, William came to Nora in a dream. Her dad was standing at Sullivan's graduation party wearing his khaki pants and a blue button-down shirt, no tie. He was so proud, standing in the back of the room with a sidecar in his hand. Nora was running around the party, looking for all the guests. No one was there except her dad. Frantically, she continued looking, searching for party-goers. There were none. She went to her dad and cried. She hadn't spoken. In her dream, much as in life, her dad had simply read her thoughts.

"You can do hard things, sweetheart. You can do hard things," he'd said as he pressed a worry stone deep into her palm.

Nora slept soundly for most of the day. When she awoke, Joe was gone. This time, a note on the bedside table marked his exit.

Nora, I didn't want to stay longer than I was welcome. I left your bottle of pills here on the bedside table with a glass of water. It's okay to use them, they will help. No one should go through what you did today, or what you've been through this summer. I made you risotto—I know it's your favorite and lucky for me it's the one dish I can cook ;) It's on the stove. Please call if you need anything. I'll be back in a heartbeat. Thank you. Thank you for asking. Love, Joe

Nora held the note in her hand and picked up the bottle of pills and turned them around in her hand. She'd slept in her own bed—and slept soundly. She'd asked for help when she needed it—and Joe was there for her. In fact, he had been there for her this afternoon in ways he hadn't been for her in years. Because she'd asked.

She set the bottle back down on the bedside table. Nora didn't intend to be a martyr. Perhaps she had been in the past, but she'd also tried to be perfect and that hadn't turned out well, either. She'd been afraid to take the pills because taking the pills meant she couldn't handle the anxiety on her own. Taking the pills would be admitting her life wasn't perfect. But now she saw things differently.

No, she still wasn't going to take the pills just yet. Instead… she was going to ask for help. Nora could see now that her reluctance to take the pills had been an exercise in vanity and perfection, but her refusal had also served a purpose. By not getting the help she needed the anxiety had broken her down. She has no option except to accept she isn't perfect. She has no choice other than to accept she needed help. And Nora did need help, there was no doubt about that.

The panic attack had been by far the worst one she had experienced. She supposed the panic and the fear that came with it had become familiar—but she now knew in a way she hadn't yesterday or the day before— that it didn't have to be. Nora pulled the covers back on her bed and walked to the closet dressed in a cape of her blue blanket. She could still smell Joe's cologne. She decided not to decide what to wear. Instead, she simply dressed herself in the first pieces of clothing she saw. She pulled on her favorite pair of yoga pants and one of Joe's old U of M hoodies he'd left behind, and then ate the risotto.

The rest of the evening she spent researching online. She needed to find a counselor. Joe had been right about that two years ago when William died. While she knew hindsight was twenty-twenty, Nora couldn't remember why she'd been so resistant to go when Joe had asked. Because he suggested it? Because counseling didn't pass the perfection litmus test? Probably yes to both. Seeing her father—if only the dream version—had fortified her. He was right, and so was Joe—she could do hard things. In the morning she would make an appointment with Dr. Bateman to further discuss the panic attacks and to get a referral for counseling.

She went on Facebook and, instead of stalking Stephanie, she searched for support groups for anxiety. She quickly found two closed groups she thought might help and sent requests to join them both. She'd immediately been accepted and spent several hours reading posts, comments and shared articles. She read posts from other women, describing their attacks and while they brought her to tears, she realized, possibly for the first time, that she wasn't alone.

She wasn't the only one who struggled, the only one who was overwhelmed. She wasn't the only one who ached with sadness and couldn't control her anxiety. Relief came from releasing the notion that she had to confront all her problems alone. Comfort came in waves—she was *not* alone. Of course, logically she supposed she knew that all along. It's inevitable to feel alone if you don't tell anyone where you are at. So, it was time for Nora to start telling the truth about where she was at. Her life isn't perfect. It never had been.

SEPTEMBER 22, 2018

SAMMY

Nora carried two plates with healthy helpings of strawberry-pecan salad out to the dining table in the backyard. Sammy was already there with a glass of pinot grigio from their favorite winery, Bower's Harbor, in Traverse City.

"I'm disappointed Phe wasn't able to come over tonight. I know she wanted to see you," Nora offered. "But I suppose it's good she's getting back into the swing of life a bit after her hip. She had her book club meeting to go to tonight."

"Me too. I'll run by her condo—or maybe Josephine's—tomorrow before I leave," Sammy answered. "This salad looks awesome. Thank you!" Sammy touched her bag hidden under her seat. The last six months of her life were cradled in her Vera Bradley. Hours of crunching numbers at work, line sheets, mockups of web pages melded together creating her business proposal for Josephine's.

Sammy could hear the bell at the store when the door

opened as clearly as she could her mother's voice at the table. She could feel the sunlight as it poured onto the hardwood floors and could smell the rosewater and cinnamon—her grandmother spritzed the air with the rosewater and discreetly placed sticks of cinnamon throughout the space. Sammy loved the store—it was gorgeous and warm, if just a shade out of date. Nothing a fresh coat of paint couldn't fix. Maybe a pale blue? She'd seen two emerald green tufted accent chairs with a French flair at an antique shop the other day. She'd nearly bought them on the spot, they would be perfect for the vestibule near the dressing rooms.

Sammy knew her numbers were sound and she believed with a strong online presence and a rebrand of the store's lines she could make a go of it. She had a full line-up of vendors that used sustainable manufacturing practices, no child labor and she had found several designers who donated part of their profit to philanthropic causes. Coupling fashion with charity was a solid combination—both for revenue and profit and for Sammy's heart. She believed her reinvention of Josephine's would be wildly successful. She could bring Josephine's into the twenty-first century, all while maintaining her grandmother's legacy of quality clothing and excellent service.

Still, Sammy's hands were damp with nerves.

"Are you doing okay? Everything okay at work and with the girls?" Nora questioned her daughter.

"Yes, Momma. I'm okay." She smiled, but her voice

was tinged with irritation as she answered Nora's same question for the fifth time since she'd arrived home. If Phe went for the proposal, it would mean Sammy would need to live at home for a while to save money. Sammy took a deep breath, realizing it would be a little stickier than she remembered. Nora had a hard time being okay unless Sammy was okay—it was easy to pass off bad days or feeling blue or trouble at work when she was three hours away. Under the same roof, Sammy would have to up her game if she wanted to keep her mom on an even keel.

"I just worry, I'm sorry."

"I know. I wish you wouldn't. I'm fine." Sammy smiled kindly at her mom. "And even if I'm not okay, I'm plenty capable of figuring it out on my own." The weight of her mother's happiness hung heavily on Sammy's shoulders. She wished it didn't, but it always had. And now, in the midst of this stupid divorce, Nora was even more riddled with worry. Sammy felt the familiar unrest settle in her stomach.

"I know you are. I do," Nora answered.

Sammy pushed the pecans around her plate. Now was as good a time as any to bring up her ideas for the store. "Hey Mom, I wanted to ask your opinion on something."

"Sure, sweet pea—but hey before you do, have you talked to your brother much?"

"I talk to Sully every day," Sammy answered, taking a bite of salad.

"You do?" Nora was surprised. "He barely answers me. I get one-word texts. Unless he needs money. Then I tell him to text your father."

"It's only been a couple weeks. Give him a minute."

"Well I know, I just want to know that he's okay." Nora's answer was pensive.

Sammy set her wine glass down with a *ting* on the tile-mosaic tabletop. "He's struggling. He's okay. He's just homesick and a little behind with school. " She hadn't meant to say it—the wine had loosened the cap on her promise to Sullivan that she wouldn't let their mom know he had backed himself into a corner.

Nora's heart stopped. "What do you mean he's struggling?"

"School is hard. He misses home." Sammy drew a deep breath, she was irritated with herself for bringing it up and irritated that her mom had changed the subject before she'd gotten to present her the proposal. "With the divorce and Stephanie and Elise, he threw himself into the party scene a bit too much these first few months. He's gotten himself in a hole with his classes. Pretty typical of the first semester of freshman year, Mom."

Nora bit her lip. The hot wind of Sullivan struggling with the divorce blew in and burned her. "I knew something was wrong. I knew it," Nora stammered out her words.

"No offense Mom, but you always think something's wrong. Therefore, it's not that big of a surprise when you're right." Sammy looked directly into Nora's eyes, her irritation over the responsibility of her brother, her mother, and her father spilled over into her words. Nora pushed her chair back and started to stand up. "What are you doing?" Sammy asked.

"Getting my phone and calling your brother."

"No, you're not. He asked me not to tell you," Sammy said. "You're not going to do that because he's figuring it out on his own. Because he doesn't want you to know. I only told you because I suck at lying to you and, frankly, I think you *should know.* But I don't think you should do anything."

"Not do anything?" Nora took a deep breath in and blew it out through her pursed lips. "At the very least I have to talk to your father." The idea of having a valid reason to call Joe, or even just text him, gave Nora's heart a jump.

"No, you aren't calling or texting Dad about it, either. Besides, Dad already knows."

"What in the fuck?" Nora blurted out. Sammy was taken back by her mom's language—Nora Phillips did not use words like "fuck."

"Mom. You don't do this stuff well. Okay? You fly in, take over, clean up our messes. Sully needs to do this by himself. And he actually *can* do this by himself, if you give him a second before you rush in to rescue him."

"What stuff don't I do well?" Nora's voice rose three octaves.

"Let us screw up. Let us not be okay," Sammy answered with a casual shrug of her shoulders.

"I let your dad screw up huge," Nora shot back.

"Don't—"

"I know, I know. Don't put you in the middle." Nora slung back the rest of her wine and poured another glass.

"You are so wonderful. Such a good hearted, supportive, kind, generous person. It's just hard for you to see us fail. And Sully, he's figuring it out! He went to his teachers and started a study table session for each class—"

"I can get him a tutor—"

"He wants to handle this on his own. You have to let him."

"What am I supposed to do, just ignore the fact that he's living hours away from home, is struggling in *college* and his father left me for the town tramp—who happens to be the mother of a friend of his? All this just two years after his favorite person in the world—your grandpa!—passed away? Am I supposed to just ignore that the three of you 'handled' this alone, without me. You left me out! As if I wasn't left out enough already." Nora's voice was thick with emotion.

"We didn't leave you out." Sammy's voice was kind and gentle, the irritation she felt for her mother dwindling. Nora's life was upside down, Sammy knew that. Her mom needed her compassion, not her frustration. And while it seemed easiest to handle

Sullivan with her dad, Sammy could admit now that they *had* left Nora out. How could she explain to her mom that she knew her mom's intentions were good— but that Nora's desire to control everything was too much? "We didn't mean to, anyway."

"When I told you that your dad had an affair and was leaving me for Stephanie… you didn't seem surprised. Why?"

Sammy took a deep breath and stretched her arms up over her head. "I wouldn't say I wasn't surprised. I was surprised he cheated. I was surprised he left. It wasn't a surprise that you two were unhappy," Sammy answered cautiously.

"You haven't lived with us for years. How did you know we were unhappy when *I* didn't know we were unhappy?"

"You know, this isn't exactly comfortable for me. I don't want to discuss your marriage particularly. Can we go back to you yelling at me about Sullivan?"

"How did you know?" Nora's voice was quiet now, consolatory.

Taking a deep breath in, Sammy tucked her legs up and hugged her sweater around her chest. "It's not that you were fighting or yelling. Or even that I suspected he had a girlfriend. You two just felt—flat."

"Flat?" Nora repeated.

"Yeah, flat. You rolled your eyes when he talked. He ignored you when you answered. You were busy doing your thing—taking care of Sullivan, the PTO, the gym.

Dad worked all the time, always has. Dad wasn't really on your radar."

"Clearly, I wasn't on *his* radar at all."

Sammy fidgeted sideways in her chair, not looking Nora in the eye. "You were on his radar. For a while," she answered quietly. Clearly tonight wasn't going to go how she'd planned. Mentally, Sammy filed away her proposal for another visit.

"What does that mean?"

"It means nothing. It means I remember when he would ask you to go on dates and ask you to run with him and ask you to walk with him while he took pictures and you always said no." Sammy avoided her mom's gaze. So her irritation wasn't all about Nora's need to always have Sammy be okay, and it wasn't about Nora's need to control everything, or even about Nora's interference in all things Sullivan. It was in part because Sammy blamed her mother for her parent's divorce. Not entirely, but Sammy wasn't ready to let Nora off the hook.

"So this is *my fault?*" Nora was angry.

"No. Dad's affair is not your fault. Not at all. You asked me why I wasn't surprised. I told you I didn't want to answer you." Sammy turned her head and looked out into the woods that came to the edge of the Phillips's backyard. Her voice had taken the sharp edge of a young woman caught in the middle of her parents' stuff. "What he did wasn't your fault. But *why* he did it was partly your fault."

Sammy took another sip of wine and watched her mom walk into the house through the back French doors, grab her coat and leave.

NORA

"Thanks for picking me up." Nora slid into the passenger side of Molly, working the door and latch with expertise. She had come to rely on Robert's even, steady demeanor in the past weeks. He calmed her anxious nature with his quiet reserve. Nora wasn't sure where their friendship was headed, she wasn't sure what it all meant, she only knew that talking to Robert felt like coming home. He shared so many qualities with her father. He was slow-spoken and thoughtful in what he shared. He listened, really listened, and inspired Nora to want to be a better listener herself. Was there a better gift you could give someone than to take the time to really listen? To hear them and not offer solutions or Band-Aids, just simply... listen? Nora didn't think so.

Molly rattled along M119 heading north toward Church Beach in Good Hart. The trees had started to turn, the breeze was just chilly enough that Nora wished she'd brought a jacket. She pulled her arms across her chest, hugging herself for warmth. Robert reached behind the seat and pulled out a red wool blanket, just like her dad's. She smiled and wrapped it around her shoulders.

"You ready to tell me why you called to have me pick you up, wandering downtown—without Willow no less?" Robert smiled, one hand draped over Molly's ancient steering wheel, the other rested on the gear shift.

He really was handsome, Nora thought. In a completely opposite way of Joe. Robert was country, he was blue-collar, he was fruit stands on the side of the road and apple orchards and the scent of fresh-cut pine.

"My life," she answered. After she'd fought with Sammy, Nora had walked out the front door. No coat, no purse. She just left. Luckily, she happened to have her phone in her hand, and after walking for half an hour she'd called Robert to come pick her up.

"That's it? Easy fix," he chided.

"Sometimes I feel like I've lost too much. That I can't recover. I can't find myself," Nora continued. "I know that sounds ridiculous to say out loud. It sounds even more ridiculous to say to you. You've lost so much more than me." A gentle tear slipped from Nora's eyes.

"Loss is loss, Nora," Robert said.

"I suppose. It just seems like I should be better than this. I should be bigger than this. I don't understand why this is breaking me."

"Because you're human? Because losing your father is hard. Because your husband having an affair is hard. Because your last kid moving out and going to college is hard."

"I should be stronger than this. I should be braver. I used to be the one with the answers, I was the keeper of their secrets and the one whom they came to. Now they avoid me, they keep things from me. What is wrong with me?"

"There's nothing wrong with you, Nora."

Guilt washed over Nora as she turned and looked at Robert. Would his brown eyes carry the sadness of losing Katie forever? Would her death always be reflected in the beautiful laugh lines that softened his face? She had no right to complain, no right to break.

"I don't know what it feels like for you to lose your marriage or to become an empty nester, or to lose your father. But I do know loss. No one should decide whose loss is greater. It's better if we empathize with each other instead."

"Loss is loss," Nora repeated. "Have you ever thought about What Ifs?"

"What do you mean?" Robert swung Molly into the old church parking lot and wrenched the old girl into park under the canopy of a giant oak with leaves gently painted in strokes of fall colors. He turned his attention toward Nora after he pulled the keys out of the ignition and slid them into his pocket, right next to his worry stone. Nora followed Robert out of the car and walked behind him along the trail to the beach.

"Do you ever wonder, what if? What if I never married Joe? What if I never moved to Ann Arbor? What if I had a career? What if I never came back to Harbor Springs? I wonder if there's any combination of What Ifs that would have led me to a happier life, to a place where I wasn't so… broken."

"For the first year after Katie died, I imagined the 'What If my wife didn't die' scenario every single day. Sometimes I lied to myself and pretended she was away on vacation or at her sister's in California just to convince myself to get out of bed."

"What do you think your life would have been like if Katie hadn't died?"

"I'd like to imagine that we lived happily ever after, walking hand-in-hand into the sunset. But we had our troubles too, and life is never without its heartaches. We always wanted kids—but we waited too long and then she was diagnosed. Our dream of having a baby was over before it ever really started. I imagine if she were alive, we would have found some way to be parents. I imagine a little girl with auburn hair and freckles on her nose." The breeze had picked up and even though the sun was shining, he was just a bit chilly.

"Katie made me promise to live a full life without her. She wanted me to find someone new to love, she wanted me to be a dad. She wanted me to love and laugh." Robert's eyes were wistful. "It hurts to think about moving on and it hurts to think about staying deep in the loss forever."

When they got to the water, Robert kept his shoes on, but Nora slipped hers off and slung them over her fingers. The two of them walked high up the sand past the waterline. Their path made two sets of footprints in the sand, one of the soles of shoes the other the soles of feet. Robert reached for Nora's hand and held it. The warmth traveled up her arm and into her heart, soothing the pain of her fight with Samantha.

"I guess I wouldn't want to live my What If, even though my marriage ended this way. I wouldn't have Sammy or Sullivan, and that's just unthinkable." Nora stopped and turned toward Robert. "Truthfully, I can't imagine my life without having married Joe. We had many good years."

The tangerine sun was settling into the dip of the horizon, shining brightly in her eyes. Nora pulled her free hand up to shade her eyes from the glare, so she could see Robert's face. "And if it wasn't for the affair and the divorce, I wouldn't have you," she added quietly.

"What If I kissed you?" Robert asked.

Nora's hand slipped from Robert's and came to rest on his cheek. She reached up to her tiptoes and their lips touched. A gentle whisper of their friendship, the kiss was a gift, a secret given to each other. His lips were soft and warm, she wanted to crave them. She wanted to want him. Her hand fell to her side and Robert slid his hand behind her neck, under her hair and pulled her into a hug. If she had wondered if she was over her husband, she had her answer. Nora tucked the moment quietly in her heart.

"What if we stay the best of friends?" Robert whispered into the soft skin on her neck.

Nora smiled and closed her eyes against the sun. She soaked in the feel of Robert's protective arms encircling her. She listened to the waves gently lapping up on the sand. As much as she wanted to move on, leave the mess her life was behind her, Robert was right. She wasn't ready—and she knew he wasn't either. Their friendship was built on the bridge of Katie and William and Nora was more interested in preserving that love than she was in creating a new one.

The two turned to walk farther down the beach. Holding hands and trying on the definitive boundaries of their relationship. It felt good to know that they would be there for each other. It felt good to know that they would each have the space to recover from their lost loves within the friendship they had built.

"You know my dad left me an inheritance when he died," Nora offered. "I had forgotten about it, really. I hadn't wanted it when he passed—I just wanted my dad back—so I kept it invested and haven't given it a second thought."

"Until now?" Robert asked.

"I've been wondering what to do with my life next. I have spent all my life catering to what my family needs, but they don't need me in that way anymore—I'm not really sure they ever did, actually. What if... what if I do something different? What if I go back to school or help my mom with Josephine's?"

"What would you do, if you could do anything you want?"

"I don't have any idea. I've never even thought about it."

Robert pulled his hand away from Nora and bent to pick up a rock, throwing it out into the water and skipping it three times.

"That was pretty good! Bet I can beat you." Nora searched the rocks at her feet for the perfect skipper—smooth, thin, and flat. When she found just the right rock she snapped her wrist and sent the beauty skipping off the water six times before it coasted under the surf. "My dad was the king of rock skipping. He taught me well." She smiled.

Robert and Nora dug around in the rocks, finding a few more perfect skippers. The two tossed the stones into the water, watching the circles ripple out from where the rocks landed.

"Your life doesn't have to be perfect, Nora. It just has to be yours," Robert said. Nora nodded silently. "Did you ever replace your worry stone? After you gave yours to Katie?"

"No, I didn't. I don't think I have even gone looking

for Petoskey stones since my dad died. I lost track of a lot of things these past two years."

Robert sat down, digging his hands into the sand and pulling them up like a sieve. Nora smiled and sat down to do the same.

"There aren't a lot of Petoskeys on this beach," Nora said. "I don't know if we'll find one."

The two friends sat together, digging in the dense, heavy sand on a beach with the sun sinking in a slow, golden orb toward the skyline.

"We'll find one," Robert said. "We'll find one."

SEPTEMBER 23, 2018

NORA

A smile spread soft as butter across Nora's face. She turned her new worry stone around in her hand inside her pocket. She'd forgotten how much strength she'd drawn from the stones. Robert and Nora searched the beach quietly until dusk settled around them, finding her a new worry stone just as they had been about to give in. This morning, she was feeling more herself. She had a lot to think about on her walk this afternoon. She'd come to look forward to her walks, the active meditation and time to let her mind wander toward solutions or feelings that were harder to find when she was sitting still.

The sign for the store was just a few feet ahead. At first, she'd hesitated to stop by, but after turning her new worry stone around in her pocket a few times she decided she was done hiding.

As she walked through the door of Josephine's, the chimes of the bell above her head reminded her of her childhood. Nora loved the smell—rosewater and cinnamon. It'd been the same since she was a teenager and worked in the shop after school and over the summers. Her foot landed on the sweet spot, the creak of the floorboards just inside the front door. She laughed as Willow pulled on her leash, rushing directly for the box of treats saved just for her in the back of the office. When she was young, she had loved to come with her mom to the store. She colored in the back office, hid in the middle of the racks of long dresses, sorted jewelry in the display case, re-arranging them in pretty designs. She loved to be spoiled by The Ladies. They braided her hair and let her experiment with the hair combs and crystal barrettes. Phe was magical in the store, always dressed in the latest fashions, hair perfectly in vogue, she floated from customer to customer and hung shirts and dresses and pants with a ballerina-like grace. In her early years, Nora loved nothing more than watching Phe… *be* Phe. It wasn't until she was older that she began to resent Josephine's and what it stood for—everything she wasn't. She had been selfish, she'd supposed. She had wanted more of her mother's attention and it was hard to compete with Josephine's. Everything Phe touched was beautiful.

"Nora! Hello, dear. What brings you down here?" Phe stepped out from behind the counter to greet her daughter. Sammy was standing just inside the office door, eating a Guerny's sub.

"Hi, Mom. Hi, Sammy! I didn't know you were still in town." Nora hugged Phe—not the warm, inviting hug Nora gave her children, but the proper, appropriate-for-public hug that her mother had always given her. Phe gave her daughter an extra squeeze as she pulled away, and Nora turned her head in surprise.

"I stopped by to talk to Grandma on my way out of town." Sammy walked out of the office and smiled cautiously at her mother. Nora lurched forward and swallowed her daughter in a hug. Always, always happy to see her girl, but even more so after their disagreement the night before. When Robert had returned Nora from the beach, she and Sammy had spent the night quietly chatting with each other until Sammy had left to catch a drink at High Five with a friend.

"It's getting a little late, shouldn't you head back to Lansing?" Nora asked with concern.

"It's fine, Mom. I'm twenty-six, I can handle a three-hour drive no matter how late it is," Sammy answered with just a touch of snark. "What are you doing here, anyway? The store's not even open." She smiled.

"Willow wanted to go for a walk and I wanted a change of scenery—so we drove into town and walked here. When we passed by the door, I noticed the lights on in the back."

"Sammy's been helping me!" Phe's smile was dynamic, almost technicolor as she spoke to Nora.

"Oh really, what are you helping your grandmother with, Sam I Am?" Nora asked, lazily flipping through a sale rack of Donna Karan and Eileen Fisher summer cast-offs. Nora wasn't quite sure what size she was currently, it seemed ridiculous that her size eight pants now fell off of her. Willow, happy with the treat Sam had dispensed, curled up at Nora's feet.

Samantha and Phe looked at each other. Phe smiled and nodded at her granddaughter.

"Well, I came up with a plan to help Grandma with the store. You know when Danielle took over, things didn't go well. Sales declined—just a touch—but she wasn't able to make the last few payments." Sam sounded like a professional. She sounded like one of the consultants that go on the reality shows that highlight failing businesses—she was the business coach giving Phe a plan to reinvent Josephine's after Danielle's bad run. Nora couldn't help but smile—her Sammy helping her grandmother out. In some ways it was just too much to ask for.

"That's wonderful, darling! What does the plan consist of? What are you going to have Grandma do?"

"Actually, it's not just a plan for Grandma" Sammy hesitated.

"It's not?"

"No… the plan involves me coming home and taking over Josephine's. I asked Dad to co-sign on a loan and I'm going to buy Josephine's from Grandma."

"What?" Nora stopped looking through the rack abruptly.

"I have the money Grandpa left me and I asked Dad to co-sign for a loan to buy into Josephine's. Grandma is going to work with me until I am totally on my own! Based on my projections, I will be able to take over fully within a year." Sammy smiled, hesitantly looking in Nora's direction—taking the temperature of the air between them before saying another word.

"Oh," Nora said. "Oh. Okay. Dad co-signed a loan for you without telling me?"

"You aren't married any—"

"Yes, actually we are still married. He isn't supposed to make any financial decisions without my consent and approval," Nora answered.

"Well, he didn't sign the loan today, obviously. We have a lot to work out. He only *agreed* to co-sign a loan."

"Like I said, he agreed to co-sign a loan for you without telling me?" Nora turned to look at Phe. "How long have you been working on this?"

"Nora, dear. I am thrilled Josephine's is going to be run by a Sullivan woman after all!"

"Of course you are," Nora spat. Phe didn't deserve that. Whatever mistakes Nora had believed Phe made in raising her family, Nora knew now that those decisions were much harder to make than she once believed. She wasn't even sure what had made her so angry. Sammy surprising her with a complete career change, Phe and Joe keeping it a secret? Feeling on the outside—again?

"That's not fair. I just brought the proposal to Grandma this morning. We hadn't even gotten a chance to go over all of it, yet. There may be something she doesn't like about my ideas—"

"I am very intrigued by your proposal and even more thrilled by the fact that you want to continue the legacy of Josephine's! I am sure we can iron out any sticky details." Phe smoothed her hands down the side of her gray capri pants. "Nora, you should see what our girl has done. She has come up with a lineup of designers that are committed to sustainable practices and safe working environments. You should see these lovely bracelets she wants to bring in that are part of a charity that provides micro-loans to women who want to start businesses in rural areas! It's brilliant. Samantha will save my store *and* the world all at the same time!"

Nora's insides twisted in a peculiar knot. How could one feel envious of her own daughter? But there it was, all kinds of envy floating around like butterflies in her stomach. Not even bothering to try and disguise itself as worry or concern or patience. No, it was jealousy as pure as cane sugar. Sammy had just done the one thing Nora could never do: make Phe proud of her. Sammy was taking a risk, changing her life. Wasn't she supposed to be the one who taught her daughter, not the other way around?

"Of course she will. This is a huge move, sweetheart. Are you sure this is what you want to do? You love your apartment and your job in Lansing…"

"But I don't, Mom. I really don't."

"You always tell me everything is so good. You *said*

you loved your job. You *said* you loved your roommates and your loft." Nora was bewildered as she spoke back to her daughter.

"I did. But I told you those things so that you wouldn't worry. All my life I have wanted to be here, in the store. I have always wanted to run Josephine's. Remember, I used to play shop in my room and pretend to sell my clothes? It's what I have always wanted."

"You wanted to move to Lansing! You wanted to leave this little town, you said so..." Even as Nora produced the she-said, he-said argument with her daughter, she knew in her heart what was true. Sammy had told her what she wanted to hear. Sammy had been trying to live Nora's dream for her, not Sammy's dream for herself. Just as hard as Nora had rebuffed Josephine's as Phe's wish for her daughter's future, Sammy had accepted Nora's vision for her life instead of following her own.

Nora took a step toward her daughter. "Where will you live?" Nora asked carefully, afraid of the answer.

"I thought maybe I could stay with you, until I get my feet on the ground? I have a small nest egg of money saved up for my own expenses—I've worked really hard on this proposal. I have researched and researched again, I've crunched the numbers. I even took a website class last semester at Lansing Community College so I can run Josephine's site on my own and not have to pay anybody else to do it. This is what I want. I want to run the shop."

"Of course you can stay with me. You sure this is really what you want?"

"Yes. I'm more than sure." Sammy smiled back at her mom.

Phe put her arm around her daughter's waist. Nora felt the shame of envy gently dusting the edges of her thoughts. How could she have done to Sammy what she was always so resentful of Phe doing to her? Without even *noticing?*

"You did a good job with her, Nora. You should be proud," Phe said, her eyes wet with age and emotion.

"I am proud. I'm so proud of you. For this proposal, for your grit, your guts. I'm most proud of you following your heart, even when you thought I wouldn't support you."

"To be honest, I expected more of a fight," Sammy answered quietly.

"I don't have a lot of fight left in me," Nora said, her voice heavy with emotion. "I'll leave you and Phe to work. Come on, Willow, let's go girl!" The bell rang behind her announcing her departure. Nora needed to walk. She needed time to process Sammy's news outside of Josephine's.

Nora and Willow had gotten half way down the block walking toward the city marina before she heard Phe yelling her name.

"Nora! Wait, please!"

Nora stopped and turned toward her mother, who was shielding her eyes from the bright autumn sun with her hand in a salute toward the blue sky. "Did I forget something?" Nora asked.

"No, dear. I did," Phe answered. Nora's hand dropped from its perch. "Can we walk together a minute?"

"Sure, Mom. What's up?"

"You know, when you were a little girl you loved clothes. You loved to dress up, put on makeup and hats and loved my 'white fancy gloves.' You carried around my purses and asked relentlessly for lipstick. It tickled me that you enjoyed what I did! You used to cry when I went to the shop without you. So when you decided you *didn't* want to work at Josephine's, you didn't want to run my shop, I was hurt. I told myself I had spent all my life building Josephine's for you."

"I remember the 'white fancy gloves,'" Nora answered with a smile, her mother's humility and candor disarming her.

"When you were in the sixth grade, the store had a tough year. The summer had been rainy and the winter was dry. There weren't many tourists and my sales dropped. I laid off all the girls who worked for me and kept the shop open for sixty hours a week on my own just to keep it afloat."

"I remember that, too. Well, I didn't know about the financial piece, but I remember you being gone. A lot."

"I was. Too much. I let my pride get in the way. I had worked so hard I just couldn't see my life's work fail."

Nora suddenly felt the weight of her childhood

wish—to have her mother around—from her mother's perspective. What Nora had seen as selfish, her mother had seen as self-preserving, as a legacy, a gift.

"Mom, listen…"

"Let me finish. You were right, I didn't put my family first. I was never good at balancing work and home life. Being a mother to you was my greatest joy, aside from being your father's wife." Phe's eyes sparkled with emotion and sunlight.

"I knew that. I did." For the first time in her life, Nora admitted her childhood hurt wasn't based in fact. Nora had believed that if Phe loved her enough, was proud of her enough, liked her enough, she would spend more time at home. She would leave the shop work to The Ladies and stay home with Nora. She would pay more attention. To Nora. After four decades, Nora could finally see that thought wasn't true. What was true was that there were days, many, where Nora missed her mom. There were days when Nora felt neglected and unimportant. But Nora's long-held belief that Phe was disappointed with her simply wasn't true.

"I could have done better, my dear. I could have. I suppose one of the blessings of old age, and quite honestly the death of your father, is the time and desire to reflect." Phe grabbed ahold of the crook of Nora's elbow as they walked. Nora snuggled her mom's tiny hand in toward her chest, grateful for her mother's words and the warmth of her touch.

"We do the best we can, Mom. I am learning that the

hard way. It may not feel like it or look like it, but we do." The pair continued walking together in silence, their footsteps falling in perfect sync. For as much as Nora believed herself to be the exact opposite of her graceful, beautiful, elegant mother she now saw their similarities. Sure, they were different in many ways. But as the sun cast their shadows long into their path she could see it. Their shoulders held the same slope, their steps followed the same cadence (even with the hitch in Phe's get along), their arms held the same shape. Nora smiled into the comfort of her mother's presence.

"Have you spoken to Joe?" Phe asked.

"Not much. Just logistics. I'm a little irritated I didn't know about the loan to Sammy. But I suppose she is right. It's not my business anymore." Nora began to cry.

"Have the two of you sat and talked to each other about what happened? The affair? Why he left the hospital?"

"No." Nora thought of Joe carrying her covered in her blue blanket back to their bed. She thought of him laying curled next to her atop the covers. She thought of the risotto. *Thank you,* he had said.

"I think you should. I think there's a value in finding the ground of forgiveness."

"I could never forgive him. I can't. He left me. Twice."

"Don't focus on forgiving Joe. Focus on forgiving

yourself."

"Forgiving myself." Nora let out a Willow-sized sigh as her pup lazily pounced on a fallen leaf skittering across the sidewalk. The sun warmed her face and for a moment, she felt peaceful. Peaceful in the reality of her divorce. Peaceful in the pain of being alone. Looking out over the few remaining sailboats tied up in their slips, the sun shining and the autumn warmth a blessing, Nora felt the weight of what Phe was suggesting. "That may be harder than forgiving Joe."

"Oh, I understand." Phe took Nora's arm as the two continued to walk in step. "The year I almost lost the store? Your father had an affair."

Nora stopped in her tracks. Phe turned and looked at her daughter. She gently reached up and traced the scar on Nora's face.

"I never wanted to tell you that, because I never wanted to taint your view of your father. But he was human. And I wasn't around. He needed a partner and I was so focused on my business that I didn't pay attention. He begged me to do things with the two of you, but I couldn't let go of my dream, didn't ask for help. I was so afraid to lose Josephine's that I nearly lost my family."

Nora was silent. The sunshine that had been the messenger of peace just moments before now felt garish and obtrusive.

"I am not telling you this to break your heart. I'm telling you this to try and help you heal your own. I was so angry with William. Just furious. I kicked him out at first—just like you did with Joe. I told him I could never forgive him, that we would never be a family again. I told him it was his fault and I had been nothing but faithful! How could he?" Phe nodded her head at the memory. "We told you he went on a business trip for a few weeks—I couldn't bear to tell you the truth. That's when I knew I wouldn't end my marriage, when I couldn't tell you that your dad wasn't coming back. So… I let William come home."

"I never would have guessed." Nora was too stunned to cry.

"Oh everyone in town did. It was awful. I felt like everyone was always looking at me, staring at me, laughing at me."

Nora nodded, tears slipping past the surprise.

"But I got through it. I got through it when I decided to forgive myself for putting William and you last. I forgave myself for being too wrapped up in my career and not paying attention to my marriage. Then, it was easier to forgive your father. Of course, he also had to forgive himself—and he had to learn to live with who I am. He married a woman who wanted a career—I had never been shy about that. We worked together to put our marriage back together, and in the end, it was stronger than it would have been if we hadn't broken it to begin with."

"So are you saying I should take Joe back? Because last I knew he was still living with Stephanie." Nora's voice was sour.

"No, I'm not. I don't know what's going to be the best thing for you to do. Only you know that. What I do know is that either way, forgiveness is part of the equation. No way around it."

"Now I need to forgive my dad, too," Nora said.

"No, not at all. That was between me and him, not you."

"It must be hard for you to talk about, especially now that he's gone." Nora wrapped her arm around her mother's tiny frame.

"Talking about your father always squeezes my heart now that he's gone. But talking about his affair doesn't hurt any more than talking about how he used to shine the pennies for his penny loafers every Sunday." Phe smiled. "It's part of who we were. And if I don't take time to remember the disappointing and painful times, I won't ever remember the good times with as much clarity."

"Mom, you said you forgot something?" Nora asked.

"I did. I forgot to tell you how proud I am of *you.* You have handled yourself with grace and dignity through the last several months—well, other than Martini Night, but that was well-deserved! I am proud of your strength and your resolve."

Nora cried. Small, silent tears slipped their way down her cheeks. Phe had given her all she had ever wanted.

JOE

Joe worked the lock with the key he'd found under the flower pot next to the back door. At eighteen years old he had promised himself he would never move back to Beachside. Now here he was, suitcase in one hand and takeout from the new Chinese place south of town— Lucky Duck—in the other. Of course, this wasn't the first promise he'd broken to himself.

The sticky lock gave way and the solid walnut door swung inside, a few stray leaves from the river birch tree out front blew in ahead of Joe. He took a deep breath, sucking in the crisp September air before heading inside. He envisioned himself scuba diving underwater as he walked into the back butler's pantry, sliding his oxygen mask over his face.

If Joe had thought he was filled with relief after Nora found out about the affair—it was a scant comparison to the relief he felt *ending* the affair. When they first returned to Stephanie's condo from the hospital, Stephanie had gone immediately into care-taking mode. She'd played nursemaid to his patient and he had been exhausted. The days bled one into another and Joe hadn't made a move until tonight. He had become paralyzed with guilt and shame, he'd left Nora for Stephanie and then wanted to leave Steph for Nora again. What was he a sophomore in high school?

The conversation with Stephanie had gone just how Joe anticipated it would. He told her not to drive by the house again. He hadn't phrased it as a question and she hadn't denied it. He told her it was over, he was sorry. He told her that he hadn't meant to hurt her. She'd sworn at him, called him a liar and a cheat. How ironic, he'd thought, that Stephanie would be the one to call him a liar and a cheat. She had abided those lies and helped him cheat. His heart was heavy with guilt for both women. One, the love of his life. The other, the fleeting passion whom he'd used out of weakness. He wished the best for Stephanie, he really did. She was worth more than he'd given her, and more than she'd accepted. Joe knew he hadn't been the first man to break Steph's heart, and he wouldn't be the last. She'd taught him he was not above piety and in turn he hoped he'd taught her that only she could stop her heart from breaking.

The man he thought he was—the upstanding physician who was above reproach, above his father's example—was not the man who looked back at him in the mirror this morning. He was his father's son. No better than the man he promised not to emulate. His father had used women to numb the disgrace and disillusionment of being married to an alcoholic. Of course, it was impossible from Joe's angle to decide— or to even have an idea—which came first, the disease of alcoholism for his mother or the addiction to women for his father. Either way, their behaviors and patterns had been destructive. They had printed permanent scars on Joe's DNA.

In the end, Joe could not stay with Stephanie. He hoped Nora would take him back, but even if she didn't, it was time he required more of himself than the easy way out. It was time to return to who he was meant to be and figure out what had led him down his father's path.

Joe was awash with guilt—and shame. He knew his relationship with Stephanie was wrong from the beginning but he had still invited it. Sure, Steph had pursued him—that was not a lie—but he had not offered a robust rebuttal. He had not once mentioned his wife would not appreciate their friendship, and as the friendship and then affair progressed he had only spoke of Nora in terms of what she *wasn't*. He had failed to remember his wife had raised his children, supported his practice, volunteered in the community and had given support to her parents in ways he could only hope to garner care from his own kids. He hadn't mentioned how his dry cleaning was always picked up, dinner always on the table and there were always clean, matched socks in his drawer. In the end, whether Nora took him back or not did not weigh into the decision to end the affair. He had to leave Stephanie for himself. He had to start living like a man Sammy and Sullivan—and even Nora and Phe—could be proud of. A man *he* could be proud of.

Joe walked over to the thermostat, turning it up from fifty-two to sixty-eight. It was chillier in the house than it was outside. Flipping on the light, he took a quick inventory. The furniture was shrouded under ancient white sheets. Collections of dust blew across the weathered hardwood floors as the stagnant air patterns in the house adjusted to Joe's presence. Underneath the thermostat sat his mother's mid-century drink cart. Half a bottle of Tanqueray gin, a crystal decanter, and four crystal rocks glasses sat positioned in perfect alignment. Just as they had been when he was eight years old and learned how to mix the perfect gin and tonic. His mother had taught him, at first he had been excited! His mother's drink cart had previously been off limits, and this new-found responsibility made Joe feel older, important.

His father had been angry with his wife. "Eleanor, do you really think he should be learning how to do that?" Even Joe had understood the condemnation in his father's voice.

"Oh it's fine, Charles! It's fun! Isn't it, Joey? It's like a science experiment!" Eleanor's words were slippery, mushing together in her late-afternoon haze. His mother praised his still hand as he measured out the gin and his precision in cutting the perfect thin lime slice.

Joe touched the decanter now, the deep grooves of the Czechoslovakian crystal rigid under his fingers. His excitement over being given the new responsibility of becoming his mother's personal bartender faded quickly. While she was pleasant when she was only one or two cocktails in, her requests for "just another," ending with giggles and smiles, Eleanor Phillips was not a nice drunk. The more Joe served his mother, the worse she treated her son.

No, with each drink Joe watched as his mother descended into the pit of cruel barbs and self-indulgent, arrogant platitudes regarding his father's moral compass and the boring, tedium of being his mother. Of course, his father was nowhere nearby, so the words were left for Joe to hear. It changed who Joe was. Her drunken complaints turned into Joe's thoughts and fostered feelings of resentment and sadness, shame. Nora's love had been a sweet antidote to his mother's cruelty and when that seemed to disappear, Joe had found another woman to ease the burden of carrying his mother's sins.

Now, forty-some years later, Joe was overwrought with anger at a half-empty bottle of gin. Before his composure could contradict his fury, Joe spiked the Tanqueray off the floor in a trauma-infused touchdown celebration forty years in the making. Shards of green glass sparked off the ground and into the air like embers from a fire. Satisfaction flooded seven-year-old Joe as surely as forty-nine-year-old Joe felt compassion for the child who grew up soaked in gin.

"Joe?" Nora's voice floated through the closed up, chilly rooms.

Joe shook his head, dislodging his prickly memories and realizing the mess that now soaked the floor.

"Nora? Is that you?"

Nora walked through the butler's pantry into the

living room, weaving around the broken bottle of gin, understanding in a way only a woman who had been privy to his pain could be. Willow pulled at her leash, eager to greet Joe with a sloppy lick across his cheek. Joe smiled, scratching the dog behind her ears.

"I just walked in. Haven't even had time to uncover the furniture. I turned the heat up and that's about it," Joe offered.

"No problem. I was just walking Willow downtown. I walked by and saw your lights and the Jag. I was at Josephine's a little while ago. I spoke with Sammy and Phe. So you're going into the women's clothing business?" Willow barked at the loons she watched through the window. The pair of birds were swimming in the shallow water just a few feet offshore. They gracefully swam in tandem, mirroring each other's movements. A picture of synchronized perfection with their reflection bouncing off the still water. Nora swept her hair from her face with her left hand, exposing her scar.

"Are we going to fight about that, too?" Joe asked, his eyes cutting to his wife's ring finger. Her wedding ring. It was gone. In its place was a small indentation the ring had worn over their years together.

"I would have thought you would have asked me. At least gotten my opinion before you loan our daughter a rather large amount of money. That's all."

"Ahh… am I to take it you don't want Sammy to be involved with Josephine's?"

"I want Sammy to do what *Sammy* wants to do. Not what she thinks my mother or anyone else thinks she should do."

Ignoring her obvious bait into an argument Joe said, "I'd offer you a drink, but the only thing here was a questionably aged bottle of gin…"

Nora nodded her head, acknowledging the mess. "I thought you weren't allowed to make any financial decisions while we are processing the divorce?" Nora pressed.

"I didn't move a penny. The loan docs won't come around until after our divorce is final."

"Oh, OK," she countered. "What are you doing here? I still have Gatsby hired to take care of the house…"

"You can cancel that," Joe said as he leaned down and scratched Willow between the ears again.

"I can cancel it?"

"Sorry. If you give me the information, I will make the call. I'm going to stay here for a while, so I won't need Gatsby."

"Oh… I wasn't aware you were staying. I'm going to go before Stephanie gets here, I guess. I just stopped by to ask about Josephine's—" Nora turned to go back out the door.

"She's not coming," Joe said.

"She's not coming? Here? Tonight?" Nora's voice lilted upward.

"No. She's not coming here at all. I'm staying here by myself. On my own."

"Oh… oh…" Nora stopped talking. She leaned down and untangled Willow's leash from around her paws. Willow circled up at Nora's feet and thumped down, sighing as she rested her head on Nora's foot. "You know, you may want to keep Gatsby on for a bit. You are so busy. He can do the yard, get it ready for winter."

"Thanks, but I think it's time for me to take care of some things myself."

"So you're going to mow the lawn and winterize the gardens?" Nora smiled.

"Why is that funny?" Nora's smile, although it didn't quite spread across her face, warmed Joe's chest.

"I'll text you Gatsby's number, don't fire him until you're sure. It's hard to get on his schedule.," Nora tugged on Willow's leash, Willow's interest again scanning the water for the loon pair. "Can I ask you something?"

"Anything."

"Why did I not know about the pictures?"

"What pictures?"

"Your pictures. The pictures in the photo box in our—my—closet."

"I showed you some of them, through the years."

"Joe, I never saw any of those photos."

Joe walked across the room and pulled on the white sheets covering the furniture. This was the first civil conversation he'd had with his wife in months that didn't have to do with Sullivan or Sammy. Sure, it'd started off uncertain. They were likely a moment away from another scalding argument. He folded the sheets after he exposed the crushed blue velvet sofa, two wingback chairs upholstered in cream damask fabric and a weathered brown leather ottoman with toothpick legs held out at an angle—relics of Eleanor Phillips. He didn't answer Nora's question.

"Joe? Why didn't you show me?" she repeated.

"I tried," he said.

"Oh... I see." It was unspoken that she had been busy, she hadn't been interested.

"Look, it's fine. They're just pictures. It's not a big deal."

"Are you still taking pictures?" Nora asked.

"I do. I still use the camera you gave me." Joe smiled, gentle with the tenuous connection he was forging with his wife. "Can I ask you a question?"

Nora nodded.

"You seem to be spending a lot of time with Robert..."

"Is that a question?" Nora asked.

"No, I suppose it's more of an observation. I was just wondering..."

"Robert and I are just friends. Just friends."

"Ok..." Joe's heartbeat took an uptick.

Nora wandered through the room with Willow following on her leash. She brushed her hands down the back side of the davenport.

"My mom told me my dad had an affair when I was younger," she said.

Joe stood statue-still, holding the furniture covers close to his chest with his arms crossed. He looked at Nora, her eyes open and willing to listen. "I am so, so sorry about what I did, Nora. I haven't told you that yet. Out of everything that I have done, I am most ashamed about that."

Nora nodded her head. "I better go. Willow and I have a date with Netflix and you..." Nora looked around the dusty, stale room and smirked. "You have a lot of work to do."

"I'm sorry I didn't talk to you about Sammy. She was excited. As excited as I've ever seen her. I wanted to support her. I'm trying to do better in the father department."

"I understand. I do. I think it's the right thing to do. I guess I just have to get over not being a part of your decisions. It hurt me that nobody told me or asked my opinion. Sammy didn't tell me. You didn't tell me. My mom didn't tell me. But that's on me to figure out why, I guess."

"I'm not sure there really is a why, Nora. Other than we are all trying to navigate a new way. Phe without William. Me without you. Sammy without us together."

"I suppose." Nora slid her sunglasses over her teary eyes.

"Was I that bad of a father?"

"No. When you were there, when you were really with us, it was all we could have asked for." Nora's voice was heavy with memory.

"Well, I'm trying to really be there now."

"Better late than never," Nora said.

"Is it? Better late than never?" Joe repeated. "Can it be better late than never?"

Nora took a deep breath and walked to the cupboard where the broom and dustpan were kept. She grabbed a roll of paper towel and bent to her knees to start cleaning up the gin and the kaleidoscope of glass. Joe leaned down with his wife and the pair cleaned up the remnants of a forty-year-old bottle of gin, together.

OCTOBER 8, 2018

NORA

Nora peeked her head around the corner. An old storefront door with six glass panels was propped open the width of two paint cans, drips of rustic red and burnt orange paint licking the rims. A cool breeze blew stray leaves in through the door. She heard Willow whine from her car's parking spot just outside the building.

"You're okay, girl. I won't be long." She blew a kiss in the direction of her pup. "Hello?" Nora's voice echoed into the empty space. She peered through the dusty, fingerprinted glass of the windows and cautiously snuck her slender frame through the open door. Sunlight poured in through the high transom windows fronting the building. The fourteen-foot ceilings lined with the original tin and the exposed brick north wall charmed her instantly. The floors—original hardwood!—were stained with water spots and scuffed with scratches and dents.

This space was like the lone firework that sprouts off

of the main show—the one most people ignore, but the one that shines the brightest as it casts its light across the inky black sky alone. Nora was enamored.

"Hello?" Nora repeated herself. She heard the slap of a ladder collapsing followed by a series of footsteps.

"There you are, Nora." Robert leaned in for a welcome hug.

"Hi! It's so beautiful in here…"

"Well, she will be. Work in progress right now." Robert scanned the open space, a look of satisfaction with his progress so far.

The building had been owned by Robert's grandfather, Elliot Wolf, who used the space for his hardware business, Wolf Hardware. In the late eighties, Elliot sold Wolf's to a chain hardware store and the original location closed down. Elliot and his wife, Lovely, rented out the building, and over the years it had been reinvented as an ice cream parlor, a bike shop, a vintage clothing boutique, and a kitschy up-north gift shop. Robert had inherited the building from Elliot a few years ago, following his death. After the last renter left a few months ago, Robert began renovating the space on his own.

Nora stood in the space where Wolf Hardware once lived and imagined wet work boots slogging in from the street to find a needed screw or bolt. She could see the display racks—rows of screwdrivers and hammers, paint and lightbulbs. Metal bins full of galvanized nails, washers in all sizes, finishing nails and screws would have lined the back wall. She could smell oil and paint and rubber with a deep, nostalgic breath.

The building had endured a lifetime of reinventions. Not just endured—survived. Thrived. Nora felt a kinship to this building—she was as scarred as the floorboards.

"I just had the brick wall reworked and sealed. I have a contractor coming to change the wiring over so that it can be exposed, will do the same with the plumbing. The floors will get sanded down—"

"The floors?"

"I am going to sand them down, polish them up—"

"You can't do that!" Nora surprised herself. "The stains and the dents and the scratches are what has seasoned them! They tell the history of this place! You can't erase them—they are a part of the character!"

"They are also pretty nasty in some spots." Robert smiled. "So you like it?"

Nora nodded, still wide-eyed, taking in all the details.

"I'm enjoying doing the work on my own. I don't owe anything on the building and the coffers are full at the moment. That's why I brought you here." Robert stopped.

"Me?"

"Let's go grab a cup of coffee and I'll tell you my idea."

Nora took one last look around the space, soaking in the light and the possibilities, then followed her friend out the door to Bay Bean.

ROBERT

"So what's this grand idea, Mr. Wolf?" Nora smiled, her fingers tapping rapidly on the table. Robert and Nora sat with Willow curled up under their bistro coffee table at Bay Bean, each sipping a steaming full-milk latte. Robert loved the bitter smell of roasting coffee and the tink and taps of the baristas working behind the counter. He had come here often after Katie died, the noise and bustle of the shop comforting him when he was lonely.

"Well, I've been thinking. Remember how we were talking the other night about What Ifs?"

"Of course…" Nora's eyes squinted in question.

"What if…" Robert paused. "What if you opened a design studio in my building? You can help me finish the renovations. Pick the paint and lighting, design the offices?"

"Me? Me. Open a business?" Nora laughed out loud. "I don't know the first thing about opening a business—"

"Hold on there for a minute." Robert chuckled. "You don't have to know everything about opening or owning a business today." He reached down and scratched Willow's head.

"Not only do I not know anything about owning a business, I know *less* than nothing about owning a business! And I'm not even a real designer."

"You know a lot about design. And I know about

owning and running a business," he said as he looked Nora square in the eye. "You always tell me you were the CEO of your family for decades, you ran Joe's office project. You can do this."

"I can't do this, Robert. I don't have a single clue."

"I can help you. We would be in it together." Robert spun his latte cup around on the table.

"You would help me?" she asked. "What about your appraisal business? You won't have the time!"

"I think I need a change. I'll still do appraisals, but I also have my general contracting license. I'd like to get back into construction, we could combine the two businesses—I build, you decorate and design."

"You really thought about this?" Nora's head tipped sideways, just like Willow's did when Nora spoke to her.

"I have actually thought about it a fair amount. I have the space—and it needs some help. You have the talent. I think we can make something special happen." Robert tapped his foot underneath the table. He hadn't expected to feel nervous, or to worry about his friend's response. He just now realized how much energy this idea gave to him. Robert Wolf had been floating, just getting by since Katie died. There was a reason Katie had sent Nora back into his path and it wasn't for love. It was to help bring him back to life.

"I may not be all that easy to work with," Nora questioned. "You know I'm a recovering perfectionist…"

"I'm aware." Robert smiled.

"Do you think this is why we crossed paths again? After the worry stone?" Nora wondered out loud.

Robert took a sip of his latte and rubbed his hand across his mouth. "Katie never believed in things happening for a reason. She believed things happened and we were supposed to find a way to grow from them. I have been trying for years to figure out what in the hell I was supposed to learn from losing my wife so early." Robert took another long slurp of his too hot latte. "She would love this idea. Katie was a supporter. You starting a design business? Creating something of your own? She would admire your courage. She'd be all in, especially if we could help. And I know she'd be all in for me to be your business partner. Because I need something new, too. I think the reason we crossed paths was to help us both get over what we lost. And to start again."

"I'm scared. I don't know." Nora's brow came together in a tight pull of worry.

"Is being scared a bad thing? Is not knowing what to do a bad thing?" he answered.

"Of course it is!"

"Is it? Is it a bad thing, if what you're going to try and do fills you up? Is it a bad thing that you don't know today—when we can figure it out and learn tomorrow?"

"No. I guess being scared isn't a *bad* thing. I am the most risk-averse person you have ever met. This is really stepping out of my box. Like, I'd be dancing on top of it."

Robert laughed out loud at the visual. "You don't need to dance. You just need to design. And you don't need to decide right this minute. You just need to decide to think about it. Talk to Phe. Talk to Joe. Talk to Sammy and Sullivan," Robert suggested.

"Katie would admire my courage?" Nora repeated waiting for the thundering derby horse to break out of the gate. He never came.

"Absolutely." Robert smiled.

"And she'd be all in?"

"Without a doubt."

NORA

"What do you think, Mom?" Nora asked.

"It's a beautiful building. I remember when it was the old hardware store, I think it was an ice cream shop after that?"

"It was!" Nora's face brightened. "And now it will be the home of Petoskey Stone Designs."

"What a perfect name. Your dad would be so proud of you. He *is* so proud of you." Phe's eyes sparkled with joy.

"I know he is proud of me. And actually, I am so proud of myself."

"I'm proud of you, too." Phe's smile shone up toward her daughter, warming them both from the inside out. "Both my girls doing big, new things!"

"I'm not as brave as Sammy or you. I'm scared to death," Nora admitted.

"You think I wasn't scared to open Josephine's? Or that Sammy's not scared to take it over?" Phe looked at her daughter.

"Courage isn't about not being scared. At all. When your father had the affair I closed myself off for a long time. It took me a long time to be able to open up to him again. But when I did, it was with the knowledge that I could—and would—be hurt. I don't believe I knew that when we were first married. That made letting go and letting your dad in even sweeter. It was the same with the business and it will be the same for yours. You will be hurt, I guarantee it. But I also guarantee you have the courage to withstand it."

"You are braver than me," Nora said.

"Oh no my sweetheart. That's where you are wrong. I made a lot of mistakes raising you, but perhaps the biggest was believing I always had to be strong. I thought you needed an example of a powerful woman. What I gave you was an example of a reserved, closed-off woman. That's not courage. Real courage comes in being real. You are the mother I couldn't be." Phe took a deep breath and walked toward the exposed brick wall, running her hand down the details of the mortar and brick. "When your father died, I realized I don't have as much time left as I used to, and that I want to be real."

"Is that why you told me about dad's affair?" Nora asked.

"Nobody's perfect, Nora. Not me, not you. Not your father. Not Joe. I'm so proud of you for finding your footing. For being bold. For trying on a life different than what you imagined. For letting go of perfect and being real. I told you about your father's affair because you needed to know it's survivable. You needed to know you weren't alone. It wouldn't have been fair of me to stand by and watch you suffer without offering my experience."

"You were a good mother," Nora answered. "You *are* a good mother."

"I guess that's the real challenge of motherhood. To evolve. To change. To realize what your children need—not what you need or what you would like to give them. To be who they need you to be so that they can grow into everything they have the potential to be."

"I'm trying," Nora said, her eyes wide as they took in the landscape of her new challenge. The wide plank wood floorboards, the exposed brick, and the open ductwork all represented possibility.

"That, my dear daughter, is all we can do."

OCTOBER 31, 2018

NORA

Nora walked out of the house and took a left toward the walking route she'd taken since Robert suggested it. He had been right, the water was always a welcome sight. Willow wound her way through town, past the quaint shops and restaurants, the buildings stacked together like a shelf lined with library books, under the bridge and out toward the marina, knowing the way by now. The leash tugged quickly, she always did for the first mile or so. The sun was out, the breeze was gentle and unseasonably warm. Nora preened her face up like a duck on the water, letting the warmth of the day drape over her furrowed brow and tight shoulders. A deep breath in pulled Nora's chest up toward the sky. *Stay in the moment*, she thought, *be here now. No fear.*

Her steps fell lightly. She walked quickly toward the marina following the light shining off of the water, glinting like diamonds. She'd had a counseling appointment with Mary this morning. The panic attacks were lessening, and although Nora had decided not to take any medication right now, she was open to the idea if she needed it. For now, she and Mary were working on mindfulness. Not allowing the fear Nora carried with her to interfere. Walking was also working. Working on the building with Robert and creating her business had given her a reason to get up every morning. She looked forward to it! It gave her that gentle rush of excitement—the one that didn't quite scare her but propelled her forward. The one that resembled the start of a panic attack, but instead took a track that felt healthy and stalwart. It felt honest.

Nora traveled along the bay and down the Wheelway trail. Despite the early morning hour and late autumn weather, she passed fellow walkers, runners and bikers. Willow trotted along, not much bothered by any of the company. Today Nora stopped at every turnoff, breathing deeply and taking in the view of the water. Anxiety threatened to creep in, her worry for the future and her regret of the past still rose like the tide. Closing her eyes, she continued to allow the sun to warm her, and she pushed the anxiety down. She could allow herself an hour to walk and not slide down the negativity rabbit hole. She would hold on to the sun and the breeze. She would not allow the fear to intrude. Nora was a work in progress. She was realizing that honesty with herself was as important as honesty with others. Some days were harder than others, this just happened to be a harder one.

She turned back toward town, the reverse in direction behaving like a Sunday afternoon, spiking her thoughts about the day and what she needed to accomplish. A woman was poised, sitting carefully on a bench looking out at the water just ahead of her. Her chest rose and fell with deep breaths, her edge of composure was ragged and Nora could feel her struggle. Nora slowed her steps. She was drawn to the young woman, who was not much older than Sammy. As she stepped closer, Nora could see the woman's hands holding her gently swollen stomach. The woman looked up and their eyes met. Nora smiled. The woman smiled in return and a single tear slipped down her cheek.

"Are you all right, honey?" Nora asked, her hand reflexively touching the scar on her eyebrow. Not in embarrassment, more acknowledgement. A nod to what was real.

"I'm okay, thank you." Still, the young woman did not look away.

"When are you due?" Nora asked. Normally Nora would never pose that question to someone she didn't know. But today, this morning, with honesty on her mind, Nora was certain she was *supposed* to ask.

"February." The woman smiled.

"It's such an exciting time, isn't it?"

"I'm scared to death," she admitted. Nora smiled, remembering that feeling. The fear of not being good enough, the fear of not knowing enough, the fear of making mistakes. The fear of loving someone more than yourself. How ironic that Nora had spent the morning holding back those same fears, decades after she had become a mother.

"Oh I'm still scared to death and my kids are adults." Nora and the woman laughed together.

"Oh great." A smiled dead-panned across the woman's face.

"My name is Nora." She offered her hand to shake.

"I'm Tess. It's nice to meet you."

"Do you live in Petoskey?" Nora asked, wondering if Tess had known Sammy. They looked to be the same age.

"No, I am originally from Chapel Corners, near Covington?" Nora nodded yes, she knew where that was. "But my husband and I live in Chicago now. He's here for work for the week, and I just came up for a few days to join him." Tess wiped the few damp tears from her cheek.

"Is your husband excited about the baby?"

"He's beyond thrilled," Tess answered. "My in-laws are thrilled. I am too, I just want to do it right and I don't know if I have it in me."

"I remember that feeling. Would it help if I told you I never met a mom who *didn't* feel that way?"

The two women chatted about restaurants Tess should try during her short visit, other trails she could walk. Tess had been married last May, and the pregnancy was a surprise. Nora told Tess about Sullivan and Sammy. She stayed away from the standard-pregnant-mom joke urging her to get some sleep because she never would again. Instead, she tried to listen. Really listen. In the past she would have lavished advice on this young woman, she would have been sure she had the answers Tess was needing. Today, she listened, waiting for the lesson she herself needed to learn.

"I don't know how to be a mom." Tess's voice quivered as she spoke. "I didn't have a mom, she passed away when I was young. I'm not sure I know how to do this. I don't want to mess her up."

Nora nodded her head as she listened to the young woman. Life was full of insecurities and changes, even those blessings we pray for come with discomfort and pain. Nora realized then how foolish it was for her to have believed that her life's course had been charted and complete. That there would be no more decisions, no more challenges. That there would be no surprises or change in plan. Nora smiled at the sunshine, at Tess, and at this moment in time.

"Honey, no one knows how to do motherhood. Sure, there are a million books and everyone has an opinion, but nobody *knows* how to do it." Nora was pleased with her answer. "You just do the best you can. Someone told me once that if you were worried about doing it right you were doing just fine. I think that's true."

"Do you have any advice for me?"

"Do I have any advice?" Nora took a deep breath.

Just when she thought the lesson she was supposed to learn was to be quiet and listen, things changed again. "I don't know if you want my advice." Nora's eyes cast downward. The fight to keep the sadness at bay was so difficult. The loss of her family and her marriage came crashing in as strong as a Big Lake Storm. Nora looked at Tess, this young woman she'd just met. This young woman with a new marriage and a surprise pregnancy. She both envied her possibilities and was grateful that she didn't have to do it again. It's true as you get older, your energy wanes. Tess looked out at the water for a few moments, then turned her gaze to Nora, waiting to hear what she would say.

"You will want to forget yourself. You will immerse yourself in diapers and feedings and rashes and teething and crawling and walking. You will make your own organic baby food and you will read to her every night. You will make sure she's happy and full and all her needs are met. And someone will ask you how you are and you will answer, 'The baby is great, she's teething... she's walking... she's reading!... she's playing tennis... she's starting high school... she's graduating!' And then you will realize that in all that time you never answered the question. You never answered how *you* were.

"You will realize you were tired, you were thrilled, you were in love, you were lonely, you were angry and you were sad. You were disappointed and proud, you were happy and joyful and everything in-between. But no one ever knew because you didn't tell them."

Tess leaned into Nora's words, her hands cradling her belly.

"And then the baby will be grown and you will realize that what really mattered... what really mattered was that she was loved. And that you loved yourself." Nora smiled. "I don't mean to be all sentimental on you... but I've been there, where you are. And if I could tell myself anything, I would tell myself to be kind. Be kind to the kids, be kind to myself and be kind to my husband." Tess nodded, soaking in the motherly advice.

"And Tess, pay attention to your husband. Even when the kids and your job and the laundry and the house demand your attention. Pay attention to the two of you. Pay attention to who you are. If you don't... you'll wake up and he'll be gone, and you won't have a clue who you are without him."

NORA

William would have loved Nora's new studio. The building renovations were coming along. All of the wiring and plumbing had been finished. The natural light would help reflect the true colors of the walls and the furniture. The space was wide open, except for two small offices in the back—one for her! And one to use as a meeting room with clients. Next to the offices there was a restroom and a small kitchenette, with a small fridge, a sink, and countertop. She would serve refreshments to her clients when they came in for appointments. Clients! Nora was giddy with the idea of having clients, of having a business. Her mind swirled with fear and excitement.

Tonight she was confirming the paint samples she had picked out. Robert had painted a few squares on the walls so she could see the true colors. She had loved them during the morning and evening light. Now she was here to see them in the dark.

She flipped on the switch and saw the light fixtures

she had chosen were hung. Oh, she was so excited! Most of them were small globes hung from fine vertical rods, nondescript. Functional not distracting. But there was one large light fixture that was the center of the room. A crystal chandelier hung in the heart of a wrought iron orb. The light danced off of the crystals and played on the hand-laid brick wall and exposed utilities.

Yes, her dad would have loved this space. He would have been proud.

When her dad died, Nora had been bereft. Phe and Nora sat holding his cold hands. Phe on the right, Nora on the left. Nora had wept openly, sobbing actually. Phe had been numb, her mind protecting her from the gravity of the loss. The only words Nora could manage to say were, "I'm sorry. I'm so sorry."

Nora had felt responsible that her father died. Logically, of course, she knew no amount of color-coordinated calendars or three-ringed binders or delivered meals or medication pick-ups would have saved him. He'd been diagnosed with Stage 3 pancreatic cancer. At seventy-two years old. They were lucky to have had the two years with him that they did. Still, the lingering regret of not saving William hung around like an old coat in her closet that no longer fit but no one threw out.

The panic attacks started shortly after her dad died. While Nora had known that academically, it had been Mary, her counselor, who had helped her see the connection. William's death—or more accurately William's absence in Nora's life—uncovered insecurities and worries Nora had forgot she owned. Being connected to William had been enough to connect her to her mother and her world. Without her father—Nora felt adrift, lonely. William had smoothed out the edges of everyday life, he helped Nora—albeit unknowingly—believe she could create a perfect life. Her father, the man she had put on a pedestal all his life, the man who had had an affair, asked for forgiveness, and worked to heal his family, was not perfect. In a strange way, this fact helped Nora to accept that the house of cards she had built on the uneven platform of perfection was always going to fall, regardless of Joe's affair. It hadn't been built on reality or hard work, it had been built on falsehoods and inauthenticity.

"Perfect isn't real, Nora," her counselor had said. How strange that in almost fifty years, Nora had never considered that perfection wasn't attainable.

It was with Mary that Nora realized she had been angry with Phe. William had died and Phe hadn't shed a tear. Nora had been overwrought with despair and Phe appeared to glide through. "Is that your assumption or do you know for a fact that Phe isn't affected?" Mary had asked. "Is there a reason she had to grieve the way you do for her grief to be valid?" Point taken.

Nora thought back to her conversation with Phe

while they walked down by the marina. Nora missed her dad every day. But without William, Nora could feel her relationship with Phe begin to blossom. They had stood so long under the protective canopy of William's branches they hadn't had enough sun, and now they were growing on their own. Nora would stop by her mom's on her way home tonight. That felt good. It felt right.

"Hey there, what do you think about the lights?" Robert surprised Nora coming in the back entrance.

"Oh my gosh, I love them! They're just lovely. I love the simplicity of the pendants in contrast to the chandelier. I love how the light is gentle, but abundant. I love how it shows the shadows from the mortar stuffing out from between the bricks on the wall."

Robert laughed. "You like them, then?"

"Yes. I love everything about this building," Nora gushed.

"Katie would have loved it. She would have wanted to come work for you!"

"I am pretty sure I would have loved Katie, too." Nora smiled at Robert. Their friendship was unconventional, they knew. It grew under their mutual affection for the building, their understanding that both Robert and Nora were still in love with their spouses, and the idea that friendship and love aren't mutually exclusive. It grew from a small stone into a brick building and Nora was proud of that.

Nora enjoyed Robert's company, and she enjoyed

stories of Katie. How she rescued a puppy running across the road on their honeymoon—a three-legged one at that! Or how she insisted that they needed to foster the set of kittens she'd found on the beach tucked in the dune grass. Nora wished that instead of meeting her as her time on Earth grew thin, she had met her at the Bean over a chai latte or maybe on a walk with Willow and Lucky.

"Everybody loved Katie." Robert smiled. "So, what's left on our list, Boss Lady?"

"The paint! A few small details in the bathrooms and offices. But I will take care of those. The furniture is being delivered next Monday. The racks for the fabric samples next week as well—those were on backorder." Nora pulled her hair back with both hands and let it go to fly in her face as she consulted the list she had in her planner—still so much to do.

"I think we are on track for the grand opening the first week of January. Sammy sent out the invitations today, so I sure hope we are!" Nora took in a big deep breath. The grand opening of her design business just a week into the New Year. Yes, William would be proud of what Nora was doing with the inheritance she had received from him. He would be very proud.

"Are you still set on not refinishing the floors?" Robert asked. As an appraiser and contractor, it nearly pained him to not sand down and refinish the narrow planks, so they had compromised. A few of the really difficult spots would be replaced, a few others sanded for incongruity in the plane of the floor, and the rest would be refinished clear to show the wear.

"Yep, I sure am," Nora answered. She was certain she wanted to be reminded of the life the building had before her. She wanted to remember the spilled motor oil in the hardware and the grooves and scrapes cut into the wood from moving ice cream coolers. She understood it went against design principles and even may cost her a client or two—but the floors looked like she felt. Weathered, worn. Worse for the wear. But still beautiful. Still useful. Still worth saving.

"OK, you're the designer." Robert smiled.

They finished up the last decisions for the paint and reviewed the schedule for the following two weeks in detail. When the last of the items were crossed off the to-do list and the plan for the next day set, Robert suggested a cocktail.

"Come on, I'm hungry. And thirsty. Want to hit the Twisted Olive? Gatsby's working tonight, I think."

"Gatsby? How do you know Gatsby?" Nora asked.

"I'm a regular at the Olive. He's a good kid. You know, he's started making handmade furniture—you should check it out, see what he's got. May be perfect for the shop."

"I heard that, actually. He is the caretaker of Joe's parent's place in Harbor." Nora hesitated. A glass of wine and their cheese plate sounded lovely—but she hadn't been back there since Martini Night. Could she do it? Nora looked around the building, taking in all she had accomplished in a few months. She looked outside and snow had begun to fall. The street lights, draped in evergreen and white lights with festive red bows, highlighted the white flakes against the night sky. She felt like she was in her own private snow globe.

"Let's go."

"The last time I was here I threw a drink in my husband's girlfriend's face. Well, not the glass. Just the vodka," Nora said. Lifting her glass of pinot up for a sip, a small smile playing on the corners of her mouth.

"You threw a glass in someone's face?"

"Not someone's face. Stephanie Laredo's face."

"Ouch. I guess she probably deserved more than a drink in the face." Robert chuckled. "Actually, I knew that story. Gatsby told me."

"Lovely, it's so nice to be a topic of gossip," Nora chided her friend.

"Ahh… he tells me all the crazy stories to cheer me up," Robert playfully elbowed Nora in the ribs.

There were days Nora felt guilty on behalf of Robert and Katie— Joe was alive. He wanted to try again. They had talked a few times via text and Joe had pulled his divorce petition from the courts. She wasn't convinced she wouldn't file her own papers, but she was giving herself time to focus on the building, her business, and figure out Joe later.

"Katie used to love to come here. She loved a Woodford Manhattan. Strong on the Woodford, thin on the vermouth. And she always ordered the sea bass. It was funny, she was so adventurous. Always taking risks, doing spontaneous and crazy things. But when she found something she liked, she never wavered."

"Which must be why your marriage was so strong. She found you, and never wavered."

"Maybe." Robert smiled. "What are you going to do about Joe?" Robert asked. While Nora enjoyed hearing stories of Katie, she also took comfort in sharing details of her marriage's demise. She was learning it was helpful to talk about it—to be real. To let people she cared about know where she was at. It was lovely to not pretend to be perfect. Nora felt her energy being restored every time she was honest, truly authentic, with herself, with Sammy, with Phe, and with Robert. And with Joe.

"I can't forgive him."

"Hmm. Then you have your answer, right? If you can't forgive him, you have to file the divorce papers yourself." Robert stirred his Manhattan with his index finger. "You ready to do that?"

"No. Not ready to do that either." Nora picked up a piece of blue cheese and put it on one of the fresh baguette slices with a pickle.

"Why have you decided you can't forgive him?"

Nora sat quietly for a minute. *Could she forgive him? Could she find it in her heart to forgive the man who destroyed her?* She had never considered forgiveness. Even after talking with her mom in the marina, she hadn't considered it. Her counselor had asked her the same question, wondering if not forgiving Joe was an antiquated tenant of her old life. The perfect husband would not cheat, and the perfect wife would not forgive if he did. Nora supposed that was true, it was also true that she was afraid to be hurt again.

"I don't know that either," Nora said quietly. She was sitting in the exact seat at the bar that she had sat in last summer when Joe had brought Stephanie here for dinner. Nora could almost feel the tug of her red dress across her thighs, she could feel Gatsby's eyes on her full of pity. Stephanie had looked at her with condescending disdain. She was so happy to have stolen Joe. So happy to have gotten him away from Nora. Or was she? Was Nora assuming Stephanie's intent the way she assumed she knew how Phe should grieve? Or that Joe didn't want to parent? Or that William had been faithful? Stephanie had slept with Nora's husband and there was no denying that. Still, questions played at the sides of Nora's mind.

"Maybe I do know why," Nora said suddenly. She took the last sip of her wine and gathered her purse and coat from the rack behind her. "I have to run. Thank you for the wine and the cheese—I will pay next time. See you tomorrow?"

"Of course," Robert answered. "Are you okay?"

"Yes. I am, actually. I just thought of something I have to do. And I need to do it before I lose the courage."

Stephanie knocked on the front door of Nora's new studio. Even though she had agreed to meet, Nora was still surprised to see Stephanie there, standing on her beat-up hardwood floors.

Nora had called Stephanie on the walk back to her car after she left Robert at the Twisted Olive. She had thought about asking Stephanie to her house, but Nora wasn't comfortable with that. That was her safe space, it harbored memories of Joe and the kids in happier and even difficult times—it was *their* space. To allow Stephanie there would allow her too much real estate in Nora's mind. The building, however, was ideal. It was under construction, much like Nora felt. But it was also Nora's. Not Joe's. It was the place where Nora Phillips was finding her rebirth. She was redeeming the one life she had on the planks of the dented, scratched and stained floorboards.

The building was going to be a public space—one that Stephanie could easily walk into of her own will in just a few months. Memories of seeing this woman here wouldn't haunt her the way they would if Nora sat and had a conversation with her in the kitchen on

Trillium Drive.

Nora nodded that the door was open, and Stephanie walked in, the heels to her Toms boots marking her steps toward Nora. She unwrapped her black-and-gold woven infinity scarf from around her neck. She was beautiful, her long dark hair cascading down her back, her small petite frame swimming in her oversized winter coat.

"Thanks for coming," Nora said.

"I suppose I owe you that," Stephanie answered. She stomped her feet on the entrance run, kicking off the collected snow. She crossed her arms across her chest.

Nora had to give her credit for showing up.

"I wanted to apologize to you." Nora licked her lips. "I wasn't always the nicest person to you. I could have included you more, not repeated stories about you behind your back. I could have been kinder. And for that I'm sorry."

Stephanie stood under the spill of light from a single downrod globe, her face frozen.

Nora continued, "Can I ask you something?" Taking advantage of her opponent's confusion.

Stephanie allowed her arms to drop by her side, tucking her hands inside the pockets of her long, down coat. "Yes," she answered quietly.

Nora momentarily wished she had planned more for this meeting, not run it on an impromptu idea. She was still in the jeans and boots she'd worked in all day, a long Cabi sweater tucked around her middle, her coat tossed over the work table along with errant screws and scraps of fabric, paint swatches, and furniture catalogs. She hadn't looked in a mirror in hours and she was certain her makeup was a mess. She took a deep breath. She wasn't perfect. She was real. This is what a woman who had worked all day looked like. This is what a woman who is recreating her life looks like. Not perfect. Real.

"Why are you here?"

"What do you mean why am I here? You asked me here."

"It's not like we're friends, I'm the wife of your ex-lover. Why are you here?"

Stephanie stood still for a moment. Her hands shifted inside her pockets. "Curiosity, I suppose. Are you and Joe back together?"

"No, Joe and I are not back together."

"Yet?"

Nora refused to answer. She was willing to show Stephanie grace, but she was not willing to show her hand.

"Is that why you are here? To find out if Joe and I are back together?"

"No." Stephanie took a deep breath. "Maybe. I guess. I just wanted to know."

"Well, it may surprise you, but it's actually none of your business." Nora smiled. Grace was one thing, but so was taking back her power.

"It wasn't like I asked him to leave you."

"I don't really care how that all went down, Stephanie. I don't."

"Can I ask *you* a question?"

Nora nodded.

"Why did you ask me here?"

Nora walked toward the front windows, looking out at the street. The snow had continued to fall, gently landing atop the crust of snow that had been left behind from a winter storm three days earlier. The ski hills would be happy. The flakes came in a soft comfortable rhythm. It was beautiful outside. "Despite your affair with my husband, if we are together or not has nothing to do with you. I suppose I wanted you to know that. I hate what you did. I hate what he did. But I also won't allow it to hurt me anymore."

Stephanie smiled. "Joe and I will always have a history."

"You're right about that. And Joe and I will always have the thirty years we shared together, our two kids, our family. Sleeping with my husband doesn't make him yours and it doesn't erase me or what we share."

"What you share?" Stephanie snarked.

Nora hadn't realized she had used the present tense. She turned to look at Stephanie again.

"I will tell you one thing. You can chase any married man you can find and it will never give you what you want—unless what you want is just sex. My guess is that's not the case. No man will give you what you want until you decide to give yourself some respect."

"I respect myself! I'm a better woman than all of you bitches who won't ever speak to me at school. You look down your nose at me because I'm a single mom, I work the night shift. I'm *friends* with my kid. I have had to work hard and make it on my own! I didn't have a perfect life like you did!"

"Be proud to be a single mom. Be proud of working the night shift. Be proud of your kid. Stop sleeping around. Stop being the other woman."

Stephanie stood stone-still, a statue with a shadow reaching out across the imperfect floorboards.

"And for goodness sakes don't believe for a minute if someone tells you their life is perfect." Nora stopped talking, taking in a deep breath. Her hands suddenly itched to pull out Stephanie's hair, to gauge out her eyes, to take that stake to her chest like she'd imagined a million times before. But her heart... her heart had settled. It had settled into the knowledge that if Nora and Joe had taken care of their marriage, there would have been no room for Stephanie Laredo. No matter how hard she would have tried, Stephanie would have found no purchase.

"I'm sorry," Stephanie said quietly.

"Thank you," was all Nora could answer.

When Stephanie left, Nora stood still under the light of the crystal chandelier. A cascade of emotion fell like the snow outside the window in the still night. Forgiveness. She thought about her mother's words. She looked at the good times and the difficult times with William with equal gratitude. It was the imperfect times, the difficult times, the times where you had to grow and learn to change, to forgive—both give and receive—that gave life its beauty.

Katie came to mind. Robert's auburn-haired, free-spirited beauty. The woman whose spirit still lingered long after her passing in the life of her great love. The woman who refused to live life in the prison of perfection but rather relish in the beauty of life. The woman who didn't believe everything happened for a reason, but rather that we needed to find the lesson we were intended to learn with what life gave us.

Nora could see it clearly now: losing her father, Phe's health, Joe leaving, Sullivan going to jail, the car accident, Sammy moving home, the panic attacks. They had all happened to stretch Nora down to where she could learn. Learn to embrace love and the vulnerability to feel that love down to her bones. Even—and perhaps especially—when it meant also feeling disappointment.

Nora picked up her coat and walked to the front door. She flicked off the lights and stood in the dark for a quiet moment.

Perfectly imperfect.

JANUARY 4, 2019

NORA

"Mom, the caterer is here! I'll just show her where to set up, okay?" Sammy peeked her head around the corner of Nora's office where Nora was dressing. She was perhaps more excited than Nora about the Grand Opening of Petoskey Stone Designs.

"Thanks, honey. I'm almost ready." Nora finished clasping the back of her earrings to the diamonds Joe had given her for their twentieth anniversary. They were square, half-carat and she hadn't worn them since Sullivan's graduation. They felt good. She smiled at her reflection. Her red dress was a little big these days. But still, she wore it with a long, black cashmere sweater and black Manolo Blahnik heels. They were an extravagance—but Nora justified it with the fact that she was wearing her old red dress and a sweater from Josephine's that Sammy had picked out. And... they made her happy. Nora smiled at the realization that those moments of happiness were deeper and more plentiful here in this imperfect life than they ever were in the stifling days of perfection she'd cultivated.

Nora tucked her purse into the bottom drawer of her desk. She ran her hands across the smooth glass, straightened the piles of catalogs and invoice slips in the corner. Life did not look anything like what she thought it would even a year ago. In some ways it was utterly unrecognizable, and in others it was so familiar her heart ached. It was as if she had excavated her own future, taken the tools and sifted away the perfection and the unrealistic expectation to find hidden treasures underneath.

She smiled as she felt the sweet sensation of happiness surround her. She'd been looking for it for so long. Those little moments where life seemed good, content. Those moments between life's chaos and sadness, sometimes the moments in the midst of them. She was learning to recognize the beauty in smaller, tangible moments rather than looking for long, uninterrupted stretches of happiness. When she'd see a blazing red cardinal darting through the woods behind her house and be reminded of her dad, or in the quiet of the morning as she drank her coffee alone and the sun warmed her shoulders and gifted her space with light. Or how she felt when she walked—one foot in front of the other, her legs strong and her body capable. In the end, Phe was right, the beauty is in the imperfections of life. Beauty was even more brilliant when it *wasn't* perfect.

There were moments—many of them, if she was

being honest—when Nora was still sad. She was far from having everything figured out. She thought she'd wanted to find a solution, a resolution, to the challenges of the past few years. But now she knows there is no solution, only ever-changing ways to move through life. She carried sadness with her every day. She was still, and probably always would be, melancholy that her kids were grown, sad for the loss of her father, bruised from Joe's dishonesty. Instead of ignoring or trying to force perfection she had learned to lean into those moments. To really feel them, to allow the feelings to soak into her. It was then that she could move past them. They were becoming less intense, less frequent. Giving up perfection had been difficult, but giving up perfection had given her the greatest gift: authenticity. There was so much magic to be had at the hands of truth and honesty. And today, today Nora Phillips was truly grateful. Katie and Robert had blessed her with the lesson to embrace her imperfections. To give her imperfections the glory of being what makes her unique. This was perhaps the best gift she could give her children and Joe, the best gift she could give herself. The gift of freedom from the weight of perfection.

Nora looked in the antique oval mirror that hung on a corner wall of her office and outlined her lips with crimson liner, then filled them in with matching lip shade. She puckered her lips and put her hands through her hair. Her fingers ran the length of the scar just above her eyebrow. She'd disguised it with makeup but was surprised to find that when a peek of the scar was still visible Nora was grateful. She wasn't anxious and didn't feel pressured to fix it. In fact, she was oddly proud. Nora had been hurt. And she healed. Her scar was a symbol of her healing and she found she didn't want to hide it in its entirety. The palm of her hand patted the pocket of her sweater, ensuring her new worry stone was safe. There were many ways her dad was with her today—but this one, the worry stone, was the most important.

Another knock came to the door just as Nora was opening it—Gatsby.

"Did you get what I needed?" Nora asked hopefully.

"Yep. It's all set."

"Thanks, kiddo. I appreciate it." Nora smiled at the young man.

"I'm going to go see if Sammy needs any help with the catering table. Let me know if you need me to do anything else."

Nora smiled and squeezed his elbow, then watched him walk toward her daughter. Sammy's smile spread out as wide as a sail at full mast as Gatsby walked up. The two of them touched shoulders, leaning in as Gatsby whispered in Sammy's ear.

Nora walked out into the gallery area of the studio. The lights reflected around the room. The evening sky already purple out the front door and windows. The holiday decorations were still hung by the street lamps, spilling spotlights on the falling snow. Across the street Nora could see that Northern Lights, the jewelry store, still had their Christmas window display up—Petoskey was known for the elaborate, festive hometown tradition of Christmas window displays. Nora smiled, realizing next year she could design one, too. This was more than the Grand Opening of her new design business. This was Nora's love letter to the people who had helped her find happiness in her imperfect life. She wanted everything to be perfect, or at least as close as she could get.

Sullivan ran his fingers down the ragged side of Gatsby's table, then knelt down to look at the joints of the legs and top. It was a gorgeous piece of walnut with a live edge. Gatsby had crafted it seamlessly into a river table with small Petoskey stones embedded in the nooks and crevices of the wood, covered in a thick, silky epoxy. Nora loved it enough she had commissioned Gatsby to make a line of the tables to sell at PSD.

As Nora had noticed Sully's interest in the table, Gatsby did too. Sullivan's eyes were fierce, concentrated—as she heard Gatsby use the words like "plane," "draw knives," "chisels," and "wood grain," Nora stopped and watched. She saw her son asking questions, admiring the detail of the grain in the wood. Sullivan had decided not to go back to CMU this winter semester. Last year that would have sent Nora into a cascade of anxiety and stress, worrying about his future and trying to impose a traditional path on his plan. This year, Nora saw the imperfect path for what it was: *Sullivan's* imperfect path. Not Nora's, not Joe's. Maybe he would go back to school, maybe he wouldn't. For now, Nora found joy in hearing Sullivan finding excitement in Gatsby's trade.

Sammy was busy organizing the caterer, setting up the wine and cocktail bar. The website for Josephine's launched this week and her daughter had secured two more designers' lines for the shop, and was talking with a third whom she was most excited about. Nora had to admit that her girl was as happy as she'd ever seen her. Of course she hadn't seen her much, she spent sunrise to sunset at the shop and loved every minute of it. Sammy had given Nora a bracelet from Josephine's from a new jewelry designer she was carrying.

"It's made from Labradorite, which is the stone of transformation," she'd said. "It balances the seven chakras and attracts luck, abundance, good fortune, wealth, and success. I mean it's no Petoskey stone, but it's pretty!" Sammy had teased.

Nora touched the mineral stones now. They brought her calm and grounded feelings. More moments of beauty.

The racks of fabric samples were full, the shelves of the design corner were lined with catalogs brimming with ideas and potential. Hope. Nora's design table— a gift from Robert—was another Gatsby original. The top was made from black walnut with a smooth edge, it was supported by sturdy natural-cut log legs. The hand-rubbed oil finish gave the wood movement and texture. Nora ran her hands over the smooth, gentle surface. The table was a perfect reflection of her friendship with Robert—its hand-chiseled craftsmanship a reflection of time, trust and teamwork.

"Nora, dear." Phe smiled and hugged her daughter. "I am so proud of you. Your father would be thrilled. Look at how beautiful it all turned out!"

"It is beautiful, isn't it?" Nora said. "It was a lot of work, and there is a lot of work to do… but it is beautiful."

The space *was* beautiful. The walls were the color of caramel, bold enough to make a statement, but subtle enough to be a canvas for the rest of the room. The lights—oh, how Nora loved the lights!— brought the northern skies inside. The pieces Gatsby made fit perfectly around the four leather chairs she'd arranged. There was a console made of glass and wrought iron, a pair of rocking chairs bent from raw hickory and handmade by the Amish up the road. Candlesticks made of Petoskey stones (classic not kitschy), and frames made of white birch. Nora had wanted to design and create a space that celebrated Northern Michigan, a place that was as much outside as it was inside and would inspire people to make their house a home by using nature, the lake, the hills, the forests and stones around them for inspiration. And she'd done just that.

"Mom! Are you ready? I'm going to open the doors!"

Sammy said. Her excitement was contagious!

"Open them up, Sam I Am. I'm ready."

The party was lovely. Alicia and Steve were there, Fran and her husband, too. Jason Dodds and his wife Shelly not only talked to Nora about redecorating their living room, but were also chatting with Gatsby about his work. Phe made her rounds, chatting and charming everyone. Nora was proud.

Joe had not arrived yet, although he said he'd come when Nora had invited him. She tried to let go of the nugget of worry his absence gave her. There was beauty all around her—friendship, potential, family—and Nora tried to focus on that. Whether Joe made it or not, she had done this. She had helped Robert renovate this building, she had started her own business. She would be okay.

"Well, you did it, Boss Lady. Open for business!"

"Robert! There you are, I was wondering where you were at."

"Oh, I've been here. You've just been busy."

"Did you see?"

"I did see, thank you. So much. How did you get it?" Robert looked toward the cove between the office and the conference room. A picture of Katie hung in a gold-gilded frame. She was wearing a large, floppy beach hat, her auburn hair blowing in the breeze. The beach stretched out behind her, her head was turned just slightly, looking out toward the horizon. Nora loved the photo—and loved that a piece of Katie was here in the building. Reminding them to live life well.

"Gatsby helped." Nora smiled. "He's a pretty resourceful kid. Thank you for sharing your beautiful wife with me. I know it may seem strange, since our paths only crossed once. But… I do feel like I knew her. Through you. I appreciate your friendship so much. I wanted to honor that. Katie's all in, too."

Although Nora had rehearsed the words and had been certain Robert would appreciate the honor to Katie—her voice grew quiet.

Robert reached toward Nora and wrapped his long arms around her in a deep hug. His body felt warm and comforting, safe and secure. Nora was proud of their friendship and grateful for their partnership. She looked up at Katie and squeezed her eyes closed.

"Thank you," she whispered.

"Sorry to interrupt." Joe's voice was quiet.

"Joe…" Nora let go of Robert, squeezing his arm as he patted Joe on the shoulder and walked toward the party.

"These are for you." Joe handed Nora a dozen red roses. "You look fabulous. I always loved that red dress."

"Thank you so much." Nora reached up and kissed Joe on the cheek. "Did you see?" she asked, looking away from Joe.

Along the exposed brick wall were Joe's photos. Hung in gallery style, with lights to accent and matting to match. The images of Petoskey and Harbor Springs, Sammy, Sullivan, and Nora were windows into the life they had shared together, snapshots of their life and love. "I hope it's okay that I hung your pictures. I didn't include your name—but I certainly will if you'd like. I wanted you to be a part of this, and that was the best way I knew how."

Joe's eyes filled with grateful tears. "They're perfect." He smiled.

"I thought maybe you couldn't make it. The party's almost over," Nora whispered. She hadn't realized she'd been holding her breath, waiting. Waiting for Joe to come.

"Better late than never?" he said, his voice thick with emotion.

"Better late than never." Nora smiled and kissed her husband.

"I brought you something else." Joe reached inside his coat pocket and pulled out a familiar black box. Inside nestled in a pillow of velvet was Nora's original wedding ring. The small, quarter-carat diamond sparkled with new promise and decades of history.

Nora nodded her head and Joe returned the ring to her left hand. They would do better this time.

They'd disappointed each other and lost sight of what was important. They'd forgotten that the story of a marriage is written on Tuesday evenings and Sunday mornings. It's written in the monotony of laundry and mowing the lawn and shoveling the sidewalk and dirty dishes. It's written around the big days—the days that mark passing time: the wedding, the birthdays of their children and anniversaries. A marriage is written in the cracks and small spaces of tacos for dinner, laughing at inside jokes and holding hands because you still can. They'd been caught up in work and duty, perfection and the past. They had forgotten to look for the beauty hidden deep inside moments of velveteen imperfection. A pair of cowboy boots. A dozen red roses. Gently falling snow. A red dress. Photos framed on the wall. A plate of warm risotto. Well-worn hardwood floors. A heart-shaped Petoskey stone. And the promise of a ring. In a life well-lived, that is where the beauty is.

BOOK CLUB DISCUSSION QUESTIONS

1. *Where the Beauty Is* is ultimately a story of a family. However, Nora is the main character. Why do you suppose the author chose to begin the story with Phe's perspective?

2. Nora uses FamilyFind to track Sullivan. Ultimately it is what causes Joe to be caught in his affair. Do you think the use of technology to track your kids or spouse is helpful or harmful?

3. When Nora confronts Joe about his affair, why do you think he immediately admits his infidelity?

4. Joe and Stephanie begin their affair as friends. What do you think drew them to each other?

5. Sammy confides in Phe that she is unhappy and restless living in Lansing and working in insurance. Why do you think Sammy didn't confide in her mother? Why do you think she was drawn to confide in her grandmother?

6. "At first Stephanie wasn't sure why—until she caught her own gaze in the rear view mirror. The look in Nora's eyes was familiar. It was the same look Stephanie saw in the mirror every morning. Nora Phillips and Stephanie Laredo had something besides Joe Phillips in common. They were both lonely." Why is Stephanie lonely when

she is living with Joe? Why is she surprised that she and Nora are both lonely? Why do you think Nora was successful in making Stephanie believe she was living a perfect life?

7. Officer Gray becomes an unlikely confidant for Joe. What impact does he have on Joe? In what ways does his story impact Joe and his decisions?

8. Nora and Robert are perhaps an unlikely pair. Do you think men and women can be platonic friends? What do you think draws Nora to Robert? Robert to Nora? Did you find yourself rooting for Robert and Nora to find their way together?

9. Nora carries around a bottle of pills to treat her anxiety, yet she doesn't take them. Why doesn't Nora use the pills? Why has anxiety become such a problem for Nora?

10. After the car accident, Nora is left with a scar on her forehead. When Nora opens Petoskey Stone Designs she is adamant that the floor is not sanded down and refinished. What do Nora's scar and the floor have in common and how does Nora relate to both?

11. Is Sullivan a kid in trouble, or is he experiencing the angst of growing up as most teens do? Is Nora's concern for him warranted or overreacting?

12. Nora invites Stephanie to Petoskey Stone Designs to confront her about the affair she had with Joe. Why do you think Nora felt the need to speak with Stephanie? How do you think that helps Nora forgive Joe? How important is forgiveness in a happy, well-lived life? Why do you think Nora apologizes to Stephanie first?

13. Nora gave up having a job or career to raise her family. In what ways did that contribute to her belief that she and her life needed to be perfect? How did that belief change over the course of the book? What did Nora gain by giving up the idea that she needed to be perfect? What did she lose?

14. The worry stone that Nora gives Katie ultimately connects Robert and Nora. Do you have an inanimate object that connects you to someone you've lost? Do you have a belonging that you carry with you that helps you in some way?

15. The premise of *Where the Beauty Is* is twofold. One, that perfection isn't real, and two, that beauty is found *in* the imperfections of life. What unexpected places do you find beauty in your life? What has helped you find joy and gratitude amidst the struggles in life?

Would you like Lara to join your book club discussion? Contact her at lara@laraalspaugh.com for availability!

ACKNOWLEDGMENTS

On all days and in all the ways that I am blessed, this is just a small list of my gratitude.

Thank you to my first readers this round: Tamara Stout, Courtney Hofbauer, Kira Quick, and Mo Parisian. You were invaluable. I hope you can see the sparks of our conversations, emails, and texts manifested in the pages. Thank you with all my heart.

Susie Poole at Poole Publishing. I thought I couldn't love a cover more than I loved the cover of *Last Turn Home*. Until you gave me this. Your vision of the message of this story was perfect. Thank you for your help and guidance.

Jesse Waldron, Carrie Reynolds and John Martin for willingly sharing your expertise in furniture making, appraisals and renovation respectively. Thank you!

To the women in my life who laugh with me, cry with me, sit in the pit with me, stand on top of the mountain with me, encourage, inspire, challenge and drink wine with me. I am so grateful God put you in my path.

I am blessed with a family, both given by birth and marriage, that are always in my corner. There is such grace in my heart simply knowing that no matter what—if I think I can or I think I can't—they are there for me. Always.

My Boys. My why for every last thing. Momma always has your back. I love you.

My E. You make me a better person, and that is perhaps the best compliment one can give another. I love you more. Every time.

This past year has been full of struggle for me personally and in my writing life. This story was born of my desire to challenge myself to find the beauty that resides in the truth of pain, struggle, joy, and peace. Because in a life well-lived, that is where the beauty is.

Take care,

Lara xo

Lara Alspaugh is a retired nurse, former teacher, and figure skating coach. She is the mother to three boys and recounts the adventures in parenting them on her blog, "Confessions of a Daughterless Mother." *Where the Beauty Is* is her second novel, and is the first in the coming series, *The True North Collection*. She lives in Michigan with her husband and Labrador, Lulu, who she loves to take for walks.

You can find her on Facebook, Instagram, Pinterest, Goodreads, and her website laraalspaugh.com.

Photo Credit: Capital Area Women's LifeStyle Magazine